Was t

Tess wondered if she ~~really~~ impromptu date with another drink. It was Monday and she needed to be at work early. But, even though Graham had a kid and felt not so much her normal type, she had this crazy, weird connection with him. She couldn't *not* stay.

And it had been a long time since she had no-strings-attached fun with a hot guy.

When their round of drinks arrived, Graham clinked his glass against hers. "I'm glad you stayed. Feels as though we're dancing around—"

"Hooking up?"

He gave her a serious look. "Is this what we're doing? Hooking up?"

Heck, she didn't know. But this night with Graham felt right. It felt like something more than just fun. It felt like magic. Like Graham was her perfect match. "Maybe."

Moving slowly he lightly brushed her lips with his. Her pulse sped at the first touch, and she leaned in for more. She knew with absolute clarity that she didn't want just one night with Graham.

Dear Reader,

Ever been to Mardi Gras? Well, if you have, you know. And if you haven't, well, you gotta get down here and "laissez les bons temps rouler!"

I can't remember which was my first Mardi Gras parade—it was a small one in Metairie on a weeknight. But I remember the sheer joy in the air that night. I know—sounds hokey. But there it is. Mardi Gras is about reverting to being a kid again and hugging joy against you tight. It's about tossing one's cares into the background and becoming a part of a centuries-old tradition of... pretty much begging for beads. There's laughter, music and dancing in the streets. It's magical and nearly indescribable. So I knew I wanted to write a book that revolved around Mardi Gras.

Problem is there's not much written on the companies that create the dazzling floats. There's plenty of history, but hardly any information on the business side of things. So this book took a bit more research...although it was fun research. Once I understood how things worked in that fascinating world, Tess and Graham came together much like those magical floats.

I hope you enjoy the story of the Ullo family and the man who shakes things apart for his only daughter. This book is set against Mardi Gras, but at the very heart, it is about family and love. Yes, it always seems to come down to family and love, doesn't it?

I'd love to hear what you think. Feel free to pop by www.liztalleybooks.com—send me a note, sign up for my newsletter or read about what I'm up to next.

Happy reading!

Liz Talley

LIZ TALLEY

—

His Forever Girl

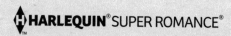

HARLEQUIN® SUPER ROMANCE®

Recycling programs
for this product may
not exist in your area.

ISBN-13: 978-0-373-60826-3

HIS FOREVER GIRL

Printed in U.S.A.

TM www.Harlequin.com

ABOUT THE AUTHOR

A 2009 Golden Heart Award finalist in Regency romance, Liz Talley has since found a home writing sassy Southern stories. Her book *Vegas Two-Step* debuted in June 2010 and was quickly followed by four more books in her Oak Stand, Texas series. In her current books, she's visiting one of her favorite cities—New Orleans. Liz lives in north Louisiana with her hero, two beautiful boys and a passel of animals. She enjoys laundry, paying bills and creating masterful dinners for her family. She also lies in her biography to make herself look like the perfect housewife. What she really likes is new shoes, lemon-drop martinis and fishing off the pier at her camp. You can visit her at www.liztalleybooks.com to learn more about the lies she tells herself, and about her upcoming books.

Books by Liz Talley

HARLEQUIN SUPERROMANCE

1639—VEGAS TWO-STEP
1675—THE WAY TO TEXAS
1680—A LITTLE TEXAS
1705—A TASTE OF TEXAS
1738—A TOUCH OF SCARLET
1776—WATERS RUN DEEP*
1788—UNDER THE AUTUMN SKY*
1800—THE ROAD TO BAYOU BRIDGE*
1818—THE SPIRIT OF CHRISTMAS
1854—HIS UPTOWN GIRL
1878—HIS BROWN-EYED GIRL

*The Boys of Bayou Bridge

Other titles by this author available in ebook format.

Special thanks to the Elsensohns at Mardi Gras Decorators for sharing the business aspects of Mardi Gras.

This book is dedicated to my nieces and nephews—Audrey, Ava, Sam, Davey, Mikayla, Byron, Christian and Devvin. I don't always see you, but I carry you in my heart.

CHAPTER ONE

TESS ULLO SLID ONTO a stool and knocked her knuckles against the weathered bar. "The usual, Ron. Stat."

The bartender with ripped biceps and a sweet smile sauntered over. "That kind a day, hon?"

"God, yes." Taking Granny B to the doctor and running all the errands the older woman had piled up on her list wasn't for the faint of heart. Tess's Italian grandmother wasn't of the sweet variety— more like the salty-with-a-side-of-vinegar kind. For seven hours, Tess had "helped" her grandmother find a bath mat the perfect shade of periwinkle. All that running around came after hearing Granny B tell the technician doing the mammogram about her sex life with Tess's long-departed grandfather. Tess would never look at the picture of the stern-faced man dressed in his Navy uniform in quite the same way. *Scarred* wasn't even the word for what she felt. "Took Granny B out today."

"Yikes. I'll make it a double," Ron said with a twinkle in his eye.

Tess gave a wave to Petra Ostrav who worked in

the paint department at Tess's family company. The diminutive woman sat close to her lover, Paola, a beautiful Chilean dancer who headlined at a top-notch gentleman's club. Otherwise there were not many patrons on this late Monday afternoon. Maybe it was the weather—misty rain fell outside the open plantation windows of the bar located not far from the French Quarter in the Marigny district. Or maybe the small crowd was because it was Lent and the devout were being, well, devout.

Two-Legged Pete's was a regular joint for the employees of Frank Ullo Float Builders—owned and operated by Tess's father—so she usually knew someone when she dropped by. Of course, she'd been a more frequent patron at Pete's recently since Mardi Gras was over and she'd stopped seeing her on-again-off-again boyfriend, Nick. She'd caught him with Merri Wynn right after Christmas. Nick had defended himself by claiming they weren't exclusive, but Tess didn't care. Still felt like a slap after they'd spent the previous weekend talking about a possible future together.

Her phone buzzed and she slid it from her purse. The text was from Gigi Vastola, her best friend.

Can't get away from the office. Sorry, babe.

Damn it.

Tess had wanted some girl time with her bestie,

but she understood. Gigi worked with a law firm on Canal Street, climbing the ladder toward partnership, which meant her friend often got trapped after hours preparing cases. No biggie. They'd catch up later. Tess would have one drink then maybe head to spinning class…or home to watch *The Bachelor.*

The door opened and Tess caught the movement out of the corner of her eye. She cocked her head and looked—like everyone else in Two-Legged Pete's—at the man in a raincoat shouldering his way in. A navy suit and a conservative tie showed beneath the black trench. He sported a fresh haircut and had a jaw of granite.

Nice.

But very out of place for a casual joint like Pete's.

Tess snuck a peek at her middle-of-the-week jeans and long-sleeved sweater. Although the sweater had a pinprick dot of bleach on the hem, the bright green made her eyes look deeper. And she'd worn her UGG boots so she didn't look totally sloppy.

Jeez. Why was she taking stock of herself? Because a good-looking dude walked in? Or maybe it was because Granny B had pointed out she needed to do something with her hair and wear more flattering shoes.

She glanced at the table of women who looked like bank tellers. Every woman stared at the guy, too. One woman tucked a curl behind her ear, and another wiped the mascara shadow from under her eyes.

Even Ron sucked in his gut.

The stranger nodded at the bartender, who in turn gave him a quite charming smile. The man slid onto a stool three down from Tess as Ron flew toward him like a magnet toward a metal pole.

"Hello, there," Ron said, showing his dimples.

Good Lord.

"Hey," the man said, reaching into the open coat for what she presumed was a wallet. "I'll take a J.B. and Coke, easy on the ice."

Ron lifted an eyebrow. "J.B., huh? My kind of man."

Tess snorted. She couldn't help it. She hadn't seen that kind of bad flirting since Gigi got drunk and tried a top-ten list of bad pickup lines on every man at the Columns on Valentine's Day. Okay, that was only a month ago, but still Ron not only took the cake…he'd already licked the spoon.

Typical Ron.

"Hush," her friend said, slinging an arm her way, but not daring to take his eyes off tall, dark and hewn-from-granite.

Tess giggled. Yes, she actually giggled.

Damn it.

The man looked over at her and smiled.

Oh, hell, no. She'd pull out dimples, too…if she had any to use. She smiled as if they all shared one big joke.

"Ron's a consummate flirt," she said, jabbing a finger at her bartender bud. "You'll fall prey if you stand too close."

"Oh, please. You stand closer than anyone, *mon amie*. You love my flirting." Ron grabbed a bottle of the amber liquid from the back shelf and held a glass to the light.

The stranger laughed and the sound tickled Tess's stomach.

Whoa, girl. Down.

"True," she said, pulling her own drink toward her. Ron made her gin gimlet just as she liked it— simple syrup, muddled cucumber, tarragon and Hendrick's. Delish. "When it comes to flirting, you're the don."

"Ron the Don? Sounds like a wrestler." The stranger quirked an eyebrow. He turned toward her allowing his gaze to travel lightly over her. A shiver ran through her. Dear Bessie, he had the prettiest blue eyes that would exactly match the bathroom rug her Granny B had spent eons searching for. Good humor twinkled in the periwinkle depths, and Tess felt more than the warmth of the gin in her girl parts.

Dang, he looked good enough to sop up a biscuit with, and Tess didn't even eat biscuits. Carbs were the enemy, after all, but this man made her want to change her mind.

"What brings you to Pete's? We don't get much tourist traffic," Ron asked, pouring a generous amount of whiskey into the tumbler then topping it with soda.

"Job interview. Someone at the company mentioned this place when I said I wanted a local pub." The man pulled the drink to him, sipped and nodded in satisfaction.

"Really?" Ron said, swiping at the bar with a towel and sliding a surprised look at Tess, keeping her in the conversation. "Good to know we're getting recommendations around here."

The stranger made a sound in the back of his throat that sounded like an agreement, and Tess sipped her drink, trying not to out-and-out stare at the hotness mere feet from her. She had to be ovulating because her hormones had shifted into overdrive and clamored for her to put on some lipstick and sidle closer.

She ignored her hormones because they made bad decisions. In fact, last time they'd led her to a strange bed, overly polite note and a cold cup of coffee the morning after. Tess had stopped letting her girl parts dictate her love life.

The man glanced at the TV that was broadcasting something with racing dirt bikes. "Any way I can talk you into turning to the Rangers game? Wanna check the score."

Ron looked like someone had farted. "Hockey?"

"Nah, baseball. Preseason."

Despite her declaration to keep her distance, Tess

slid onto the next stool. "Feliz is pitching. They're checking out his arm after rehab."

The man smiled at her.

God, his smile was good.

No, not good. Sexy. And not just sexy but up-against-a-wall-naked sexy. Tess was certain she'd seen such a smile only twice…and the aftereffects had resulted in its moniker. Though up-against-the-wall-naked sex wasn't as hot as it sounded. Required a lot of balance.

"Ugh, baseball?" Ron groaned but lifted the remote. "The only thing good about baseball is the way the players look in those tight pants."

"I'll concede that point," Tess said, dragging her purse over, telling herself she moved closer to the man only because it gave her a better view of the TV.

"That's what all the ladies say," the stranger said. So was that a message to Ron? Or to her? "And, uh, I guess some guys."

Ron found the right station. Texas was up 5–2 in the third inning. The Rangers' designated hitter was at the plate, swinging and missing at low and inside.

"Shamburg's gonna throw that pitch at him all night," Tess said.

"A lady who knows baseball." The man looked pleased at the revelation. But, really, there were lots of girls who liked baseball. Okay, maybe not *lots*. But others.

"I'm not obsessed but I watch."

Ron nodded. "Yeah, she keeps stats."

The stranger raised an eyebrow. "Really?"

"I like the Astros best," she said, tugging a notebook out of her purse. "I've gotten into a habit of studying batting averages and making predictions. My brother was a bookie during his college years and paid me to help him. Old habits die hard… and now I like the whole challenge of dissecting the game."

"Bookie? Does he still—"

"Nah, he's a priest."

The man's laughter made her stomach twitch. He looked even better laughing and the bar lights caught the rain droplets in his dark hair. Her hand rose to wipe them away, but she caught herself in time and instead lifted the pen, jotting down the starting pitcher and his ERA.

"I'm Graham." Hotness extended a hand.

"Tess." She tucked the pen and pad into her purse and took his hand. It was damp but warm. "Nice to meet you."

Now that they'd introduced themselves she definitely wanted to keep the conversation flowing, but couldn't come up with a topic. Maybe more baseball?

"Hey, there. I'm Angela," a woman drawled from behind Tess.

Graham spun on his stool. "Oh, hi."

The woman who'd earlier tucked her hair and put

on lip gloss stood behind them with a gleam in her eye. Like a predator.

Graham pulled at his tie.

"Would you like to join me and my friends? We're celebrating a promotion, and we've ordered stuffed mushrooms and smoked oysters." Angela gave Graham a come-hither gaze that made Tess shift on her stool. Jeez, the woman was good.

Graham looked ambushed and his eyebrows lowered a fraction. Tess could almost hear the wheels creaking, turning, churning, trying to figure out how to respond to the overt invite.

"Well, I'll take some of those stuffed mushrooms," Tess joked.

Angela shot her "the look"—the one that said something needed to be stuffed, and it wasn't the mushrooms.

Graham looked like a man who had swallowed a lemon. Okay, maybe not that uncomfortable or sour, but Tess could tell he didn't want to go with Angela and couldn't say so without being rude.

Aw…he was a sweet guy. Tess should help him.

"Actually Graham and I have been catching up," Tess said.

A few seconds tripped by and finally her handsome stranger nodded. "Yeah, it's crazy and such a coincidence, but Tess was my blind date to Sadie Hawkins back in '97."

Tess rolled her eyes. She had been eleven years old in '97, but she wouldn't correct him. If Graham said they went to Sadie Hawkins together, they went to Sadie's together. "Small world, huh? All because he asked Ron to turn to the Rangers' game."

Graham gave Angela a small regretful shrug and then gave his attention to Tess. "You know, stuffed mushrooms would be good before we go to dinner."

Dinner?

Well, all righty then.

"Perfect," Tess said, with a sunny smile.

Angela stood there for a moment, looking unconvinced. Graham turned back to her. "Thanks for the offer, Angela, but I don't want to crash your girls' night out. Go celebrate, and I'll send a round of drinks for you and your friends."

Angela gave a shrug and fake smile. "That's sweet of you."

"The least I can do after that nice invite."

"Send the waitress. She's been on break for fifteen minutes and we're empty," she said to Ron before sashaying to her friends.

"You're the nice guy my mom's been begging me to find," Tess cracked, admiring the way Graham's dark hair brushed the collar of his white dress shirt. The tugging at his throat had loosened the striped power tie and he'd unbuttoned the top button showing gorgeous tanned skin at his throat. His five o'clock shadow gave him a rakish air. "But you don't have to feel obliged to take me to dinner."

"Of course I don't. But come to think of it, you do remind me of Ainsley Braddock, my Sadie's date."

Huh. What did that mean? He wasn't taking her to dinner?

Disappointment stung her. Which was crazy. She didn't know this man from Adam. Which she always thought a stupid saying because she didn't know Adam. Okay, she had a cousin named Adam, but—

"I would love to take you to dinner. That is, if you're free."

Tess nodded, wondering if it was a mistake to look so eager. Her stomach growled and she decided dinner was dinner. And if it were with a handsome stranger, she'd have news to share with Gigi when she called her later. There was something appealing about being spontaneous, something exciting about having dinner with Graham of the power tie and wing tips. "A friend was supposed to meet me after work but couldn't get off. I haven't eaten yet so…that sounds fun."

Graham lifted his glass and clinked it against the one she held in her hand. "Then it's a date."

They both drank and Ron shook his head. "How do you do it? Any time I go to a bar, I go home with a tab and that's it."

Tess laughed. "Joanne would be pissed if you came home with anything other than a bar tab."

"Pregnant women are such downers. She used to be fun," Ron grumbled.

A perplexed expression gathered on Graham's face.

Tess helped him out. "Ron isn't gay. He's just an indiscriminate flirt. Always chasing that tip."

Ron lifted a shoulder. "I never said I was gay."

"You implied it," Graham said.

"No, you made an assumption based on my comment regarding men in baseball pants." Ron's eyes danced with laughter. He loved flipping stereotypes.

"Ron has a twisted sense of humor," Tess said, finishing off her gimlet. The crisp taste and slight buzz made her feel invincible. Or maybe that was due to the fact she'd picked up a hot guy in a bar. Okay, only for dinner, but even so, she felt better about her crap day with Granny B who had ended it by declaring Tess would never see a single piece of jewelry in her will. "Do you want to order stuffed mushrooms? If so, we better put in an order. Daryl's slow."

"Hey, good food requires patience," Ron said.

Graham centered his attention on her. "Let's roll. I'm hungry for more than an appetizer."

"Meow," Ron purred, before moseying toward a customer at the other end of the bar.

Tess's cheeks blistered even though she knew it was a joke.

Graham's gaze slid over her, lingering particularly on her mouth. Tess licked her lips before she could catch herself—and he definitely noted the movement. "I'm not familiar with the Marigny area so I don't know any restaurants close by."

"I'm not dressed overly nice, so we better stick to casual." Tess glanced outside. "Looks like the rain is gone and the stars are out. Why don't we walk toward the Quarter? It's not far and you know there's something there to tickle the fancy."

Tess hopped off the stool, tossing a ten and five on the bar to cover her drink and give Ron a decent tip. Joanne had only a month to go until she delivered their first child, and money was tight for the couple.

"I'll defer to the local." Graham withdrew a credit card and drummed his fingers on the bar while Ron slid the card through the machine. Then he stood, lifting an attaché case. "Let me lock this in my rental and we'll head out."

"Have fun, you two," Ron called holding up his bar towel and giving it a wave.

And so Tess walked out of Two-Legged Pete's with a good-looking man and the expectation for good food, good wine…and maybe something more.

Or maybe she wanted it to be more than what it was.

Either way, it was better than watching *The Bachelor*.

CHAPTER TWO

Graham Naquin popped the trunk of the Chevy Malibu and placed his briefcase inside, slamming the lid with finality.

So…he'd picked up a random chick in a bar.

Outside his current comfort zone in a huge way. In fact, it was something he'd vowed not to do for a while. His focus was on getting his crap together.

In the past couple of months, he'd abandoned the impulsive, carefree Graham, electing to play everything safe. Hadn't worked all that well for him so far, but he liked thinking he was a man who considered every decision thoroughly before moving forward. But tonight he hadn't even tried to apply the brakes. Nope. He'd tossed out that white lie about Sadie Hawkins and backed it up with re-extending the offer for dinner.

He almost felt like himself again…like lady luck winked at him and dealt him a winning hand. Like things were going his way finally.

Smiling at Tess, trying like hell to convince himself an impulsive dinner date was a good idea, he waved an arm in the direction of the French Quarter. "Lead on."

In the damp air, Tess's beach-streaked hair had curled around cheeks scattered with freckles. Her eyes were the color of wet moss, and not much about her implied overt sexiness. More like friendly puppy or kid sister.

Okay. Not exactly friendly puppy. Or sister.

Tess also had full lips and a stubborn chin. Her perfectly-proportioned breasts were nicely outlined in her sweater and her caboose was tight. She wore those weird brown boots all the teenagers wore and jeans that looked comfy and trendy at the same time. She smelled like apples—sort of fresh and fruity. She had an all-American vibe, but there lay a promise in the sway of her hips, a hint of mystery in her smile. Tess reminded him of that one Christmas he'd found a forgotten present beneath the tree.

She'd sucked him in, stretched him outside his intentions…and damned if he wasn't intrigued by the connection between them. It felt like something he'd never felt before. Or maybe he was on a high from nailing his interview.

"Wish I were dressed nicer so we could go somewhere swanky," she said as they fell in step on the deserted sidewalk.

"I see how you roll," he said, laughing when her eyes widened.

"No, I'll totally pay for my own dinner. It's just

you're dressed nice and if it's been a while since you've been to New Orleans…"

"I come to New Orleans often enough…just not since November. Besides, New Orleans is a city where even the cheap eats are good." Graham looked back toward the edge of the Marigny District, spotting the huge warehouse he'd toured that afternoon in the distance. Something warm and right settled in his gut at the thought of returning to his first love. The sound of tugboats blowing their horns on the Mississippi echoed the certainty in his soul.

"So a job interview brings you to the Big Easy?" Tess asked. The puddles along the worn streets tossed back reflections of the buildings. Occasionally someone rode by on a bike or a cab passed as the rhythm of the city reestablished itself after the early spring rain. The squeal of brakes, the rev of engines and the occasional shout of laughter accompanied the music spilling into the streets. The earthy smell of New Orleans which had once been like bacon and eggs to him filled his nose.

"Yeah, I worked for NASA for six years, but with all the federal cuts, my project was canned. Since I have to relocate, I wanted to come home. Something called me."

"That's almost romantic," she said.

"Except it was an actual phone call," he said, with a wry smile. No one had ever accused him of being romantic.

Her laughter tightened something within him. He glanced at her profile. Her nose tilted up, button cute. He liked that. Cute. Like he could drop kisses on it all night. Then and there, he revised his earlier impression. There *was* something sexy about Tess.

"Did you get the job?"

"Not yet, but I have a good shot because I have experience in the field. Years ago I started a company doing what this guy does, plus I got my MBA on top of my engineering degree. But who knows? Felt like the interview went well and the guy's pressed to find someone soon."

"Good for you," she said, tossing him a smile. "Where do you live now?"

"Houston."

"So you'll be transferring here?"

He nodded. "I have some job leads in Houston, but my family lives here. Well, my brother lives on the Northshore, but that's essentially here. You originally a New Orleans's girl?"

"Born and raised. Can't you hear the accent?"

Each region of the Crescent City had its own dialect. "Not from the Westbank or New Orleans East. Uptown?"

"Close enough. My parents still live in Old Metairie."

"I went to Jesuit. You?"

"Country Day." Whoa, swanky, yet Tess didn't give off that vibe.

"Class of '93."

Tess whipped her head around. Obviously the woman excelled in math. "Then why did you tell Angela you took me to Sadie Hawkins in '97?"

He laughed. "Because you didn't look old enough to have gone in 1993."

"So you thought you looked young enough for 1997?" She laughed again. Her laugh was low and raspy. Another thing he liked about her.

"Touché," he conceded as they turned on Decatur Street, skirting the edge of the eclectic, high-rent neighborhood. "So where shall we eat?"

"You have a favorite?"

"I have lots of favorites." And he did. Galatoire's. Dickie Brennan's. Elizabeth's. Irene's. GW Fins. And on and on and on. "Somewhere with a good po'boy? Haven't had good Nawlins bread in forever."

"Central Grocery is closed but we can try Maspero."

"Let's go for it."

She turned her head again and he wondered if she thought he'd meant on some level other than dinner. Maybe he did mean it that way. Things had been so stressful lately with being out of work, depleting his savings and dealing with Monique's demands he'd pulled out of the dating scene months ago. He hadn't been to dinner with a woman in a while...not counting his brother's girlfriend the night before.

What would it hurt?

Tess had nice curves, a good sense of humor and

kept baseball stats. Not to mention she'd agreed to go to dinner with a stranger. Many would think her actions dangerous, and maybe to an extent they were, but something about her spontaneity and her self-assurance struck admiration in him. He liked a woman who knew what she wanted, who didn't shrink from the fray, but waded in bold and in control of herself.

She reminded him of his ex-girlfriend Monique in that way—decisive and thoroughly modern. But that's where the comparison ended. Tess had a sweetness and honesty Monique lacked. He patted his breast pocket where he usually put his phone. Thinking of Monique reminded him of their daughter—he needed to call Emily before nine o'clock.

As they got closer to Maspero which sat across from Jackson Brewery, almost on the corner of infamous Jackson Square, the crowds thickened. Tourism reigned supreme in New Orleans. Here and there tourists gawked at street performers while others swigged beers in foam cups and eyed the open storefronts selling offensive T-shirts and Mardi Gras beads.

When they arrived at the restaurant, they found a short line. Graham gave the hostess his name and then motioned to the bar with a raise of his eyebrows.

"Yeah. Abita Amber," Tess shouted, a warm smile curving her mouth.

That smile made him forget all his troubles. He

needed to recapture his previous mood. He'd nailed the interview—he'd read that much in the old man's face. Graham had been in the zone, dressed to impress with the knowledge to back up his proposals. Everything in New Orleans was falling in place. Including getting his social life on track.

Stop overthinking and walk toward good things in life, Graham.

He paid and went outside, handing the icy beer to Tess, clinking the bottle with his. "To new beginnings."

"And to your new job."

"I'll drink to that," he said, lifting the bottle to his lips. In that instant he felt something swell in him he hadn't felt in so long, not since he'd left New Orleans six years ago. Maybe it was joy. Or freedom. Or both. He wasn't sure which it was, but he embraced the warmth, that feeling of possibility. All that lay withered inside him revived, swelling to life with sweetness.

After cashing out his 401K last month so Emily could continue going to the Montessori school she'd been attending for the past two years, he needed to feel good about something. To chase hope of a better future and pin it down.

Ten minutes later his name was called and they slid into wooden chairs at a table facing the floor-to-ceiling doors looking out on Toulouse Street. Passersby strolled, collars up against the wind sweeping in with the cool front. A slight draft wafted in but it wasn't enough to keep them from picking up the menu.

"I already know I'm blowing my diet on a shrimp po'boy," Tess said licking her lips, a move that heated his blood.

What would she taste like?

Apples?

Or something spicier perhaps?

"And maybe some gumbo, too. Suddenly I'm starving." She looked up at him.

Yeah. Him, too.

He cleared his throat and tried to tame his desire for her. This wasn't a date...or maybe it was. He wasn't sure what they were doing.

"You don't have to buy my dinner," Tess said, with a little shake of her head. "This isn't really a date."

"It's not?" he asked.

"I don't think so. Maybe it is." She gave a wry twist of her lips. "In all honestly, I don't know why I said I'd go to dinner with you. You're a total stranger."

"It's not that different than meeting someone from a dating website if you think about it. In fact, it's almost like an old-fashioned date. Two people meet, they're attracted to one another, and then they—"

"You're attracted to me?" she asked. A faint pink bloomed in her cheeks and the refreshingly honest question made him like her even more. And he already had a healthy like for her. "Yeah, that sounded sort of middle-schoolish. Been hanging out with my nephews too much."

"Actually I thought it was understood I'm attracted to you. Otherwise I'd be sharing stuffed mushrooms and wings with Angela and the girls."

"Well, good to know. I'm pretty hungry but I'd hate to think this was a mercy date."

"Far from it," he said, unable to contain the desire he had for her.

His salacious gaze didn't put her off. In fact she smiled wider before turning to the waitress.

After they ordered po'boys and a cup of gumbo, a comfortable silence descended. He took the time to study her. Her eyes weren't really the color of moss so much as the color of a magnolia leaf: rich, fertile green. The freckles weren't overly pronounced, merely sprinkled across her rounded cheekbones. She had delicate eyebrows and small earlobes from which winked simple solitaire diamonds.

Tess cleared her throat. "So if this is a *date,* you should tell me more about yourself. I know you went to Jesuit, grew up here and worked for NASA, but what about your…hobbies?"

"Hobbies?"

Tess made a face. "That lame, huh? Guess I have issues with uncomfortable silence."

"Felt like a comfortable silence to me."

"Really? Hmm…" She smiled, opening a package of crackers from the bowl on the table. "Sorry.

Should have taken Angela up on the appetizers. I'm starving."

He'd been eyeing the crackers himself, so he mimicked her. "Me, too, but I didn't want to look like I had no self-control."

"No sense in standing on ceremony. As my nephews say, *YOLO*."

He crooked an eyebrow.

"You Only Live Once," she clarified.

Perfect reason to ignore the flicker of logic edging in on his good time with Tess. YOLO. He liked that. "Okay, a little about me. I read the newspaper every morning, don't have a Facebook account, like dogs over cats, have a seven-year-old daughter and I'm a Scorpio."

"You have a daughter?"

"Somehow I knew that would stand out to you. Yeah, Emily. She's beautiful, smart and can tie her own shoes. Big accomplishment. She lives here in New Orleans with her mother and I don't see her often. Another reason I want to move back."

"Wow, a kid, huh?"

"Deal breaker for you?"

"No, I've just never dated a guy with a kid. Not that we're dating. This is a special circumstance. Or something."

"Or something. But we're going with it, right?"

"Definitely. I'm having fun."

The waitress arrived with their gumbo, and with

unspoken agreement they dug in. The gumbo was decent and minutes later both cups were empty.

Graham pushed his bowl to the side. "So tell me about you."

"Nothing special. Graduated from Carnegie-Mellon in industrial art design, work for my dad's company and live in a loft in the Warehouse district. I ride a bike to work most days and I do the *New York Times* crossword puzzle every Sunday even if it takes me until lunch. I don't have children, pets or a lactose intolerance. Big Italian family, no ties to mafia, though my brother likes to infer it."

"The priest?"

"No, the surgeon."

"Accomplished family," he murmured.

"Exactly what my father expects. I'm the baby of the family and the only girl. I have three older brothers who excel at their careers, but I'm the only one who followed in my father's footsteps."

"*Three* older brothers?" He feigned loosening his collar.

She laughed as the waitress set huge po'boys in front of them. "You don't have to worry. They're all my size and busy with families. I see them only at Sunday dinner. Now Granny B, she's the one you should worry about. She once accosted the mailman for being cheeky."

"Cheeky?"

"Yeah, had something to do with Publishers

Clearing House and apparently he didn't take Granny B seriously. The woman is a menace."

"But you love her," he said as she crossed herself and then dug into her meal.

"That's required, too," Tess joked, but the warmness in her eyes said differently.

He picked up the sandwich and took a bite. "Oh, mmm."

"Yeah," she agreed wiping cocktail sauce from the corner of her mouth. "I forgot how damn good these are."

Graham couldn't stop thinking about how good it felt to be home…to be with this cool chick. He really liked her casual openness along with the mystery. Tess was like a box his grandfather once had. On the outside simple, smooth lines but once the key turned, the inside held carvings of exquisite beauty.

And he really wanted to open her.

And do bad things to her.

The waitress delivered the check and they both reached for it.

Tess grabbed the small purse she'd hung on the back of the chair. "Let's split, okay?"

"I like to think of myself as a gentleman," he said, reaching for his wallet.

"How are you not a gentleman? Really, I feel more comfortable splitting the check."

"But next time I pay and we do this for real," he said, surprising himself with the offer. But why not? He'd get her number and when he next came to New Orleans—whether it was in a moving truck or merely to visit his family—he'd call her.

"Deal. Next time we dine, I'll wear an LBD and heels."

No clue what LBD was and his face must have given it away.

"Little black dress," she said.

"In the words of Ron, *meow*," he joked.

They smiled at each other, possibility hovering over them.

"Want to have a drink at the Carousel Bar?" she asked. "It's not far."

He thought about his rental car and wondered how safe it was. He'd thankfully purchased rental insurance—this was New Orleans, car theft capital of the South, after all. Then he looked at Tess's lips. She'd swiped them with lip gloss and he caught a whiff of strawberry or something similar. Yeah, he wouldn't mind dessert. "Sure. I'm not ready to go back to my hotel room."

Hotel room. That sort of sat between them.

This time Tess's smile held a secret…and a challenge. "So don't go back. Come with me instead."

CHAPTER THREE

TESS LOOPED HER PURSE STRAP over her shoulder and wondered if it was a good idea to extend the impromptu date. As the person in charge of scheduling the Mardi Gras float rotations, she had a 9:00 a.m. meeting with the art director of Bacchus regarding the 2016 theme. Plus she had to start on the proposal she'd promised Miles Barrow, the captain of Oedipus, too. But, even though Graham had a kid and felt not so much her normal type, she had this crazy, weird connection with him. She couldn't not go. "Let's roll."

They strolled out the door and down Decatur until they reached the street that would take them to the Monteleone Hotel and the infamous bar slowly spinning like a carousel. Through the windows she could see they weren't busy. Monday night wasn't ideal for partying in the Quarter, but New Orleans never felt deserted. The city still moved around them, lights flashing and the streetcar making a run down Canal.

They slid onto stools and ordered cocktails.

"I love this place," she said, turning to him and

trying to decide whether she wanted to take him home. It had been a long time since she had no-strings-attached fun with a hot guy.

"Yeah," he commented with a self-deprecating smile. "I'm glad we extended the date. Feels as though we're dancing around—"

"Hooking up?" She smiled, taking a sip of the drink sat before her.

"Is that's what the young kids call it?" His gaze lowered to her lips.

"Oh, please. You're gorgeous and single—don't even pretend you don't take a girl home now and again."

"Me?" He grinned, with a shake of his head. "I'm just a lowly computer-geek-turned-engineer. My idea of a hot night is *Dr. Who* and a pint of Ben and Jerry's."

"Geek?" She snorted, taking in his perfectly tailored suit and frat-boy tie. "Even if you qualified, don't pretend you haven't been thinking about getting into my jeans."

He jerked his gaze to hers. "Into your jeans? I've been thinking about how to get you out of your jeans."

She mocked a shocked expression.

Graham's eyes widened as if he might have gone too far. "I didn't mean to imply—"

Tess laughed before pressing one finger to his lips. "Please imply. I've been pretty much contemplating the same thing. You without that jacket, tie and no doubt plaid boxers."

"I'm wearing boxer briefs," he drawled, his eyes dipping again to her mouth.

"Goodie," she purred with a flirty smile. "I'm not used to hooking up with a guy when I'm this sober."

She hoped like hell he didn't think she was so capricious she'd screw any man who bought her a drink. She wasn't. She expected at least two drinks. Laughing at herself and the sudden case of nerves, she picked up her martini and took a gulp.

"Is this what we're doing? Hooking up?"

Tess glanced over at him. She didn't want to seem too eager. Heck, she still wasn't sure if hooking up with Graham was a good idea. It had only been at Christmas she'd dumped Nick. Maybe she needed to give herself some time…or maybe she needed to have a nice little rebound fling.

Or maybe this was neither of those two things. Maybe this was something more than just fun. Felt that way. Felt like magic. Felt like Graham was her perfect match. "Maybe."

Graham watched her, his Nordic eyes sliding down and dipping briefly at her neckline. "I've wanted you since you told me Feliz was pitching for the Rangers tonight. I think we'd be fantastic together."

Tess leaned toward him. "Wanna find out?"

His lips looked soft. She'd never thought such a thing about a man before, but at that moment she wanted to feel them on hers. Why not see if the tension between them was as electric as she suspected? Why waste time wondering what they could know in seconds?

Graham set down his drink and leaned close to her, pushing an errant strand of hair from the corner of her mouth. "You talking a little chemistry experiment?"

Her breath quickened and her eyes dropped to his mouth. "No sense in taking this any further if we're not…compatible."

Lightly he brushed her lips with his and she caught his taste. Yeasty and warm with beer. Her pulse sped at the first touch, and she leaned in for more.

But Graham was a tease.

He dotted little kisses along her jaw, making her stomach flutter with excitement.

"Oh," she breathed, the warmth spreading as he moved steadily back toward her mouth.

But then he decided to stop teasing and covered her mouth with his, sliding a hand around her neck to clasp the back of her head, tilting her so he could gain better access.

Like rain on the parched earth, Tess welcomed the onslaught of desire. She opened her mouth, only slightly, her tongue flitting out to taste him, evocative and flirty, but Graham tasted rich as expensive wine or fine chocolate. Addictive.

He responded to her invitation and hot desire

slammed into her like a midnight train eating up track when his fingers stroked the nape of her neck and his tongue stroked hers.

Tess didn't want to stop, but she did.

Because if she didn't stop now, she might not be able to. Because if she didn't stop now, she might straddle him right there on a stool in the Carousel Bar.

Wouldn't be the first time, but nothing had ever come of any guy she'd hooked up with randomly… and for some reason she didn't want Graham to go down as a guy she'd never meet again. She wanted to wear a little black dress and killer heels she didn't need but had to have because they made her legs look long and lean. She wanted moonlight and champagne…or at least a really good pinot grigio. She didn't want just a one-night stand with Graham.

And that surprised her.

Pulling back, she whispered, "I think I got my answer. You?"

"Oh, yeah. I'm definitely going to need your number." He touched a finger to her nose in a move that should have been corny but was anything but.

"So you want to walk me home?" Her voice was thick…almost seductive, so she cleared her throat.

"Some water," the bartender said, setting down two icy glasses in front of them. "So I ain't gotta call the fire department."

She picked up the glass and toasted the bartender

who winked at her before moving on to a guy waving a twenty on the other side.

"He has a point. We can't do that again without charging people admission," Graham said, looking as if the kiss had shaken him down to his wing tips. His smiled at her and picked up his water, a tinge of awe in those blue eyes.

And like a hit of smack, he made her suddenly crave more of him. She wanted to inhale him, taste every square inch and lose herself in something primal and good and irresponsible.

Maybe meeting Graham at Two Legs was a moment-in-time thing. What if there would never be a black dress, nice dinner and moonlight? What if Graham didn't get the job? Never walked back into her world again?

Would she regret the missed chance to immerse herself in him?

Yeah, she would. So...

"When are you leaving?" she asked.

He gulped down the ice water, his strong throat moving as he swallowed. She wanted to kiss him there. Where the pulse beat in his neck, right above the loosened tie. "Tomorrow morning."

Indecision.

She hated when she felt this way. Hot and fast? Or slow and...?

"You want another drink?" he asked, nodding toward her half-finished pomegranate martini.

"Not really."

"Oh," he said, sounding disappointed. Grabbing the hand she'd tucked in her lap, he cradled it. Stroking her inner wrist, he contemplated his empty glass. She could tell he didn't want the evening to end…and neither did she.

"Pay for the drinks, Graham," she said.

Hooking an eyebrow, Graham turned to her.

"Unless you don't want me to see you in those boxer briefs?"

Like magic, his wallet appeared. Tossing enough cash to cover the drinks and tip on the bar, he pulled her to her feet. "You sure?"

Tess slid her hand up his lapel, cupping his jaw and dropping a light kiss on his lips. "We're not going to overthink this."

He pulled her toward the door. "Cab?"

"My place isn't far. Let's walk."

"Or run." He spun her into his arms, pressing her against the rough brick, not caring a homeless man slept in the alcove a few yards away.

Tess tugged his head down, her mouth eagerly meeting his. This time she wasn't stingy with opening her mouth and it inflamed her even more. He pressed himself against her, sliding his hands down to her hips in order to pull her against his erection. Warmth turned to frenzied fire.

"Oh," she breathed, her hands knotting in his short wavy hair. "Maybe we better hurry."

He smiled against her.

"Yeah, y'all should," the old bum squawked. "Unless you want a little company."

"No, thanks," Graham called, wrapping an arm around Tess and pulling a five out of his pocket and dropping it in the man's tipped-up hat. "Something for you, sir."

"Not as good as what you're about to get, brother," the man cracked.

"True," Graham called out over his shoulder, not slowing up as they crossed Canal Street. Several blocks later she pulled her keys from her purse, struggling to keep her hands from shaking. Right before she pushed through the front entrance of the building, Graham caught her elbow. "You sure?"

She looked up, surprised he'd try to stop now. "You trying to talk me out of having hot, uncontrollable, slightly dirty sex with you?"

He swallowed, his teeth flashing in the darkness. "That's what's on the menu?"

"It'll be better than the stuffed mushrooms you turned down. I promise." She held the door open with no regret.

"I like your confidence."

GRAHAM ROLLED OVER and glanced at Tess asleep in the moonlight. Long lashes lay against her upper cheeks. The smattering of freckles were more pronounced against her luminous skin. Wild locks of dark gold mixed with light brown caught in the light. She looked so innocent.

And not so much like the hellcat who had pinned him down, taken control and brought him the most excruciatingly pleasurable orgasm he'd ever experienced.

And it wasn't just the skill Tess possessed in bed, it was the passion she plied it with. She'd taken his breath away as she made love to him with both reckless abandon and deliberate focus. Her girl-next-door vibe hid a consummate lover.

Thank God he'd invited her to dinner.

She'd fit him perfectly. The projections and reliefs of her body meeting his in such a way he'd felt like a jigsaw puzzle finally completed. Sounded hokey, but he felt that way. He'd never met someone like Tess—a woman he'd had an immediate connection with. Walking into her world felt like a fate thing.

"Mmm," she groaned snuggling against his body, her lovely breasts brushing his chest as she wound an arm around his lower stomach. "That was *soooo* good."

"Beyond good," he said, pushing a hank of hair from her face.

She opened those gorgeous eyes and blinked sleepily up at him. "I fell asleep. Sorry."

"Why?" he whispered, sliding a hand down to cup her bottom. She arched against him, sliding a leg over his, fitting herself to him and giving him better access.

"I don't want to sleep tonight. I want to make love all night. That was an appetizer. Remember?"

"Right." He pulled her atop him, sighing as she allowed her legs to fall to either side of his hips. With her breasts plumped against his chest and her smiling eyes studying him, he almost believed he could fall in love with a woman in less than twenty-four hours.

Lifting his hips, he teased her with his stirring erection. "Ah, Tess, you might kill me tonight."

"Then we'll die happy." She lowered her mouth to his, dropping tiny kisses against his lips. "I don't want morning to come. Let me have these hours."

He cupped her ass and moved her against him. He wanted to be inside her again. But not yet. Not until he tasted every inch of her. Not until he made her shudder and arch against him. Not until she screamed his name, grabbed the sheets and lost every ounce of sanity she possessed.

He might be a geeky engineer, but he was a determined geeky engineer who prided himself on his attention to detail…and he was about to get it so right with Tess.

Flipping her, he pulled himself back, staring at her in the faint light before dropping his head and tugging her nipple into his mouth. He glanced up as she sighed and closed her eyes. Minutes later after making her writhe beneath him, he slid down her soft belly. "Your appetizer was good, baby."

Her only response was a moan. Graham ducked

his head and rained kisses around her belly button. "But I'm hungry for dessert."

"Oh, sweet—" Tess arched against him as he slid lower.

"You taste so good," he murmured, his hands lifting her hips.

Tess's hands slid to his hair, fisting in the depths. "Graham."

He sighed as he lowered his head and dropped kisses along her hip bone. "I'm so glad I walked into that bar and saw you. It's like getting the sweetest of gifts, Tess."

"Oh, Graham," she begged, wiggling her hips. "Please—"

And so he gave her what she wanted.

By THE TIME Tess slid from her bed, she'd managed a good hour or two of sleep and that was it. She'd be toast for her meeting, but she had no regrets.

All night, she and Graham had laughed, dreamed and made love on those new sheets, and it had been the most wonderful night of her life.

Seriously.

She'd had lovers—ever since she'd let Justin Hogue go all the way with her the night of her senior prom—but she'd never had one like Graham. She couldn't believe how good they'd been together. Everything he did felt ten times more incredible than with any other guy. Tess had hit the jackpot with the unlikeliest of guys, and it felt a little surreal…and maybe a little scary. Sex had never been so mind-blowing before.

She glanced at the suit folded on the funky polka-dot chair that matched her apple-green duvet and smiled. Buttoned-up, wing-tip boy. Who'd have thought?

Joy bubbled inside her as she walked naked into the bathroom and turned the knobs in the shower. Waiting for the water to heat, she glanced back and found Graham still asleep, sprawled on his stomach, the sheet barely covering his splendid backside.

She stepped into the marbled shower stall and sighed as the hot water coursed down her body. Minutes later she felt two arms slip around her.

"Got room for me?" he murmured in her ear, causing goose bumps to shiver down her length.

She turned, wrapping her arms around his neck and grinning at him as he brought her body against his. "Always."

"You'll change your tune when I use all your hot water."

"I have a tankless hot water heater. I don't run out." She rocked her hips against his.

"Oh, my naughty Tess. We could have some fun in here, huh?"

Wiggling her eyebrows, Tess turned and handed him the loofah. "Do my back?"

"As long as I can also do your front."

Tess sighed and the shower that normally took her ten minutes stretched into twenty-five.

Finally, wrapped in a fluffy robe, Tess stood cradling a steaming mug of coffee in her kitchen. Graham walked in, towel tucked around his waist.

"When do you leave?" she asked, pulling a carton of eggs from the depths of her mostly empty fridge. If she had some onion and spinach, she could make an omelet. But, alas, only a few cartons of yogurt and a pint of creamer.

"As soon as I take a cab back to my car."

"Don't bother with a cab. Since I have a meeting with a client today, I'm not taking my bike. I can drop you off."

He smiled and something in her chest grew warm. "Damn, I thought I would ride on your handle bars, but I guess since I have to wear my suit…"

"Handle bars? I totally have a basket you could sit in," she joked.

"Hope it's still there."

"The suit or the car?" she said, grabbing a pan from the dish rack.

"Both," he said, sliding his arms around her and dropping a kiss on her ear. "Is it going to sound totally crazy to say this was the best night I've had in forever?"

She leaned back into him. "No. I feel like we've known each other for longer than a day. It's strange, but I'm loving it."

"Yeah, I'm loving it, too. This feels right. I can't wait to come back to New Orleans. I can't wait to take you out in that black dress and then bring you back here and take it off."

Tess set the eggs and pan on the stove and turned in his arms, lifting on her toes so she could kiss him. "I can't wait for you to come back, either."

Kissing her thoroughly, Graham smiled at her, his blue eyes full with something deeper than she expected. "I'm going to get the job, and then we're going to celebrate. This is a fate thing. I can feel it in my bones."

"You think so?" Tess searched his eyes, afraid they were going too fast. After all, though she knew every inch of his body, she didn't know much else about him. There was no room for talk of something serious, right? Just because they'd fit together so well, just because he'd made her heart gallop, her body sing and her soul shine brighter, didn't mean they were moving toward the *L* word.

No. Tess couldn't allow herself to go over the cliff after one night with a man. That was movie crap. Not real life.

But when she looked at Graham, she could almost believe in love at first sight.

"I know so," he said, kissing her again, taking away any doubts she had about a guy walking into a bar and tying a girl up in ribbons of fate.

Tess pulled herself away and jogged to the bar between the kitchen and living area. Picking up her phone, she handed it to him. "Here. Put your info into my phone. Where's yours? I'll put in mine."

They tapped the info into each other's phones. He handed Tess her phone and she set it on the bar and directed him to the table. "I'm not the greatest of chefs but I can manage eggs and toast. Then I have to run. I need to go by my office before my meeting at nine o'clock."

"That's fine. I need to get going, too. I'm stopping by Emily's school and I need to hit Houston before rush hour. And you never told me where you work. Is it—"

The harsh shriek of the teakettle going off interrupted him. Tess turned around and snatched it off the burner, accidently touching the hot kettle to her wrist.

"Ow!" She set the kettle on another burner and ran some cold water over her arm. Total klutz…or maybe she was nervous about talking about taking whatever this was to another level…or maybe she was scared it was all too good to be true.

"Let me get ice," he said, scrambling to the freezer.

Thirty minutes and two pieces of burnt toast later, Tess stood outside her apartment dressed in her best go-to-meeting business dress that happened to match the deep pink burn on her wrist. Graham wore his suit, tie stuffed in pocket, shirt open at the neck. His tousled dark hair made him look exactly what he was—a businessman who'd gotten lucky…and not much sleep.

To Tess he looked terrific.

They kissed, a slow, sweet kiss laden with good-bye and tinged with possibility.

"I'll call you soon," he said.

"Good," she said, running a hand along his jaw. "I'll be waiting."

CHAPTER FOUR

A month later

FRANK ULLO SHOVED the lab report from his oncologist's office into the top drawer and spun his
chair toward the bulletin boards. Pinned up were
various sketches of Mardi Gras floats dated from
1967 to present. Elaborate plans cobbled together
into breathtaking beauty. His life's work sprawled
across a wall—a reminder of what he'd built and
sustained…and what he was about to hand over to
the man sitting on the other side of his desk.

Doubt fluttered in his gut before he centered
himself. He had to keep emotion out of this decision. Had to remember what he did now was for
the best…even if it was a bit chickenshit of him.

Then he touched the photo on his desk as he often
did. A tap for luck. In the silver frame smiled three
dark-headed teenaged boys and a fierce little girl
who snarled at the camera. Frank cherished this particular picture of his other life's work: his children.
Each boy stared back at him, intelligent, smirking
with their father's Italian temperament. Their chins
jutted out with their mother's Irish stubbornness.

And centered in the middle was Therese, his Tess.

His hellion with dark blond hair and eyes blazing a path to the heart. A difficult child, Tess challenged everyone around her as much as she blessed them with her warmth. The girl never took no for an answer and wrapped her older brothers around her proverbial pinky. Tess was never a princess…more like a bruiser in soccer cleats with a crooked hair bow and bandages on her knees. Tess—his sunshine girl with an unceasing passion for all she did.

And he felt very, very sure she would hate his guts for what he was about to do.

He tapped the photo again, making sure it faced him. Then picking up the phone, he dialed Billie. "Hey, ring Therese. I need to talk to her."

Billie gave him her usual monotone. "Whatever you want, Boss."

Frank pressed his hands against the ink blotter and looked across his desk at Graham Naquin, the man he'd hired to become the next chief executive officer of Frank Ullo Float Builders. "This ain't gonna be easy. My vice president of operations don't know about this."

Graham folded his hands across his stomach and squared his chin. He was maybe too handsome for this job, too slick and together. Doubt nickered at Frank, but he squashed it.

"It's never easy for employees to accept change," Graham said. "My coming on board will take some adjustment but I'm determined this will work. I'm a good fit."

"You are. But this employee's a little different because she's my daughter."

Mr. Spit and Polish actually grew green around the gills. "Your daughter—who is the VP of Operations—doesn't know you're hiring me to run the company? Don't you think you should have told her before you hired me?"

Frank didn't like to be questioned, but Graham wasn't altogether wrong in his comment. "Yeah, but I got my reasons. She ain't ready to run a company. I'm not saying she's deadweight or anything. She's good at her job, but she don't have the head for making tough decisions. And let's face it, we still live in a man's world."

Graham's eyes widened and he got kinda choky-looking. Briefly Frank wondered, yet again, if he'd missed the boat on the whole equality thing.

"I'm not sure I feel comfortable with this situation, Frank. You should have been up front about her earlier. I'd rather not start the job with animosity in the workplace. Transparency is always best in business dealings."

Frank shrugged. He couldn't just say "I have cancer and I'm trying to protect my daughter." But that was his main reason. Wasn't like he wanted to hand over the reins of his company to anyone, but in a few days he'd have a stent placed in his ducts to alleviate the jaundice he'd been suffering. Then he'd start weekly chemo treatments to help shrink the tumor and prevent further metastasizing, and that would make him feel like shit. He'd have to rest and stay away from people who could make him sick. The least he could do for his employees and family was to leave the company in capable hands…and Graham Naquin seemed almost too good to be true.

The kid had graduated in mechanical engineering and then started a float company with two others—Upstart thrived and was currently the biggest thorn in Frank's side. Graham could take Frank's company on his broad shoulders and free him from the day-to-day minutiae. And hopefully, the energetic engineer holding a new MBA could revitalize a business mired in its own success.

Frank didn't want to place that burden on his Tess. She already thought she could handle more than she actually could. "I wasn't trying to dupe you, if that's what you're implying. Things are delicate, you see."

"I think there is a lot you're not telling me, Frank, and that worries me. If there is something I need to be aware of, you need to be forthcoming about it. Don't set me up for failure, especially with your family."

"The only one of my children who works here is Therese, and she's a good girl even if she is headstrong. She's young, you know? But family is more important to her than ruffled feathers. Give her a day or two and she'll see she's not prepared to deal with the business end of this company. Her head's in her art, designing the floats and dazzling the krewes. We all have our talents, right?"

Graham pressed his hands down his thighs, smoothing his trousers, and then refolded them in his lap. Nervous for a man who exuded extreme capability. But Frank would give him being a little nervous. Frank had known this would be hard.

A knock sounded at his office door and Tess stuck her head in. "Hey, you wanted to see me?"

"Come on in, honey," Frank said, motioning her into the room. She wore her customary jeans and T-shirt and a flash of guilt struck at not making the meeting more official, at not giving Tess a chance to get her professional game face on. Another mistake he'd weather.

Graham's eyebrows drew together and he spun around as Tess stepped inside. Frank saw his body go rigid. "Tess?"

Tess's eyes widened and her mouth gaped for a second. "Graham?"

For several seconds they stared at one another in shock.

"Wait, you know each other?" Frank hadn't considered Tess might know the young man he'd chosen to run their family business. Graham had lived in Houston for the past six years, but since the man had grown up in New Orleans, it wasn't impossible. But this seemed more than casual.

Tess ignored his question and closed the door before advancing toward his desk, her gaze crackling. "What are you doing in my father's office?"

Graham stood. "You're Therese?"

"I prefer Tess." She crossed her arms and shot a look from her father to Graham, "Yeah. So back to the original question—what are you doing here? I assumed you didn't—" And then her mouth snapped shut as something altogether different flitted through her gaze. In that moment, Frank realized however his daughter knew Graham, it hadn't ended well. Which meant this situation wasn't going to be slightly uncomfortable. Nope, it was atomic-wedgie uncomfortable.

"I—" Graham made another choked face and shook his head. "You never told me your last name. You put, uh, Two-Legged Tess in my phone."

"Thought it was cute and memorable. Big fail, huh?" she said, voice like poison darts. Even Frank wanted to duck.

He cleared his throat. "Two-legged Tess? What the hell are you two talking about?"

Graham sat like he'd been hit by bad news. "I met your daughter at the bar you recommended to me after the interview. Two-Legged Pete's."

"Wait a sec, *you* told him about Pete's?" Tess asked, her eyes narrowing as something in her head started clicking. Her voice faded as she murmured, "At a job interview."

Her head whipped around, her arms dropped, fists at her sides as she faced the new CEO. "You had a job interview with my dad. A job interview for what?"

Graham sank in the leather chair. Or was it cowered? "Christ, this is crazy. How are you Frank Ullo's daughter?"

"Why are you interviewing for a position I don't know about?"

Both of them directed their gaze toward Frank.

"Okay, okay. Tess, have a seat," he said, gesturing to the chair beside Graham.

"I think I'll stand." She crossed her arms, her chin jutting out. "I don't want to sit for what you're about to tell me because obviously I'm the last to know about what's going down at our *family* company."

"This is exactly the reason I had to make this decision."

Her eyes glittered like icy, cold emeralds that reminded him of his wife Maggie's when she was pissed. "What decision?"

"If you'd sit, I'd tell you. But as usual you're acting like your mother," Frank said, annoyed a simple announcement and introduction could get bogged down in drama before he'd said his piece. But what had he expected from Tess? *Reasonable* wasn't her middle name.

"If it means that much to you, fine." Tess sat. "So what's the deal, Dad?"

"The deal is a change that's been forthcoming here."

"Really?" she said at a near growl. Graham averted his gaze to the sketches on the wall.

"You know I've been talking about retirement in the past several weeks. Now's the time. I wanna pull back and enjoy life with your mother before I cash in my ticket."

Tess said nothing…just stared at him. Frank nearly shifted in his chair, but refrained because he was a man, damn it. He didn't shrink under the disdain of any woman…much less his youngest child who hadn't even reached age thirty yet. Hell, she was still a kid.

"And?" she asked.

"I hired a headhunting company to look for someone who could—"

"You hired a headhunting company?" Tess arched one eyebrow. Frank felt the steam coming off her. She had never been laid-back, but she had a good temperament on most days. Everyone at Ullo liked her. She got what she wanted, but it was because she always leaned on people rather than pushed them. Honeyed words and all that. Still, when crossed, her Irish-Italian temper simmered out of control.

"That's what I said, Therese. These guys go out and find—"

"I *know* what they do. You should have inferred my question to mean *why* not *who*."

Frank had to think about that because he hadn't had a fancy liberal arts education—he'd been raised on the streets and got his business smarts from what had always worked for him. "I hired a headhunter because I can't leave the company with no one to look after it. You need help and your brothers have their own careers."

Tess slapped her hands together. "Perfect. I see where this is going now. You want a *man* to run the company instead of trusting your own flesh and blood. You're just that egotistical and misogynist."

"I don't know those words, but if you think this is because of what you ain't got between your legs, you're wrong." Leave it to Tess to think this was about gender. Okay, maybe ten percent of his reasoning had to do with her being a woman. He wanted Tess to find love, settle down, have some babies—something hard to do running a company like Frank Ullo. But mostly this was about protecting her. She couldn't shoulder the entire burden of this place alone.

Tess had amazing talent and a keen intellect, but she possessed very little business acumen. For the past seven years, ever since she'd graduated and come to work for him, they'd done wonderful things together. Tess had found better materials for their floats, and her clever design work had krewes lining up, willing to pay big bucks for Ullo to design their floats. Frank had handled the business end and thus far it had worked like a well-oiled engine. He didn't see any reason to change things. She had to understand that. "This is about doing what's best for our company."

"How can you say that?" she asked in a small voice. It was as if the anger had dissipated, leaving a shaken shell in its place. Somehow this was worse. Anger he could handle. Hurt? Not so much.

"This ain't personal, baby," he said, leaning forward, keenly aware the PET scan report he'd received from the doctor a week ago sat in the drawer beneath the blotter. It pulsed into his psyche, reminding him how little time he had to settle things…how little time he had to insure his family stayed healthy, wealthy and stable.

"Wrong. It's extremely personal." Tess stared at the family crest ring he'd given her for her college graduation. "More than you even know."

Graham had very wisely stayed out of the fray, but now he looked at Frank, something wavering in his eyes. Briefly, Frank wondered what he didn't know about Graham Naquin…and what the man had meant to his daughter.

"I shouldn't be here for this conversation, Frank," Graham said.

"Of course you should. You're going to be working with Tess. Better to clear the air and get us all on firm ground."

"No, he's right. This is between you and me,"

Tess said, her voice low. "This is about you not trusting me."

Frank shook his head. "You're being dramatic, Tess. This is—"

"No. You hid this from me because you knew what would happen. Don't act as if you didn't know I'd be upset. You created the drama, Frank."

Frank snapped his fingers. "Don't call me Frank. And this does concern Graham. He'll be working with you."

"As what?"

Frank shrugged, almost too scared to say the words. "Technically, he'll be the chief executive officer. Your job will remain the same. He'll need you to help him—"

"No." Tess slammed her hand on his desk. "I don't accept this."

Frank narrowed his eyes. "You don't have a say."

"The hell I don't. I've worked here all my life. In case you've forgotten, my last name is Ullo. You're skipping over me, your daughter, to hire someone else. I don't accept that."

"This is *my* company. Not yours."

Tess reeled back as if he'd slapped her.

Graham shifted in his chair. "I'm stepping outside."

"Yes, go." Tess jabbed a finger at the door.

Graham ignored her and looked at him. In his eyes, Frank saw frustration and something else that looked like regret. "I'll take a walk and return in half an hour."

"Take a walk off the pier, why don't you?" Tess said, before turning a frosty gaze to her father. No more defeated Tess. This was his pissed-off sunshine girl who had scored the winning goal in the state soccer finals. She didn't know the words *give up*.

Graham didn't take the bait. He merely shook his head and walked out.

The door snicked closed and Tess put her hands over her face. "Why are you doing this, Dad? I've been working so hard to earn... I thought you wanted me in this company. I thought it was understood that I would take over when you retired."

"There are things you don't understand, honey," he said, softening his tone.

"So why didn't you come to me and discuss the issues you had? Instead of doing that, you went behind my back. In fact, you interviewed him on the day I took Granny B to the doctor so you could hide it. I suppose you swore Billie to silence, too?"

"Billie doesn't know everything that goes on in this company."

"Ha." Tess sank back into the chair. "Well, the solution to all this is simple—tell Graham you were wrong. Tell him thanks, but no thanks. I'm totally prepared to run Frank Ullo Float Builders, and you can do a step-down retirement over the next several months. This is what I've been preparing for over the past seven years—an Ullo running *our* company. I'm going to pretend like you didn't say the company belongs to you."

"But it does."

"Technically, but it's ours. Our family's."

"I'm not firing Graham. He signed the contracts this morning."

Her gaze went feral. "What I say doesn't matter?"

Frank closed his eyes. *Knowing* that telling Tess would be hard was way different from actually doing it. He hadn't told his children about his pancreatic cancer diagnosis, except for his son Joseph who'd been his consult during the whole process. Frank still wanted to talk to Maggie about how to handle telling them. Hell, he still hadn't come to terms with the thought of not making it to next Christmas.

But he wouldn't use his illness to make Tess relent. He knew he wasn't the best father in the world, but he'd never resorted to manipulation with his children. He ignored the small voice that said he'd tricked Tess to get his way in the first place. "You matter to me more than you know, but in this instance I will stand firm. You're not ready to run the company. Plain and simple."

"But why? If you knew you were going to retire this soon, you should have brought me in and prepared me. You should have taught me what you do. None of this makes sense. You were always so

proud I followed in your footsteps. I just thought…"
Tess covered her face again with her hands.

For a few moments neither of them said anything.

"I'm not staying if you hire him." Tess dropped
her hands, her gaze resolute.

"So you'll quit?" Frank had never even contemplated the possibility his daughter would leave if
he didn't give her the wheel. "Like a child taking
her toys and going home, huh?"

"No. I'm not being unreasonable in leaving a
place where I have little respect."

"You know that's not true."

"Doesn't feel like it, Dad." Tess swallowed hard.
"I refuse to remain where there is no future for me."

"Tess, there's always a place for you here. This
is your home, your family."

"No. This isn't how family feels. Instead it feels
like I don't matter at all. Feels like you gave me
some shell of a job to keep me in New Orleans, to
keep me under your control."

Now Frank felt as if he'd been slapped. "You love
what you do."

"Yeah, I do. I love this company, but I'm not staying while you wrap it in a bow and give it to some
jerk a headhunter found for you. Really, Dad? It's
like a frickin' nightmare, that's what this is." She
rose. "But that's the way it's going to be. As you
pointed out, this is your company and you can do
what you want with it, but you might as well have
disowned me."

"Don't be unreasonable, Tess."

"Call it what you want, but I don't work here any longer."

"Tess," he said her name like a prayer. Never had he wanted to hurt her. Why couldn't she see that?

Because she didn't know his reasons. She didn't know he had one foot in the grave and the other in quicksand.

"Consider this my notice. I'll finish out the day and gather my stuff."

"Don't do this. You're in the middle of designing for Bacchus and we've got props in bay that need your direction. What about the meetings you have this week? What about our customers?"

Tess shook her head. "Dave will see the designs through, and you now have Graham to figure out the rest."

Like a soldier, his daughter squared her shoulders and marched to the door.

"Tess, don't do this. Everything will be the same as yesterday. I promise. Graham is a good man."

She paused, her hand on the doorknob. "You're wrong, Dad. It'll never be the same again because you don't trust me. Good luck with Graham. In my experience he's not so much a man of his word."

She gave him a sad, sad smile. And then she walked out.

CHAPTER FIVE

TESS STALKED OUT of her father's office feeling like she'd entered a boxing ring with a world champion. One punch and she was out. Her mind couldn't wrap around what had happened moments ago.

How had her Tuesday gone so wrong?

It had started well with new bodywash in her shower, a good coffee from Cuppa Joe's and the sun on her shoulders as she biked through the awakening French Quarter. Fog had burned off the river by the time she'd reached the warehouse, and every line on her sketches that morning had been true. It had been a banner morning that had turned to hell in the blink of an eye.

Graham Naquin.

Bastard. Usurper.

The irony of the man she'd thought her forever guy being the person taking the helm of Ullo was like someone shoving a spoonful of crap into her mouth and expecting her to say "mmm." But this was one spoonful she wasn't going to swallow.

How dare her old man hire him? *Him.* The very person who had almost broken her heart. Okay.

Had broken her heart. Which sounded strange since she'd known him for such a brief time, yet for a while it had felt every bit as real as what her parents had.

She'd eaten a lot of ice cream trying to get over the false start with Graham. In fact, she'd wolfed down a half gallon in twenty-four hours. That's how much cream and sugar she'd needed to soothe the hurt of rejection.

And now this. She would have to run to California to work off what was likely about to be spooned down in mourning of the thing she loved most about each day—her job.

Dear God, she was no longer employed at Ullo.

As Tess pushed through the metal door into the stairwell, her knees gave way. Sinking against the cold cement steps, she struggled for a breath.

This wasn't happening.

No way.

She was an Ullo. She'd grown up skipping through the phantom floats hulking like huge freighters bobbing at a wharf. Tess had worked summers perfecting sculpting foam, schlepping papier-mâché onto props and wiring fiber optics. She'd taken extensive art lessons, chosen a major in industrial art and ignored the tryouts for the Junior U.S. Soccer team…all so she could work for her family's business. All because she wanted to be the one child who pleased their father by caring more for Frank Ullo Float Builders than for herself. She'd sacrificed so she could do what was right, what would be best for their family business.

And it had been for nothing.

Unshed tears gathered in her throat. She wanted to cry, wanted to lie down right in the dusty stairwell and sob until she ran dry. But she wouldn't give the world the satisfaction of knowing her disappointment. Of the betrayal.

Her father didn't think she was good enough.

"Damn it," she whispered into the air around her.

"Tess." The door opened with a whoosh, nearly nailing her in the shoulder. Billie's head popped into the stairwell.

"Hey," Tess managed to say, hoping like hell the tears in her eyes weren't noticeable.

"What in the name of Sam Hill is going on?" Billie asked, darting a look at the inner recess of her office. "Your father said you quit."

"I did."

"Why?" Billie looked like someone had run over her cat.

"Ask my father."

"Don't you think I did? He buttoned up his lip like a preacher in a whorehouse. Said you no longer wanted to work here and to send a note to Accounting so you could collect your last check. Sister, what's going on?"

"Nothing you need to worry about, Billie. This is between my father and me."

"It has to do with that good-looking guy Frank

hired, doesn't it? I knew something was going on when your dad got all secretive, wanting me to show him how to use the fax machine and getting all those calls from Texas."

Tess pulled herself from where she slumped. "Yeah, you're about to be working for that good-looking guy." The words hung in her throat. She didn't want to think about Graham Naquin. She'd spent far too much time thinking about the son of a bitch already. She'd just stopped longing for him. Or mostly stopped moping around waiting for his call.

"Huh?"

"Dad's retiring. Might as well be the first to tell you."

"Retiring? No. He hasn't even made a peep about—"

"Well, he is. Soon."

"I had no idea." Billie's face crinkled as she soaked in the ramifications. "So Frank basically hired this guy over you? His own daughter?"

"You're a sharp cookie." Tess gave Billie a half smile that hurt like hell to deliver.

"Smart cookie. Not sharp," Billie muttered, sadness etched on her face. "I can't believe this, Tess. I'm sure he has a good reason. Something's wrong. I've had this weird feeling. He's been saying strange things, and I wondered what was up. But this?"

"Not a good enough reason. I don't know what's

going on, but I'm not about to watch him give Frank
Ullo to some asshole."

"He seemed okay to me. Together, polite, nice
ass."

"Yeah, well, he's an ass all right. Good luck,"
Tess said, giving Billie a quick squeeze. Billie had
been with her father for forty years so Tess couldn't
fathom the woman not knowing about Graham Naquin, the interview and Frank's plans. That her father had kept them from his most trusted assistant
boggled the mind. "I'll see you around, 'kay?"

"How? You won't be here. What am I going
to do without my Tess? Who's going to make
chocolate-oatmeal cookies and post pics of delicious
man candy in the ladies' room? How are we going
to function without you?" Billie wouldn't let go.

"Just like you did before I worked here."

"Don't do it, honey. It's your pride standing in
the way. Pride's a tricky thing." Billie pulled back
and looked at her with eyes the color of chocolate
chips. She had always reminded Tess of the teapot
in *Beauty and the Beast*—if it had a wry sense of
humor, a dirty mouth and a way with advice. Billie always seemed to know what to do—but not
this time.

This time Tess wouldn't be cajoled into accepting her father's decision. She was many things, but
she wasn't a blinking jackass. Her father had gotten
his point across with bloody accuracy. He had no
faith in Tess, therefore Tess had her back against the

wall. It was either give in and hate herself, or quit, get a new job…and gather together the remains of who she was.

"I have to do this, Billie. I'm good. I have to prove that. Not only to Dad, but to myself. I don't need Frank Ullo. Frank Ullo needs me."

"Of course we need you. You know that. Don't go, Tess. Work through this. Change is always hard, but when you come through on the other side, you see it's for the best."

"Hiring someone else is not for the best, Billie. Change or no change. Dad chose a stranger over me, and I got the message loud and clear."

Billie shook her head. "Oh, honey."

Tess jogged down the stairs, heading toward her desk which sat with several others in a sectioned-off area of the warehouse. Tess liked to be near the action—the place where the ideas on paper became full-fledged art ready to roll down the parade route carrying the krewes and the thousands of throws revelers begged for. She'd loved the nook she'd carved out, and though the warehouse often grew noisy, she enjoyed feeling like a cog in the machinery that created magic for millions of people during the four-week Mardi Gras season. She focused better in an area she could move around, a place where she could see her visions carried out.

"Hey, Tess," Dave Wegmann said, spinning in his chair, scratching his balding head. "Reeves Benson called about the Hera bid and wants you to call him back. Thought I'd sneak down here and take a peek at what Petra did with the globe."

"He left a message with you?" Tess asked, trying like hell to pretend today was any other day. No way would she break down in front of Dave. He'd been here for as long as she remembered, first as a sculptor, then he'd moved to painting. After two back surgeries, he'd taken design courses and started working as the art director. Tess had learned all she knew about float building at Dave's knee, and when she'd come to the company, they'd split the load of design, meeting regularly to schedule work and solidify the vision for each krewe's contracted floats.

"Your phone kept ringing and it was driving me crazy. I'm also looking for the specs on the Cleopatra sea creature. Upstart's trying to schmooze Cary Presley with some crazy hydra with motorized heads, so this float's gotta be stellar."

Any other time and Tess would agree, but she could hardly speak, much less bolster Dave on the Cleopatra bid. She sank into the squeaky chair beside the one Dave sat in and looked at the files and sketches scattering the surface of her desk.

Where to even start?

"Tess? You okay? You look weird."

"Yeah."

Dave shook his head and hunkered down, his fingers moving deftly over the face of the calculator, his eyes screwed up in concentration. "Okay, I found the file. Just…wanna…see…if…this…matches."

She probably needed to get a box to put her stuff in. She had funny pictures tacked up on the corkboard beside the huge filing cabinets that held all the past year's designs and sketches. Those designs would be systematically replaced over the course of the next few months with new designs for 2015, paying special attention to the repurposing of all the props. At Ullo they reused every part of the float, even joking about trading out toilet seats yearly. They begged, bartered and stole from last year's floats to create the awesomeness of Mardi Gras 2014 for the various krewes around New Orleans and the outlying areas. A flurry of meetings nearly a month ago before this year's parades had finished rolling had cemented projects for the upcoming season and those of 2016.

Tess picked up the bumblebee with the crazy boppy antennae Jules Roland, the head sculptor, had given her on her birthday. Tess the busy bee.

The clip of hard soles on the concrete floor interrupted her thoughts. Then she saw the wing tips.

"Tess?"

She looked up, meeting Graham's blue eyes. Damn, they were pretty eyes. Too bad he was a creep.

"What?"

He swallowed and she watched the powerful muscles in his throat convulse. She'd kissed that sweet spot at the base of his neck. He'd smelled so good—sort of citrusy and clean—and he'd tasted salty and warm. Very solid. Very sexy.

"We need to talk."

Dave looked up, tucking his pencil behind his ear. He raised bushy eyebrows. "What's going on? Who's this guy?"

Tess glanced over at her friend and mentor. "You'll understand soon enough, Dave. But don't worry. I've got this."

She stood. "I don't have much to say to you, Mr. Naquin, but what I do have will be better said in private." Ice hung in her words…. Exactly what she intended. Part of her boiled over with anger, hurt and disappointment. The other part felt frigid and empty.

Graham had caused that particular arctic front when he'd never called…and then hadn't been man enough to return the call she'd made two weeks ago.

Total asshole.

She stalked toward the exit, wishing she hadn't worn jeans and sneakers. High heels tapping on the floor would have been much more dramatic. Pushing the bar that would lead to the smokers' lounge high above the rough waters of the Mississippi, Tess inhaled not smoke, but the brackish, fetid air of the river. No one sat on the porch, but she didn't want to be interrupted, so she quickly took the worn steps down to the deck several feet below, now glad she'd worn her tennis shoes.

Reaching the smaller landing holding an ancient picnic table and two chained deck chairs, she spun around. "You bastard."

Graham stopped by the last step, shifting his gaze toward a tugboat pushing a colossal rusted barge. "I deserve that."

"Yeah, you do."

"I didn't call you."

His words were a day late and a dollar short. Didn't matter anymore. She'd decided twenty minutes ago when she'd seen him sitting in her father's office as the heir apparent she was way over the infatuation that had dominated her thoughts and body for weeks after he left her loft. That ship had sailed. Bye-bye.

"You think this is about you not calling?"

"It was rude."

"It *was* pretty rude. But what did you think I wanted? Commitment? You were a fun screw, that's it. So, no, this isn't about you not calling."

Something in his eyes wavered and she could tell he hadn't expected such a casual dismissal. "A fun screw, huh?"

"For you, too, I imagine. If it were anything more you would have called me, right?" She lifted an eyebrow, feeling the righteousness in her anger.

"About that. See, there were some things going on…." He looked away, hiding from her, but she didn't care. She meant what she said—what she felt—Graham meant nothing to her on that level. He was a used-to-be.

But on a professional level…

"What I have to say to you has nothing to do with that night a month ago. That's over. This is the here and now, and you are the bastard who slinked into my company and stole my job."

"Now, wait a minute." He held up a hand. His was a nice hand—manicured nails, strong blunt fingers, wide palm. Very capable hands that had stroked her, loved her and made her believe in something that wasn't real. "I didn't slink into anything. In fact, your father never even mentioned you. I had no idea until today that he had a daughter who worked in the company."

Knife wound. Tess clasped her chest before she could think better of betraying her emotions.

Her father hadn't even mentioned her?

"What do you want me to say? Did he mention Dave? Or how about Petra? Jules? Red Jack? Bennie B? Or Scooter O'Neil?"

"No, he went over the departments, but never said he had a daughter who headed up operations. You know I didn't sneak in here trying to steal anything from you. You can be pissed, but you have to be fair."

Jabbing a finger at him, Tess said, "I don't have to be anything. Don't tell me what to do."

Graham slid his hands into his pockets, making his shoulders beneath the poplin dress shirt look amazingly broad. Yeah, she hurt, but she hadn't failed to notice his masculine charms, which pissed her off all over again. "Fine."

For a few seconds they stood, defensive and wary.

Tess sighed. "What do you expect me to say?"

"Nothing. I don't know. It's a hard situation, but right now I don't feel I can take the job." He looked almost like a dog trying to nose the bone her way after he'd already gnawed off the fattest parts.

"Oh, please. Who passes up a job like this?" she said, trying not to hiss at him.

God, please tell me he's not that stupid. Please tell me this isn't some capricious acceptance of a job. She couldn't handle it if he treated it like it was no big deal.

Graham shrugged. "Everything's pretty much ruined. I can't be your father's pawn in a game I don't even understand."

"Pawn?"

"Well, something's up. Otherwise you would have been in on this from the beginning, right? I don't know why your father has done what he's done, but I'm wading in uncharted waters without a compass."

Tess didn't want to admit he was partly right, didn't want to forget the asshole status she'd assigned him. None of his admissions fixed anything in the world falling apart around her.

"I'm not going to lie. I need this job—it's the best thing that's ever happened to me—but I never slinked in. I never took anything from you. I'm not saying I'm blameless or you shouldn't be angry, but don't paint me as what I'm not. I was a jerk to you, but I did nothing wrong in regard to this job."

"A jerk I can deal with. This? Not so much," she said, turning her head toward the far bank of Algiers Point. She didn't want him to see the cracks in her. Didn't want him to know how much his callous disregard almost a month ago had dinged her pride, had made her wonder why she wasn't good enough for a guy to want as more than just a good time.

Why buy the cow… Her mother's voice echoed inside her head.

Maybe that was Tess's problem—she wanted to be in love, craved the touch of a man who would love her back, so much she plunged in without checking the depth.

In Graham's case the water had been about six inches deep.

Splat.

Graham moved closer, his steps sounding sympathetic, even though Tess knew that was impossible. "Don't," she said, flinging out a hand.

"What?"

"Don't come near me."

He stopped, resting his hands on his hips. "Look, it will be easier for everyone if I dissolve the contract and move on. It's the least I can do in this situation."

Tess snorted. "The least you can do? Whatever. Spare me your sympathy."

"It's not sympathy. I'm trying to do the right thing."

"Well, don't. I'm not working here. My father obviously doesn't value me enough to think I can handle our family business. I won't waste your time with how that makes me feel. He's not giving the job to me so I could give a rat's ass who takes it."

Graham searched her face with shuttered eyes of arctic blue. "I can break the contract."

"No, you can't. My father gets what he wants, and he's never played well when it comes to business. If you quit, he'll sue you, wrap you up in red tape and hire someone else."

Graham swallowed again. Hard. "Surely once I tell him our relationship—"

"Why? We don't have a relationship. It was sex. Meaningless sex. Let's not make it what it isn't. Besides, why would he care? He's a misogynist Italian who could have run the mafia but decided he'd rather screw people legally. Don't let his Hush Puppies shoes fool you. Frank Ullo's a shark."

Graham seemed to think about this. "I still don't feel right though. Doesn't feel good to me."

So now he feels bad? He should have felt bad two weeks ago when she put her heart on the line and called him, when she told him she'd never felt this way about anyone and asked him to call her.

That's when he should have been honorable and at least given her the decency of a call.

But she didn't say that. Instead she shrugged. "Too bad. You're the new boss. Might as well start thinking about who you are and how you want to be perceived by everyone here. He's not going to let you go easily. He doesn't care about 'feelings.'"

Graham shook his head and she could feel his frustration. Welcome to the club, buddy.

"How can I take your job?"

"It wasn't my job. My dad made his point—this is *his* company. Not mine. I suppose your first order of business will be to hire my replacement." Tess stared toward the door. Like a wave heading her way, she could feel the emotion inside her building. She didn't want to stay here any longer with a man who had rejected her as a woman. The man who had taken what she thought to be hers.... A man she still felt an ungodly attraction to even as her world unwound. Tess could pull off the ice-princess routine for only so long.... She was coming undone, and she'd be damned if she did it in front of anyone. Much less him. "See ya around."

She tried to slide quickly by him, but he reached out. "Wait, Tess."

"Please don't touch me," she begged, her voice almost at a whisper. She really couldn't stand the tenderness in his touch. He felt sorry for her. That was all. And something about that hurt more than if he'd been the ruthless son of a bitch she'd wanted to paint him as.

"What can I do to make this right?" he asked, his voice plaintive and so freaking sincere.

"You can't. Only I can make this right by moving on and proving I can be more than daddy's little girl. The best you can do is to take care of this company. There are a lot of good people here and they deserve better than a half-assed job by their new boss."

She wrenched her arm from his grasp and climbed the steps that would lead her to a place she loved…a place where she no longer belonged.

Quitting had been her choice and it had been one she had to make. Her assumptions had gotten her nothing but wounded pride, but she knew she wasn't part of this business merely because her name was Ullo. She was good at her job. She'd brought in new accounts and the floats she oversaw were detailed and cost-effective. She hadn't done well because her father owned the company…she'd done well because she'd pushed herself to live up to his name.

And now she would take her experience and foresight to a new company. She would show the world—and her father—just how good she was.

"Tess?" Graham's voice carried on the river breeze.

He stood etched hard against the muddy waters

and soft emerging spring green of the brush along the riverbank.

"I'm sorry."

Tess lifted her chin. "At least someone is."

CHAPTER SIX

GRAHAM TWISTED THE key in the door of the apartment he'd rented two weeks ago and pushed inside.

What a crappy day.

The dim room was hardly welcoming with an old leather couch that had a rip in the arm, a big-screen TV perched on a less than sturdy table and a single flowered armchair donated by his brother's girlfriend. The place looked pathetic, but it would have to do until he could afford some new stuff. Currently, he had bills due and wanted to take Emily camping at the beginning of summer.

The contract he'd signed had given him a nice salary, a large enough expense account and a car. Soon, he'd be back to where he once was, replenishing his meager savings and funding the retirement fund he'd depleted. The severance package NASA had given him had helped buffer the loss he'd taken on the sale of his condo. Damn housing market had tanked and he'd been upside down on the gated executive condo he'd bought five years ago. He'd been relatively smart with his money, thank God, but it still hadn't been enough to weather all the notes and student loans he'd collected over the years. Growing up poor made a man want things and Graham had been no exception—something he regretted when he'd looked at where he'd spent his money.

But this was to be his new start. Landing the Ullo job had been like gravy on the grandest of Thanksgiving dinners. Running a successful multi-million-dollar Mardi Gras company would take him back to his roots, allow him to use his skill set in a way NASA never had. While the mechanical engineer in him loved the technical aspects of cutting-edge innovation, the artist in him had mourned the loss of pushing past the boundaries creatively.

But now his success tasted like last night's dinner coming back up.

Tess.

When she'd walked into Frank's office, a myriad of emotions had galloped across him, starting with delight and ending in bitter regret.

She was right. He was a bastard.

He reached for the remote, tuned the TV to *Sports Center* merely so he could hear another human voice and then he went to the kitchen to find last night's leftover takeout.

His phone jittered on the bar.

Emily.

His heart brightened.

"Hey, sweetheart," he said.

"Daddy!" she cried, a smile in her voice. "What are you doing?"

"I had homework today," she said excitedly.

"Wow, you're already doing homework in second grade?"

"Dad," she said, using a teenage voice. "Of course. Most kids don't like homework, but I do."

"That's because you're a smarty pants."

She giggled, and he tucked that laughter into his soul. He'd screwed up a lot of things in life, but Emily had been the one perfect example of how an emotionally infantile man could grow into something better than his own father. Graham had made being a good father a vow…. Another reason he'd been adamant about returning to New Orleans. "I can't wait to come to your house. There's a pool there, right?"

"Yep, and a tennis court."

"I don't know how to play tennis," she said, her voice a little breathless. He could hear the rattle of cabinets in the background.

"Maybe you can take lessons? That would be fun, right?"

"Maybe," she said, chewing something. "I'm not good at sports stuff."

"You don't have to be good. It will be fun just to be out in the sun, moving around." Graham had noticed Emily had started putting on some unhealthy weight. Monique had laughed it off, talking about Christmas cookies and king cake, but Graham suspected Emily was left too often to her own devices after school, snacking and sitting in front of the TV glued to the Disney channel. Being here would give him a better handle on her health…a better handle on building a stronger relationship with his daughter. "Where's your mom?"

"She's with Josh. They're in a meeting or something. I'm in her office. I did my homework and now I'm eating a snack and watching *Saved by the Bell*."

Saved by the Bell?

"It's an old show. Mom said she watched it when she was little. Isn't that funny?"

"Yeah, princess, it is. Look, I'm going to pick you up on Thursday, okay?"

"Cool," she said, her attention waning, most likely caught by the campy sitcom. He thought he heard the sound of Screech's voice.

"Tell your mom to call me later, okay?"

"Mmm-hmm."

"Emily? What did I just say?"

"Uh—" She paused. "I don't remember."

"Tell your mother to call me."

"Oh, right. Bye, Daddy," Emily said, still distracted, but Graham would take it. He loved every minute of hearing her breathless little girl voice. Something about her innocence buffered the guilt floating inside him…made his day not so crappy if only for a few minutes.

God, he wanted to do better by her.

And he would.

"Bye, pumpkin," he said before pressing the end

button. Tossing the phone on the counter, he sighed and wiped a hand over his face. He had to get his shit together. That's what a good father did.

He had to be there physically for Emily, picking her up from after school care, spending weekends proving he wasn't the same as his old man. He wouldn't chase sparkly things or shirk his duty to his child. Emily was the reason Graham couldn't bow out of Ullo.

It had been so long since he'd felt confident about who he was. He'd gotten a taste of it that night exactly a month ago when he'd met Tess. That night, he'd been the man he'd once been—the man who had not only dreamed but made things happen. The man who hadn't failed with Monique, who had never been laid off, who had never paid a bill late, who had never taken medicine to pull himself out of depression. That magical night had given him a piece of himself back, cracking open the door to a new tomorrow.

But then he'd slammed it closed out of fear. Out of embarrassment of who he'd become. Yeah, it was a stupid reason to toss a chance for happiness with Tess away, but something inside him had balked about coming to her with so little to offer.

Panic had grabbed him by the throat. No matter how well he'd presented himself in his pressed suit and expensive shoes, buying drinks like he had a bankroll in his pocket, he'd known he'd been a facade of the man he'd once been.

All he could think about was his father with frayed cuffs and a shitty-ass excuse for why he couldn't afford to pay school fees. He'd looked in his bathroom mirror and seen the man who'd failed so often, who'd cared so little he'd rather take his life than get a job beneath him and show his sons how real success worked. The fear of turning into that man ate at him and convinced him to wait to call Tess until he was in a better place.

"Shit," he said to no one…because no one was there. Story of his life. "Ah, you're pathetic. You effed up with Tess. Game over."

His words echoed in the apartment and as he looked at the Chinese takeout box in his hand, he felt anger wash over him. So he lived in shitty circumstances now, and he'd blown any chance he had with a woman who had made him feel the way he hadn't felt in years—whole.

But it was a new day. A new beginning. He had a job, a challenge and a daughter who needed him. No time for feeling sorry for himself.

He was Graham Naquin—over-educated, nearer to forty than thirty and possessing all his teeth.

He was in it to win it.

The world was his oyster.

He would kick ass and take names.

Because he refused to be the man who'd raised him. He might have been down, but he wasn't out.

Graham Naquin was a fighter.

Tᴇss sɪᴘᴘᴇᴅ ᴛʜᴇ lukewarm café au lait and studied Gigi who glowered like a jail warden.

"Draw unemployment," she said, her red eyebrows drawn together.

"No. I don't want unemployment. I'm getting another job." Tess stared at her computer, trying to figure how best to position the experience she had. It was damn hard writing a resume with a single company as your only employer.

"Where?" Gigi pushed her tight red curls off her face and sucked on the straw of her iced tea. Gigi hated coffee but loved Cuppa Joe's with its bright red couches and black lacquered tables. Soft '80s rock flowed through the speakers and modern art displayed at irregular angles decked the walls. It had a cool, comfy vibe, so they met here as regularly for Wi-Fi and coffee as they did at Two-Legged Pete's for drinks with more kick.

"Not sure. I love design work and haven't been able to do as much of it for the past few years because I've been working with clients. Maybe I'll freelance."

Gigi snapped her fingers. "Didn't your father say this dude started a Mardi Gras float company way back when?"

"No, Graham told me the company he interviewed for was something he'd done before.... Wait, uh, maybe he did say he started a company, but I haven't a clue which one. There are a lot of smaller ones."

"Give me that," Gigi said, tugging Tess's laptop toward her. "Let's see what we can find on him."

Tess scooted her chair closer, wondering why she hadn't already done that. She often used social media to scan the guys she dated, but Graham had said he wasn't on Facebook.

Gigi typed away like a flame-tipped woodpecker on crack as Tess sipped her coffee and looked around at the world still turning even though hers had crashed that afternoon. How could people still laugh, still make jokes, still flirt across the room? Didn't her sadness permeate their happy, shiny faces?

"Bingo!" Gigi crowed, sitting back with a smile. "You're never going to believe this one."

Tess tipped the computer so she could see the screen. "Holy crap. Upstart?"

"Yeah, that's crazy, huh?"

Tess reeled with the news. Upstart, run by the effervescent Monique Dryden, had grown to become Frank Ullo's staunchest competition...and Graham Naquin had been one of the founders?

Gigi started reading. "Monique Dryden started Upstart Floatmakers in 2003 with her partners Graham Naquin and Josh Laborde when the three postgrad students, on a whim, created a sci-fi float for the Krewe of Vader, a satirical sci-fi fantasy krewe started by Jimmie Ray Dietzel. The three friends' collaboration led to a passionate venture—" Gigi wiggled her eyebrows "—which united a film student, an engineer and an art history graduate in like purpose. Building their floats using high-tech materials, cutting-edge light displays and fuel-efficient design has vaulted the 'Little Engine That Could' into the big leagues in float design."

Gigi stopped reading out loud and skimmed the article, her lips moving as fast as her blue eyes. "Wow, he sold his interest in the company and moved to Houston to work for NASA."

Tess looked away. She didn't want to know any more. Something about Graham having a relationship with Monique Dryden made the coffee curdle in her stomach. She'd met Monique many times at fundraisers and the occasional Mardi Gras ball and had found the vivacious brunette to be smart and gorgeous. She'd always made Tess feel a giantess next to her dark, diminutive beauty.

"All this is pretty interesting…almost coincidental," Gigi said. "You sure he didn't know who you were? This smells funny."

"He didn't. I never gave him my last name, and obviously my father didn't care to mention his daughter Tess frequents Two-Legged Pete's and takes home random hot guys. Graham didn't have any more of a clue than I did. I'm certain about that. Besides, how would it have benefited him? My dad didn't tell me what was going on."

Gigi stared out the window at the world moving by in the late afternoon light. "Know what you should do?"

"I'm scared to ask," Tess joked, trying to forget she was devastated, trying to find what little humor she had left after cleaning out her desk and passing her key to Billie.

"You should talk to Monique Dryden about a job. Bet she would love to sink her teeth into you." Gigi gave a sharky lawyer grin.

Tess made a face. "That would be…I don't know…too weird. Plus, it's doubtful she has an opening."

"Don't know until you ask, do you? And how awesome would that be? You'd totally teach your dad and Mr. Fancy Pants Naquin a lesson."

"But it's—" Tess rooted around for the right word "—treason. I'll stick with trying freelance design or something. I can't work at a rival company."

"Why not? It's a job. Your father screwed you, and Graham Naquin literally screwed you. Don't play the victim. Turn the tables on them."

Gigi didn't understand family the way Tess did. Her best friend's parents had split in a bitter, contested divorce rendering their only daughter a bone to be fought over. Finally after winning joint custody, Gigi's father moved to California and pretty much forgot about the daughter "he loved beyond himself." The whole messy affair had left Gigi cynical.

"I'm not you, Gigi. Ullo is part of my family and I can't hurt my family."

Gigi just stared at her for a good ten seconds.

Censure, and maybe disappointment that Tess wasn't jumping to get revenge on her father and Graham, clearly visible on her face.

Seriously, how could Tess work for the company that had given Frank Ullo the most competition over the past two years? Sounded too in-your-face for Tess's taste.

Then again, Gigi wasn't totally off base. Working for Upstart would be a great way to prove to her father he'd made a colossal mistake, and Tess could prove to herself she could make it in this business without her father's name. Would it really be so evil?

The hurt, bitter part of her said *no*. And the tied-to-her-family, devoted part of her screamed *yes*.

But loyalty to family went both ways, didn't it?

Her father hadn't felt compelled to keep it all in the family…so why should she?

Self-doubt gathered inside Tess. What if everything she thought she'd been was a lie? What if she wasn't as good at designing floats or hustling krewes as she assumed she was? What if everyone else had pulled Tess's weight, winking at each other over the boss's daughter's incompetence? What if she sucked?

Tess glanced at the computer. Hell, she couldn't even write a resume. What was the difference between freelancing float designs and anchoring a desk at another company? Not much.

"Maybe it wouldn't hurt to drop by Upstart with

a resume…if I can get the stupid thing finished," Tess said, gulping the last of her coffee, wishing she didn't even have to think about resumes, family loyalty or the fact she forgot to grab her favorite water bottle out of the company fridge. She couldn't think past the hurt…and Gigi wasn't helping by planting the seeds of rebellion within her.

Gigi smiled, obviously pleased Tess considered her diabolical plan for revenge. Blood in the water excited her, made her hungry rather than faint. "Bold, ballsy and very Tess-like."

"What?"

Gigi shrugged. "We're friends for a reason. You might smile and laugh more than I do, but we both have an innate need for justice, for righting wrong and bringing balance to the world. And we do what it takes."

Is that what taking a job with another Mardi Gras float builder would be? Righting a wrong? Didn't feel that way, but Tess did want to prove everything she'd done as an executive in her father's company wasn't because she was an Ullo but rather because she was good at it. She trampled the self-doubt and thought about how satisfactory it would be to work for the company Graham had abandoned. There was something deliciously wicked about turning that screw…a sort of a flagrant "suck it, big boy."

"You're right. I'm ballsy and I right wrongs. I should have a cape."

Gigi laughed. "Get a green one. Matches your eyes."

Tess rolled those green eyes. "Besides, a job is a job, and right now I need one. So I better get this resume finished so I can pound the pavement tomorrow. Hmm…never had to do that before. I'm liking the challenge of having to really earn my way. Is that crazy?"

"No. It's normal. There are very few people who have a job waiting on them when they graduate from college." Gigi shoved her glass aside and rummaged through her purse. "Hurry and finish. I want to get to The Columns for happy hour. I need a date for a company party and I want to hit up the after business crowd before they go home to their Labradors."

"Or wives."

Gigi pulled a lipstick from her purse and made a face.

The last thing Tess wanted to do was go to a bar, even as nice as The Columns was. She wanted to go home, eat some comfort food, watch *Seinfeld* re-runs and sulk about the shit sandwich life had handed her. No, not life. Her father and, to a degree, Graham. Okay, in fairness, Graham had only hurt her feelings when he hadn't called like he said he would…and being awarded her job didn't help matters. But, hey, she was Gigi's wingman just like Gigi was for her. Maybe after an hour she could leave. "Fine, but I have to go by FedEx first. No more free copies for me."

Gigi gave a humorless laugh. "Like the rest of us."

"Whatever," Tess said, wondering why her friend saw her as different merely because she'd worked for her family. Did that make her privileged? Lazy? Entitled? She had never thought so because she'd worked hard, but maybe the world thought her life had been too easy. And maybe it had been. Maybe being truly on her own would be good for her.

But her heart told her differently.

She'd loved who she was three days ago. Well, except for Graham's knock to her ego. But even that she'd gotten over. Mostly. Her life had been gravy...and now it was soured wine.

"Put on lip gloss and brush your hair. Don't forget you're available, too. Wouldn't hurt to find a little something-something to take your mind off tall, dark and deceitful."

"My mind was never on him," Tess lied.

Gigi gave her *that look,* the one that plowed through the bullshit. "You actually used the line 'I found *the* one' after that night with Graham Naquin. He was on your mind."

"I had forgotten about him until today." She lied again because it was easier that way.

"Whatever you say, hunny bunny. He's a job stealer anyway."

"Technically he didn't steal my job. According to Papa Dearest it was never mine to begin with."

"So you say. Still, it's time to find someone who will make you feel better."

A man instead of ice cream? It *would* be better for her thighs, although she didn't want a man at present. Better to stay home and get her shit together…but there was that whole loyalty thing.

Tess shooed Gigi away. "Go fix your makeup or something. I can't think while you're nipping at me. I need to put the finishing touches on this resume before I can go out with you."

Gigi huffed, but did as suggested, flouncing away, sliding a smile at a cute guy in a Brooks Brothers suit and pink tie. Tess refocused on her resume, wishing it looked a little fuller. But she was who she was.

And who was that?

She'd thought she knew. She'd been beloved daughter, tolerated sister, good friend and devoted VP of operations in the family company…but now?

Tess felt like she'd been dropped into a maze. Every turn presented a barrier. No job. No man. Anger at her father…and Graham. Self-doubt. She'd never had such barriers that required her to backtrack or climb over hurdles to reach her goal.

But Tess knew something about herself—she may have lived a charmed life, but she wasn't going to lie down and flop about, bemoaning her state. She'd find a new job even if it meant going to the competition. Nothing wrong with a modern woman taking control of her life, leaving conventions behind.

And maybe she'd even get a new man...or not.

All she did know was that Graham needed to be a memory, and Frank Ullo needed to learn his daughter wasn't a doormat.

Plugging the flash drive into the computer, Tess downloaded her resume and renewed her determination to prove to the world she could kick ass and take names.

Tess Ullo was a fighter.

CHAPTER SEVEN

GRAHAM PULLED UP to the curb in front of the house in which he'd once lived. Looked the same. Felt different.

The Orleans brick with the intentional plaster smears and the beige stucco had once seemed so modern, so very much "them." But now it looked pretty much like what it was—a new townhouse in a decent area of Metairie, crowded in like the others. Pansies lined the sidewalk. Graham only knew they were pansies because he'd planted the same flowers in that spot years ago. He wondered if Josh planted them now.

The door opened and Emily flew outside, dark pigtails flying, smile as wide as sunshine.

"Daddy!" she screamed, her sneakers slapping against the sidewalk.

Graham scooped her up, squeezing tight. Two chubby arms curled around him. "Hey, pumpkin. Jeez, you've grown a foot since I last saw you."

Emily tilted her head and grinned, one tooth missing. "I've been taking vitamins."

"Oh? That's the reason?" He gave his daughter

one last squeeze and lifted his head to see Monique approaching. "Hey."

She gave him a cool smile…as always. "Hey. As you can see she's beyond ready for dinner with Daddy Graham."

Daddy Graham?

"Yeah," Emily said, waving a five-dollar bill. "Daddy Josh gave me some money for the arcade. I'm gonna play skee ball."

"Daddy Josh?"

Monique brushed manicured fingernails across an imaginary horizon. "That's what Em calls Josh. Easier that way."

"Really?" Graham said, eyeing his former fiancée, wondering whether this new term had come from ease or a vindictive way to twist a fork in Graham. Monique enjoyed creating drama. It's what made her brilliant as an artist…and nearly impossible for Graham to live with.

She lifted a shoulder and gave him a half smile. "For Emily."

"What's wrong?" Emily asked, her forehead crinkling as she glanced at him. Her brown eyes looked worried even as her rounded cheeks were flushed with excitement.

"Nothing, sweetheart," Graham said, giving Monique the "we'll talk about this later" look. "Let's get going."

"I don't have to sit in a booster anymore," Emily

said, eyeing the sedan Ullo had delivered to him that morning. "I'm big now."

Emily had grown in the past four months. She'd always been such a tiny girl with brown velvet hair and fluffy fairy skirts. As a mature seven-year-old, she wore a T-shirt with silvery looking stuff on it and trendy teenager-looking jeans. Her sneakers had sequins on them, and the hair bow was noticeably absent. A small glittery purse hung at her side.

But he had no idea if she needed a booster seat or not—another mark against him as a father. He'd never thought to check that kind of stuff. Monique had always handed him the car seat or the diaper bag or the medicine. He didn't even know the pediatrician's name anymore.

This was why he'd had to come back to New Orleans.

This was why he'd had to ignore the ignoble feeling within him when he'd found out about Tess yesterday and make himself indispensable to Frank Ullo and his company.

"So you're the new Frank Ullo, huh? Never even crossed my mind something like this could happen," Monique said, eyeing the Toyota Avalon before lifting her gaze to him. "Highly ironic you're working for my competition. It's almost Machiavellian."

"It wasn't intentional," he said, opening the rear door. Emily climbed in, looking around the leather interior, poking at buttons. "I told you as much when we talked last month. It's a perfect opportunity for me, doing something I'm good at. It puts me back in New Orleans. Back in Emily's life as her father. Her only father."

Monique narrowed her dark eyes. "Feels like you're punishing me. Upstart was yours, too, at one time, and you're making this personal when it's not. You'll take food from the mouth of your child, merely so you can look good."

"You really believe everything is about you, don't you, Monique?" The dislike he had for Monique would forever overshadow the passion they'd shared. She always held a piece of herself back, setting barriers she protected with a crushing disregard for others. She was a faucet, hot or cold, but never both together.

Her gaze was frosty…but wasn't it always now? "Tell yourself that, Graham, but anyone can see the writing on the wall."

"This isn't revenge, Monique. It's about a job. Not allegiance. In case you didn't get the memo, I need this…and I can't return to Upstart, now can I?"

Her bitter laugh was answer enough.

"Exactly." He closed the door and faced his ex. Monique didn't step back as he crowded her slightly. No, not Monique. Small, delicate with dark arched eyebrows, a bowed mouth and wavy hair, Monique was a fiery ballbuster. Even as Graham despised her for what she'd done to him, he admired her ability to stand her ground...all five feet one inch of it. "This isn't war, so don't don the armor."

"I'll do whatever I wish to do, Graham."

"Of course you will, but I'm asking, for all of our sakes, don't make this personal. There is plenty of business for both Ullo and Upstart."

"You didn't used to feel that way," she murmured, an almost savage look in her eye. "You hated Frank Ullo. You hated that he controlled the market and squashed smaller businesses trying to take a piece of the pie. That's changed now because he signs your paycheck?"

"Upstart is no longer in the position it once was. Frank Ullo isn't, either. You know that." He wanted to get out of there before he and Monique started shrieking at each other on the street. Dealing with her had become more and more contentious in the past two months...ever since she learned he intended to come home to New Orleans. Monique liked having control and the agreement they had over Emily would change.

Josh walked out wearing a pair of dark jeans and a weirdly patterned shirt with a hot pink tab collar. Tall, lanky with a soul patch on his chin, Graham's former best friend had a wicked sense of humor, a badass restored Harley and a shitty sense of loyalty to a friendship started back at Jesuit. He'd been too weak to resist Monique...probably still was.

"Hey, Monique, we gotta jet," he called, not even meeting Graham's gaze.

Irritation flashed in Monique's eyes. "We'll go when I'm ready, Josh."

Emily knocked against the window, pressing her button nose against the glass smudging it. Graham smiled and nodded, dangling the keys.

"We're going to head out, Monique. Text me when you're through with your fundraiser and I'll bring Emily back. I'm guessing it won't be too late since it's a school night?" Graham started around the front of the car.

"I'm not finished talking about this, Graham," Monique said, smoothing the lines of a dress that was too short, but still looked incredible on her. Monique's beauty had never been in question. Even as slight as the woman was, her essence screamed "lush" and "sensual." It was her heart he questioned. As determined as she was to create an empire she could control, she had one fatal flaw—her ego. Often Monique valued her own worth above the truth. This inability to see the writing on the wall was the main reason Graham didn't fight for Upstart. Well, that and the fact Monique and Josh had started sneaking around sleeping together.

"Well, I'm finished discussing this. Everything will work better if you shut down whatever you're working up inside yourself about me running Frank Ullo. I'm not competing with you. I'm trying to take care of Emily."

"You could have done that with another company. You could have done that from Houston."

"But I didn't want to," he said, before sliding into the car. "Don't forget to text me."

Shutting the door, he shut out the dissonance Monique always created in his life, and instead focused his attention on the only reason he'd done Monique and Josh a favor tonight—the bouncing, wonderful Emily. "Ready to roll, squirt?"

"Can we go to the pet store and see the kitties?" she asked, ignoring his question.

Graham pulled away from the curb, unable to resist glancing at Monique who stared angrily after them. He wished he didn't get satisfaction in needling her. He'd have to be very careful to keep the fragile peace between them for his daughter's sake. Wouldn't be easy because Monique had never been easygoing or amiable to anyone's opinion but her own. Once he'd teased her, calling her his little general, but now that moniker wasn't teasing. "Fasten your seatbelt, Em," he said, slowing and pulling to the curb.

"I want a kitty, but mommy says 'absolutely no.'" Emily clicked her belt into place, and though the child looked big enough for the seat, Graham made a mental note to check the laws regarding child safety and cars.

"Well, pets are a big commitment, Emily," Graham said, pulling out and winding his way toward Veterans Avenue so he could take Emily to dinner and the arcade.

"I'm old enough. I can pour out its food, get it water and take care of it when it's scared."

"What about poop? You think you can scoop out a litter box? What about the vet? Pets cost money."

"I have some money. Grandy Pete gave me ten dollars last week for dusting his room and brushing Pumpkin, his big ol' cat."

Grandy Pete was Monique's irascible grandfather. Graham couldn't imagine the older man caring for a cat much less a little girl—the man had spent much of his life on the bayou, shucking oysters and shrimping. He now lived in an apartment behind a convent in the Lower Garden District, a place between Upstart headquarters and Monique's digs in Metairie. Graham had helped him find the place and move in, something that had proven easy since the eighty-year-old man had exactly two trunks of clothing, a guitar and a memory foam pillow. Colorful only halfway described Pete. "It will take more than ten dollars, Em. But we'll talk to Mom about the possibility of a pet."

"I can keep Muffin at your house," she said, brown eyes peeping over the gray leather seat.

"Muffin? Oh, no. I see your game here, missy." He laughed, deciding it felt good. The past few days had been tense, and he needed the lightness his daughter gave him. "And sit back in your seat."

"Please," she wheedled, sinking back as instructed. "She can keep you company when I'm not there."

"I don't need company." *At least not that of a cat.*

"Yeah, you do. You need a kitty."

"Wrong."

Emily crossed her arms and gave him a look that was all her mother. "I knew you'd say no. Just like Mommy."

Something inside him moved. He wished it hadn't. He wished he didn't have such guilt where Emily was concerned, but he'd missed so much in moving to Houston and going to work for NASA. At the time it had felt best for all concerned—best for him, certainly—but he'd left the raising of his daughter to Monique, being Daddy only in the summers and on a rare holiday. "How about a truce?"

"What's that?"

"It means you walk my way, and I'll walk yours. We'll meet in the middle."

Emily made a face. "We're in the car."

"It's a metaphor."

"Huh?"

He laughed. "Never mind. I have an idea. There used to be a place by a supermarket that sold fish. How about an aquarium for your room at my town-house? Do you like fish?"

"Not as much as kitties," she said.

"We'll start with fish and see how you do then we'll work up to something fluffy with claws."

"Like Nemo?"

Turning off busy Veteran's Highway into the parking lot housing a specialty aquarium store,

Graham decided an aquarium was something he could handle. Not sure how much company fish would be, but he needed things to fill up space in his near-empty apartment. And maybe he could find an actual person one day, too. He'd wanted to move forward in his life, and that meant not spending his nights alone.

Tess's face popped into his thoughts making him feel both guilty and lustful at the same time—a hard to accomplish feat but Graham obviously had that particular talent.

He should have called. But what would that have changed? Might have made it worse instead of better when he'd discovered who she was…when she'd discovered who he was and for what job he'd interviewed.

Too late to worry about it.

Fate had handed him his cards and he could play only what was in hand.

"I want three fish," Emily said, unfastening her belt as soon as he shifted the car into Park.

"Let's get four," he said.

"Cool," his daughter said, bouncing on the backseat, reminding him the present was where he dwelled. No time for past mistakes—over Tess, Monique or his failure as a father—to haunt him.

He had fish to buy.

FRANK ULLO WATCHED his wife as she rolled out the pasta, hands moving deftly as they'd done many times before, knowing the right texture, careful not to add too much oil or too much flour. Making perfection as she did each Sunday.

"I love to watch you make the cannoli," he said, sliding slowly toward her, mindful of the dressing on his side. The stint placement hadn't been bad, but he was still tired and tender. Wrapping an arm around her waist, he laid his head on her shoulder.

Maggie's deep sigh seeped into him much like the sadness that had permeated their life over the past two months. It had all started with the jaundice and stomach pain. Frank had thought it was an ulcer, but the medicine his internist prescribed hadn't touched it. It was then he'd contacted a headhunter. Somehow he'd known the prognosis wasn't good. He'd known he needed help. Not an easy thing for a man like him.

"You never watched me make cannoli before," she said, her hands never ceasing as she rolled the edges between her fingers and thumb, but she tilted her head so it rested upon his.

"Meh, I never stopped to see things before. Knowing death has caught hold of you by the neck changes what you see in life."

"Shush, Frank, don't say things like that. I hate when you talk about dying. You're not dying. We're fighting this."

He didn't have the words to protest. Maggie had set her foot down, defying the reaper to touch him.

She was a tough opponent. Old Grim didn't realize what he was up against.

"The kids will be here in half an hour. Frank, Jr. is never late." Frank looked around the place his wife felt most comfortable in. Maggie had returned the emerald earrings he'd given her for their thirtieth wedding anniversary, taking the money to an appliance center and custom ordering the huge Viking range. He'd laughed because he could never convince his Maggie she was worthy of jewels… not when she'd rather be barefoot and making his grandmother's red sauce. Maggie may be as Irish as the Blarney Stone, but she cooked like she was a fifth-generation Italian.

"Tess is coming," Maggie murmured, picking up the sharp knife and cutting the dough.

"It's Easter," he said with a shrug. "Family is family."

"She's angry and hurt, and rightly so."

Frank stepped away, picking up the flour and sealing it into the large storage container, helping Maggie where he could. But he had no words to say regarding Tess. His youngest had been difficult from the moment she'd entered the world, screaming and impossible to console. As wonderful as Tess was, nothing was easy with her. From her being allergic to disposable diapers, formula and gluten to her choosiness over schools, clothes and hair bows, Tess overwhelmed any space she occupied.

"You have to talk to her, Frank. You have to make her go back to work for the company."

He shook his head. "No. I'm not doing that, Maggie. Tess molds everyone to her, arranging her life so it fits her needs, her demands. She hasn't had much set against her and I think it would be a mistake to fix this for her. She needs to understand my side of this. She needs to see I'm not doing this capriciously or with any intention other than doing what is best for the company."

"She's your daughter." Maggie turned and prodded him with her gaze. They'd had this same conversation over and over in the past week, but Frank wasn't easily moved. On this he would stand firm.

He knew to some degree he'd failed Tess. His only girl, his last baby, she'd gotten all the petting and doting he'd held back from his boys. Whatever Tess wanted, Frank made sure she got. He'd been so proud when she'd declared she'd follow in his footsteps, even as he worried about her ability to handle a business like Frank Ullo. Tess thought she could handle everything thrown at her. Thing was, life hadn't thrown much at her. She'd lived a golden existence, and as Frank thought about his company and his daughter, he could see his child had never been tested in any way.

Tess needed to learn more than what he could give her. She had to be challenged, had to live outside of the bubble she'd been so safely ensconced within.

Maybe he was wrong. Maybe he was playing God, testing his daughter much like God had tested Job.

But he knew his Tess. She would not only survive, she would thrive.

"Yes, she is my daughter, and so I know she will make her way."

"Make her way? Frank, she's a hard worker and loves the company. Sure, she's young, but you should have made her the CEO and hired this fellow to work for her."

"I know what the company needs, Maggie. Trust me on this—it's the right thing. The rubber is meeting the road and time will tell us where we go. You understand?"

His wife of forty-five years shook her head. "You're a stubborn goat."

"Like my daughter…and my sons."

"I don't see this as you do, but I will trust you. I have always trusted you. But tread softly, Frankie. These are strange times for us."

He sighed. "Times I don't wish on my enemy, but this is what we're left with, Maggie."

"Are you going to tell them about the cancer today? Tell them about the operation this past week?"

"It's the wrong time. People want to feel joy at Easter."

"It's always the wrong time," Maggie said, turning to the bowl containing the mascarpone cheese, stirring with a furrow between her lovely green eyes. Maggie meant business when she cooked for the family. "But you don't have much more time. Next week you'll start the chemotherapy. We've already hidden all the tests, and I don't know how we managed that as nosy as this family is."

"Easy to do when your kids are busy living." Frank looked out the window at his shady backyard. Everything bloomed—the huge azaleas clustered around the sprawling live oak anchoring the landscape. A beautiful waterscape tumbled water over the stones mined from a quarry in Arkansas. Birds darted through the canopy and the world looked soft and beautiful...as if something as ugly as cancer couldn't exist.

And it made Frank angry.

Why had this happened to him? Why now? At the end of his life when things should be simple... when he deserved to sink into his recliner and put his feet up?

He'd worked so hard his whole life, pouring blood, sweat and tears into creating something worthwhile, something good. He'd come from humble beginnings, born the year after the U.S. entered World War II, his father dying that same year in the Pacific. He'd been raised by a working single mother who married a man who drank hard and hit harder. Eventually, Frank dropped out of high school and went to work sweeping a warehouse owned by a celebrated early float maker. Soon after he put down his broom and learned how to build the floats rolling for some of the earliest parades like Comus and then Rex.

Years later after a stint in the army, Frank returned and bought a warehouse with his savings and a loan from Maggie's father. He'd started Frank Ullo Float Builders, and because he loved what he did, it had grown into the international business it was today. Finally, he'd been thinking about taking it easy, traveling to Italy for the summer, duck-hunting with his sons and watching his grandkids play soccer every Saturday morning.

Irony bit a man in the ass sometimes.

A sound at the door told him his reverie must end.

"Papa Frank?" Max bellowed, feet slapping the wood floors as the five-year-old headed for the kitchen.

Frank spun as Maggie wiped her hands on her apron. "Sugar, I told you about running in the house."

Their grandson skidded to a halt in front of his grandmother who smiled through her fussing. "Sorry, Gee, but look what the Easter Bunny put in my basket." He waved a lacrosse stick in the air.

"Jeez, Max. Put that down before you break something," Frank Jr. said, entering the kitchen, snatching the stick from his youngest son's grasp and dropping a brusque kiss on his father's cheek then turning to Maggie. "Happy Easter, parents."

Maggie started the hugging and kissing as Max's older brothers poured in, looking for snacks before dinner. Finally Frank Jr.'s wife, Laurie, stumbled in with a casserole dish and a tired smile.

Frank watched this part of his family, soaking in every detail, brushing away any annoyance he'd normally feel at the boys tussling over the remote or snitching too much chocolate from the candy dish. Then Joseph arrived with his quiet wife and even quieter twin girls. Michael showed up with a bottle of Cabernet and an Easter lily for his mother. And finally, Tess rushed in to good-natured ribbing from her older brothers about being late as usual.

Frank's mother, Bella, plodded in behind his daughter, sharp-eyed and grumpy about being late to dinner.

"She shows up ten minutes late. Ten minutes I had to listen to Ira Messamer complain about his damned gout. I didn't know a man could whine so much about swollen feet."

Tess, dressed in trim pants and a cotton shirt that hugged her figure, rolled her eyes. "I told you I had to stop for rolls. You said it was okay."

"A little late, you said," Bella, otherwise known as Granny B, muttered. "Not a whole ten minutes."

Tess looked at Maggie with a tight smile. "Next time see if Frankie can pick up Granny B. Please."

Granny B shot a look at Tess. "Mind your manners, missy. I'm not too old to take you over my knee."

"Yeah, you are," Tess said.

Frank almost laughed, except his mother would swat at him, so he kept his mouth shut. Tess glanced at him, but quickly averted her eyes. The frostiness told him all he needed to know about where he stood with his daughter. Far away. Perhaps even across the ocean.

"I get no respect, especially from her," Granny B said, jabbing a finger at Tess, even as something in her dark eyes sparked with admiration. Granny B thought the sun rose and set with her Tess…not that she'd ever let on. Tough as a cornstalk and soft as a brick, Isabella Ullo hadn't stayed long with a man who hit her or her son. She'd left Mick Mac-Dougall two years after she'd married him, going to work at the Bon Sucre hotel, catering to the elite of society. She'd stayed for forty years before moving to a small retirement community in the Garden District.

Tess snorted. "You're being difficult, Granny B, because you can. Ten minutes isn't late."

"Have you ever met Ira Messamer?" Granny B cracked lifting the lid on the sauce, smelling it critically. "Too much garlic, Maggie."

"You know she can't have garlic, Mom," Tess

said with an evil gleam in her eye, "for the same reason I have to carry around a silver stake and have her at the home before sunset."

"Hah," Granny B said, "I wouldn't suck your blood if you paid me in cash. Probably half vodka anyway."

The women all laughed, and Frank sank into the moment—typical teasing Sunday banter between the women in his family. How many more of these would he have? He wasn't sure. The doctors had been blunt—his cancer would move fast. The chemo he'd start next week would only slow the inevitable—there was a sliver of a chance he'd survive longer than six months.

So he sat in the middle of his family stocking up the images in his mind, piling them into a suitcase in his memory, carefully arranging them so when the pain came, the sickness overwhelmed, he could unlock the sound of Max's laughter, the curve of Maggie's cheek, the way Joseph tried to count Tess's freckles. Tears filled his eyes and he quickly turned his head, refusing to sully even one second of this day.

He'd tell them about his cancer another day—a day that wasn't about resurrection and new beginnings.

No, he wanted today full of sunshine…full of love.

And it might happen even if he'd invited Graham Naquin for coffee and dessert.

CHAPTER EIGHT

TESS SAT AT the table with her family and tried to pretend this Easter Sunday was like every other one that had gone before—full of deviled eggs, impromptu egg hunts and at least one chocolate bunny ear. She was pretty good at talking a niece or nephew into sharing.

But it wasn't the same.

Anger and betrayal made her mother's sauce taste of ashes. Hurt laced even the green-bean casserole bland Beth had thrown together…if such a thing were even possible. Not Beth's being bland—which she probably couldn't help, being married to Joseph—but the whole green-bean casserole tasting like tears.

Same old smiles, same old jokes, same old china filled with food Tess's mother and sisters-in-law had slaved over. She should be enjoying the home-cooked meal rather than picking at the jicama-and-shrimp salad and poking at the ziti.

The frustration over what her father had done had stitched itself inside her and refused to be undone. Not that Tess wanted it undone. In one way she liked what the soreness gave her—a hunger she'd never had before, a need to prove herself. Even admitting she craved the challenge, however, Tess couldn't erase the deep hurt at her father not believing in her. His failure to hand her the keys had knocked a hole in her she couldn't see filling anytime soon.

"Cat got your tongue, Tess?" Michael asked, his dark eyes studying her over the frames of his glasses. Father Michael Ullo read people who didn't want to be read—a talent he put to use often. In this case Tess knew her mother had told him what had happened. Michael knew why she was quieter than normal, but for some reason wouldn't let her get away with it.

"Just enjoying Mom's cooking as usual," she said, chasing a noodle around her plate with her fork.

Michael took another sip of wine. "Yeah, I see. Ravenous, aren't you?"

Tess tossed him the "shut the hell up" look. As usual, Michael ignored her. God forgive her, but Father Michael could be super annoying.

"Might as well get everything out in the air before dessert, Therese," Frankie, Jr. said, taking a butter knife away from Max before he could saw a flower from the arrangement her mother had put together. "Kid table next year."

"Me or Max?" Tess cracked.

"Both?" Frankie deadpanned.

"Let it drop before you ruin today, Frankie," Tess

said, watching her brothers exchange looks. They'd always treated her like their child rather than their sister. Tess had been the ultimate surprise to her aging mother and father, throwing off the whole balance of the family when she'd arrived nine years after Michael, the youngest brother.

"We can't have every Sunday like this," Joseph complained, giving Beth a knowing look. As a neurosurgeon, Joseph usually took a backseat to his brazen older brother who chewed up district attorneys every week as a highly sought-after defense attorney. Michael always held his own—the white collar did wonders for respect in their Irish-Italian Catholic family.

Tess glared at her brothers, pissed they'd waited until everyone was held hostage by her mother's red sauce to bring up the rift between her and her father. "We're going to do this now?"

Frankie Jr. shrugged. "We're all here."

Tess's father cleared his throat and everyone stopped fidgeting and slurping their tea. "We ain't doing nothing to destroy this day, boys. Leave your sister alone. What happened between me and her is business, not of concern to the family."

Tess lowered her head. She wasn't sure if it was because she was so angry at his words or relieved she wouldn't have to slug it out over Easter dinner. Lifting her head, she stared defiantly at a cream-colored camellia in the flower arrangement.

"Feels like it's more than business, Dad," Joseph

said, tossing down his napkin. "It's damned uncomfortable is what it is."

"Well, it's not your concern. Tess is my daughter. I'm her father. Nothing changes that." Frank set down his fork. He hadn't eaten much, either, which was very unlike him.

Granny B's sharp eyes took in all that went on at the table. "What's he talking about? Of course she's his daughter. Stubborn enough, isn't she?"

Maggie inhaled and blew out a sigh. "Everyone looks ready for dessert. Who wants cannoli?"

Tess ignored her mother, jerking her gaze to meet her father's. "He's right. Nothing changes that." Tossing her napkin down, she scooped up her plate and headed toward the kitchen.

Maggie followed, picking up the empty roll basket. Tess knew her mother hated conflict at the table, but could do nothing. Her stupid brothers were responsible for the discomfort.

The older nephews and twin nieces sat at the kids' table in the kitchen and all turned wearing guilty expressions, when she and Maggie entered the kitchen.

Maggie took one look at the uncovered plate of cannoli sitting on the granite counter and jabbed a finger at Conner. "I told you to stay out of the dessert."

Conner wiped the cheese from the corner of his mouth. "I love you, Gee."

"Flattery will get you another cannoli," Maggie

said, rolling her eyes, but softening. The woman was a sucker for her grandchildren. "Sorry, Tess. I told Joseph not to say anything. You know how he hates everything wrinkled."

"Well, too damn bad," Tess said, scraping her plate into the trash. Joseph's twin girls, Margaret Ann and Meghan, gasped. "Sorry, girls."

Conner and Holden grinned, obviously enjoying the strong language—a family argument couldn't compare to middle school where naughty language wasn't so much colorful as the norm. Tess wasn't so old she didn't remember how an eighth grader rolled.

"He's trying to smooth out wrinkles in a world that's not his. He chose to be a doctor. Frankie chose to be a lawyer. And maybe God chose Michael, I don't know, but none of them are involved in the company outside of hanging out in our float stand during parades or showing up at an occasional ball, so they aren't involved in this."

"They're members of this family, and that is enough."

Tess set the plate in the sink and winced as it clattered against a soaking pot. "Dad said this isn't about the family."

"You and I both know differently." Her mother shot a frown at Holden, who wiped his mouth with the back of his hand. "Napkin, Holden."

Holden and Conner rose in silent communication, grabbed a few cannoli and headed out to the yard.

"This isn't the time or the place, Mom," Tess said, tossing her hair over her shoulder, eyeing the two girls watching them with rapt attention.

"You're just like him. That's the problem."

Tess opened her mouth to deny her mother's declaration, but the doorbell rang.

Maggie made a face. "Who could that be?"

Tess shrugged. The family was there, so had to be a neighbor or a friend dropping by.

"Girls, help Auntie Tess with the dessert. I'll see who's here and find out who wants coffee and cannoli." Maggie tucked her fading auburn hair behind her ears and headed toward the foyer.

Margaret Ann and Meghan cleared the table before coming to stand beside the stove. Tess located the serving spoon and uncovered the other plate of cannoli, eying the chocolate and pistachio coating. Her appetite hid behind the cold wall between her and her father, but surely she could summon enough enthusiasm to have her mother's Easter cannoli?

She'd just started serving when she heard his voice.

His voice.

Graham Naquin.

The spoon clattered to the tiled floor. "Shit."

Margaret Ann blinked at her.

"Yeah, I know, Margaret Ann. It's a bad word, but, baby, trust me. It fits the situation."

"Oh," her niece said, glancing at her sister whose eyes were wider than normal.

Not like Tess could explain that the guy she'd fallen at least a one-fourth in love with, had amazing sex with and lost a job to had shown up at her family's Easter dinner. Using the obscenity was mild compared to what she wanted to do, which was barge into the dining room and call him a no-good bastard. But this wasn't a soap opera, so she picked up the spoon and tossed it in the sink.

"Why?" This from Meghan.

"Huh?" Tess swiped at the tile floor with a paper towel, removing the crumbs.

"The reason you said *shit,*" Meghan persisted.

"Shh!" Tess said, slapping a hand over Meghan's mouth and looking around for Beth. "Don't repeat that word. Ever."

Margaret Ann wrinkled her brow. "So why does it fit the situation?"

"Have you ever had a best friend who you thought was super cool, but then she kicked dirt in your face and went off to play with someone else?"

Meghan peeled Tess's hand from her mouth. "Kay-Kay didn't kick dirt but she did dump my bubbles out."

"Well, that's what this is like. Kind of." Tess eyed the hall leading to the dining room and tried to decipher the hum of conversation coming from there. She couldn't hear exactly what was being said, but the vibe seemed congenial.

Pinching her cheeks and rubbing her bare lips

together, Tess tossed her hair and scooped up two plates of cannoli. "Later, gators."

"We wanna see the mean girl," Meghan said.

"It's not a girl," Tess whispered, wishing she could hold a finger up to her lips and shush the chatty eight-year-olds. "It's a man."

"Ohh," Margaret Ann said, her eyes growing wide. She gave an excited smile to her sister. "It's a boy…which is kind of gross and kind of interesting."

"Shh," Tess said again before throwing back her shoulders and sashaying into the dining room…. At least she thought it was a sashay. She'd never taken dance. Interfered with soccer.

Everyone turned and stared. Imaginary crickets chirped.

"I have cannoli," she trilled with a fake smile plastered on her face.

"Us, too," one of the twins said.

Tess set a plate in front of Michael and then one in her own place. Sinking into her chair, she refused to look at the man standing beside her father. Refused. Picking up a fork she cut into the crisp pastry with the sinful filling. "Mmm…this is fabulous, Mom."

Michael stared at his plate and tossed Tess a questioning look. She could feel the guilt emanating off her family. Why did they feel guilty? Wasn't their fault her father had invited the enemy into the fold.

"Thank you, honey," Maggie said, shifting eyes

to her husband then to Tess. Getting no help, she rose. "And who else would like some dessert?"

A few murmured responses met her mother's inquiry. Then silence fell again, hard and loud.

After several stretched minutes, Frankie Jr. cleared his throat. "So, Graham, would you care for some coffee?"

Frankie Jr. What a nice boy. So mannerly for a shark. So hospitable toward the man who had screwed his sister then not bothered to call her like he'd said he would. So welcoming to the man who would take over the family business. Did Frankie even know he extended the hand of politeness to the wolf who would eat them?

"No, thanks," Graham said. Everyone's attention was on him. But not Tess's. She was busy pretending Graham wasn't intruding on her family Easter dinner.

Why in the hell was he here anyway? Why on God's green earth had her father invited him to a family meal? If she didn't know her father better, she'd think it was designed to rub her nose in the mess he'd made of their relationship. But while her father was many things, he wasn't a total bastard. No way he invited Graham to needle her. He had other reasons.

Silence sat among them. Even Joseph, impeccable surgeon able to withstand excruciating ten-hour surgeries with a steady hand, squirmed in his chair.

Finally Beth smiled. "So, Graham. Frank told us you have a daughter who is close to our girls' age."

Not a question but an invitation.

"Emily. She's seven and with her mother today. I'm actually on my way over to her house to take Em her Easter basket. Frank asked me to stop by and meet his wife. I had no idea the entire family would be here. I hate to interrupt. Sorry."

His words were softly spoken, like an apology meant for Tess. But instead of soothing her, they made her angry. She didn't need his damn pity. If her father wanted Graham here for their family get-together and if he wanted Graham to take over their family business, fine. Tess had no say. If she had, she wouldn't be stabbing her cannoli, trying not to launch herself on the floor and pitch a temper tantrum the way Max had at the last family dinner.

Self-control—hadn't she told Graham it wasn't her strong suit? So he'd been forewarned if she launched herself at him and clawed his eyes out.

Her anger must have crackled because Michael picked up the knife nearest her hand and moved it. Tess glared at him and he shrugged.

"So you're the fellow who stole Tess's job?" Granny B piped up, tackling the cannoli one of the twins had set in front of her.

Tess shot Granny B a fierce look designed to zip lips, but, of course, Granny B didn't give a flying fig whom she offended. Never had.

"No, ma'am. I didn't steal anything," Graham

said, nodding his thanks at Joseph who had so thoughtfully brought him a chair.

"Frank gave you control of his business, control of the empire he built from a scrap of nothing into something that paid for this house, my house and a trip to Italy last year. He trusts you. He gave you what he'd give a son."

"But not a daughter," Tess said before she could stop herself. Setting down her fork, she glanced at her father. He looked miserable. Good. And ironically, Graham sat to his right, also looking miserable. Doubly good.

"Tess," her father breathed, shaking his head. "Let's not do this now. I invited Graham over for coffee and dessert last week, before our kerfuffle. This is not the time or place."

"Kerfuffle? Right," she said. "You ready to go, Granny B?"

"Nope," the older woman said, picking up a piece of cannoli and popping it into her mouth. "This is like watching *The Young and the Restless*…only better."

"Mother." Frank cast a cautionary glance to his mother.

"Frank," she replied in the same voice, pursing her lips, a vicious gleam in her eyes. "You set this in motion. Did you think your daughter would let it slide? She's a good girl, but she's an Ullo."

Tess pushed away from the table. She couldn't

do this anymore. "Mikey, take Granny B home for me, 'kay?"

For a priest, Michael knew enough about a woman not to make a fuss when she meant business. He nodded and went back to his dessert as if it were more important than saving sinners.

Tess didn't bother saying goodbye. She walked toward the living room where she'd left her purse, her sandaled feet soft on the carpet—yet another time when she could have used the angry staccato of heels to drive her point home. Damn it.

Scooping up her clutch, she headed for the door. She shouldn't have come. Should have faked a stomachache. The pain was too raw, the betrayal too recent for her to put on a smiling face and play happy family. But she'd wanted to be with her brothers and mother. Not her father—she'd planned to pretend he wasn't there, but that hadn't worked. Not when Graham had showed up looking fresh, handsome and ready to be the golden boy he obviously was.

"Tess?"

Stopping on the wide porch, she spun toward Graham who stood framed in the open doorway of her parents' home. "Don't, Graham."

"Tess, please. I didn't know you'd be here. Truly."

"Doesn't matter," she said turning toward the driveway crowded with a BMW, a Mercedes and Michael's priest mobile, aka a black Caddy. Her small Prius looked out of place…a true representation of who she was among her talented, over-accomplished brothers. Tess: quirky, trendy and socially conscious. But not successful and stable enough. Is that what her father saw when he looked at her?

No substance? Not smart enough to rise to the top? No penis?

She'd never thought so before, but now she didn't have a clue how anyone saw her. Hell, she wasn't sure how she saw herself.

Walking quickly toward her car, Tess caught sight of Graham's ride sitting at the curb. A little salt rubbed in her wound.

Reaching her car, she pulled open the door, but Graham's hand slammed it closed. "Damn it, Tess. Stop. Please."

"Move, Graham."

"No," he said, shaking his head, his blue eyes intense, apologetic and riled all at the same time. He wore a polo shirt and a well-worn pair of jeans. The blue stripes in the shirt made his eyes look brighter and his shoulders broader. Tess wished she hadn't noticed. And the scent of his cologne tickled her nose, making her long to inhale and savor his unique smell. Instead she concentrated on a scar on his forearm.

"I didn't come here for this."

"So why did you come?"

"Your father asked me to dinner, wanted me to meet your mother. I refused the family meal, but told him I'd stop by for dessert."

Tess snorted.

"Do you think I would come if I knew you were here?" he asked.

She arched an eyebrow. "It's Easter, Graham. Where did you think I'd be?"

"I don't know, but I'm not stupid. I'm not trying to cause you pain."

"You're not that important to me. You could be anyone who took over Ullo. You don't matter to me. My anger is directed at my father."

"And me."

Tess tugged on the handle, but Graham still held the door shut. "Fine. I'm pissed at you. You're a bastard, not just because you happen to be the person my father hired over me, but because you aren't a man of your word."

Graham sighed and with his other hand he brushed back the dark hair falling into his eyes. "I really liked you, Tess."

"I could tell. Enough to screw but not enough to—"

"You're wrong."

"Don't think so. You never proved any differently, and I got the message." Tess looked pointedly at Graham's hand flat against the window. "If you wouldn't mind taking your hand away, I really want to get the hell out of here. I'm tired of thinking about you, that night and…everything. So move."

"Tess." His voice was raw, full of emotion.

Her heart ached. But only for a second. "There's

no need for any more words. You've apologized.…
I just can't accept that apology right now. Things
are too shitty. Or maybe I'm too immature to be the
bigger person. I don't know, but I do know I want
to leave. Now."

"I wish things were different," he said, lifting his
gaze to hers. In his eyes she saw the regret and it
gave her a flicker of understanding. "I wasn't ready
to offer someone a relationship. I wish you understood that it wasn't you, it was—"

"Me? Yeah, I've heard that one. Might have even
used it a time or two myself. Truth is you didn't
want me enough to fight through all that stuff." She
hardened herself against the self-pity that thought
inspired. "What happened was a one-time thing—
just another one-night stand with some guy in a
moment of weakness."

"No, it wasn't," he said, pulling his hand away.
"You can tell yourself that. I can tell myself that.
But we both know it wasn't."

"Yeah?" she asked, pulling open the car door.
"But here's the question. If this—" she swished
her hand back and forth between them "—wasn't
sitting between us, would you ever have called?"

He stood silently for several seconds. "Yes. I had
every intention of calling you, and I would have
been prepared to grovel at your feet for forgiveness
for my bad behavior."

Inside Tess the tangle of emotion that had been
knotting for the last several hours rolled over, crush-

ing even her anger for a moment. She wanted to believe him. Wanted to push aside the wall between them for a moment, so they could go back to being just a girl and just a guy who had found a piece of magic on a rain-dampened night. But—

"Too late," she said softly sliding into her car and starting the engine. For some reason tears pricked her eyes and her throat tightened with emotion.

Pulling the door shut, she buckled up, put the car in Reverse and eased out, peering over the other parked cars on the shady street.

She no longer had the luxury of looking backward.

Only forward.

There were new paths to blaze and new men to love.

If only she could believe her own decree.

CHAPTER NINE

STANDING IN THE Ullos' driveway, Graham watched Tess drive away.

She hated him.

Fine.

She didn't forgive him and she likely never would.

Fine.

What more could he do?

Quit. The inner voice sounded like an echo, like something whispered to a character in a movie, carried on a breeze in the misty gloom of evening.

But this wasn't a movie and the sun bearing down on his shoulders reminded him where he stood. In the glaring now.

Trudging toward the Ullo home, solid stone and stucco with massive columns and a message of "Somebody with power lives here," Graham decided he had to move forward. Though quitting would send Tess a message, it would put him in the poorhouse. Living paycheck to paycheck reminded him he didn't have the luxury of playing the martyr. No amount of self-sacrifice would appease Tess.

She would need time to temper her opinion of him and even that might not be enough.

He'd hurt her.

Not just by taking the job Frank offered, but by not calling. Taking the job had merely pissed her off. Anger on top of hurt was never a good look on a woman…and he couldn't blame her.

Shaking his head, he closed his eyes before entering the discomfort he'd left a moment ago. He'd tried to convince himself what he'd shared with Tess that night was run-of-the-mill. Seemed a rational thing to do. Treat it like every other one-night stand he'd ever had. Tess was a random hookup—a nice one—but nothing ever amounted to anything with hookups. He'd even convinced himself she wouldn't care whether he called her back or not. But he'd fooled himself. It was easier than facing the truth.

Graham was on a short trip to becoming his father, a man who'd had so much potential but had thrown away his dream over pride. He'd left New Orleans, spent too much and lived too recklessly, all to soothe his ego…and had paid the price when he'd opened his wallet and found it empty.

Tess didn't date losers like Graham. She deserved better. So he hadn't called her.

Doubt whirled in him and the bitter feeling of failure pecked at his psyche. Sadly, he'd grown accustomed to feeling that way over the last few months, and it would be hard to repair things between him and the only person who'd made him forget his failures for one night.

It was, as Tess said, too late.

"Hey," the door opened and the priest stood there. Michael. "Is Tess gone?"

"Yeah," Graham said, trying to clear his throat of the knot sitting within.

Michael narrowed eyes that looked just like his father's. "Something more is going on here."

Graham shook his head but didn't argue. He didn't particularly like the idea of being struck by lightning or having a piano dropped on his head for lying to a priest.

"Yeah, I know Tess, and I can see right through this thing. You knew her before you took her job?"

"Look," Graham said, aggravation rising to replace the sadness in his gut. "I didn't take anyone's job…except maybe your father's. I had nothing to do with what happened between Tess and Frank."

"You had a little to do with it, but I'm not talking about that. I'm talking about something else. I know Tess."

"So you've said," Graham muttered, jerking his head toward the entrance of the house. "Shall we?"

"What?"

"Go back inside? I need to make my exit and thank your mother for the, ah, coffee."

"You never drank it," Michael said dryly.

Graham gave him a flat stare, somewhat liking the man despite his acerbic and prying comments.

"I'm watching you," Michael said, doing that double-finger jab at his eyes and then turning them to jab at Graham.

"Better mind my p's and q's then." Graham didn't try to keep the sarcasm from his voice.

"You better. The big guy is on my side."

Graham snorted. "God?"

"No, Eddie 'the shark' Russo. He's about 6'4" and cracks skulls for a living. Friend from my bookie days." Michael smiled, but Graham wasn't sure if the man was kidding or not. Where was the pious man of the cloth? Michael almost looked like a shark himself. Guess when it came to protecting little sisters from jerks like himself all bets were off.

"Right," Graham said, slipping by the man who came to his nose in height but didn't budge from his original stance. Entering the house, Graham headed directly for the dining room.

Everyone's head swiveled toward him when he reentered the dining room…except for the old bird with the naughty gleam in her faded eyes. She was digging into her dessert with a relish reserved for those under the age of ten and over the age of eighty.

"I'm sorry," he said, not sure he offered the apology for the whole craptastic debacle or for following Tess without asking their pardon.

Frank stood with a wince. "Actually I'm the one who should apologize. Making this change in my business has cast a pall on my family. Unintended, but there it is all the same. Things have been difficult lately." Shooting an inscrutable glance at his wife, Frank gestured to the chair Graham had abandoned earlier.

"Understood, and I apologize for my role in this difficult process. I had looked forward to meeting you, Mrs. Ullo, but I feel it would be better if I go ahead and take my leave."

"Oh, don't do that," Mrs. Ullo said, trying on a smile. Something around her mouth trembled, making Graham wonder if there was more to Frank's words than what had been revealed. "Call me Maggie. And please, have a little coffee. Maybe a cannoli?"

"I thank you, but no. I want to spend some extra time with my daughter today, and Monique's not patient."

"I find it odd you had a relationship with Monique Dryden," Joseph said, setting his napkin beside his plate. "But Dad told us it's one of the main reasons why he hired you."

"Because of Monique?" Graham cast a searching look toward Frank.

"Not because you share a child and not because I'm trying to take a jab at her. She's a talented woman if not a thorn in my paw. Monique's smart."

"That I can't deny. She was always the brains behind the operation. I was merely the brawn who stumbled into her world and became enraptured with Mardi Gras and building the floats. For a while it was enough."

Everyone at the table, the five-year-old included, watched him as if he'd dug up a rock, revealing what was beneath…and that was what his relationship with Monique had turned into—something crawly and dark. Something he didn't like exposing to the light of day.

"So I'll say goodbye. I wish you all a Happy Easter," Graham said, wanting desperately to do much as Tess had—get the hell out of there.

A chorus of byes met his ears as he turned toward the exit. Frank joined him on his walk to the front door. Michael had disappeared and the heavy wood door stood cracked open, allowing daylight to slash inside the darkness.

"Look, Graham. I'm sorry about Tess. Her reaction, or rather her actions, have nothing to do with you. Wouldn't matter who I had hired, the result would be the same. She's young and doesn't understand the ways of a man or the ways of the world."

"Perhaps she doesn't understand because you haven't told her why you hired me," Graham said, his voice falling like raindrops on a flat rock.

For a moment Frank stared at him. "You don't know me or my daughter."

"Perhaps not, but from the beginning you've mishandled this. You knew she thought she would be the next CEO of Frank Ullo, but you still proceeded to hire an outsider. That makes me wonder about your reasons."

"Wonder away. I did what I thought best for the

company and Tess," Frank said, his heavy eyebrows drawn together. "If that's mishandling, then so be it."

"Just my opinion, but I daresay it's one your family shares." Graham paused for a moment, trying to find the words he needed to drive his point home. "Look, this job is my dream job—I can admit that. But I took it with the expectation you and I would work together for a few months, and then once I earned your full confidence, I could take the helm. My goal was clear—bring Frank Ullo back into focus with new technology and cutting-edge design. But I can't do that if our relationship demands I measure my every word. I won't always agree with you, and this matter is a personal one, but it's also a situation that spills over. Your mishandling of Tess affects your employees and affects how they see me and deal with me."

"My employees understand. Trust me."

Graham sighed. "I've been there for four days and you're wrong. They know you're Frank Ullo, but their loyalty is to the company and Tess was part of that. Do you know how many times this week I've heard 'Tess handles that' or 'Tess knows where the info on that account is'?"

"She's worked there since she got out of college. It's going to be hard to not have her, but we'll manage. Change is hard, right? Never was going to be easy to do this." Frank pulled open the door. Laughter filled the air and Graham caught sight of a teen running with a lacrosse stick and two girls about Emily's age chasing him. He recognized one as the girl who had brought in the cannoli with Tess. Squeals and shrieks followed as a small boy chased the girls with a water gun. Frank watched with a hungry look on his face.

At that moment, something reverberated within Graham. And he knew, absolutely knew, what had been going on for the last month. A careful study of Frank's face—the circles under his eyes, the sallowness of his skin, was all it took to get a clearer picture.

"Are you sick, Frank?"

The older man jerked back as if he'd been punched in the chest. His skin turned ashen. "What makes you ask?"

"I don't know. Something."

Frank glanced around as if making sure no one had overheard Graham's question. "Let's talk later."

Graham nodded, understanding Frank hadn't told his family about his condition.

A sweet longing to lift Emily into his arms and inhale her sweetness, the pure innocence of a seven-year-old untainted by the difficulty of living as an adult in a bitter world slammed into Graham. "Sure, but until then, no matter what your answer to my question is, I suggest you go to Tess and try to heal the hurt inside her. It's not hard to say 'I'm sorry.'"

Frank's mouth set into an unyielding line. "I haven't done anything wrong. I'm a businessman, something Tess forgets. This isn't about loving your child. It's about doing what is best for everyone concerned."

Graham stepped outside. "Just think about it, Frank. Life's too short, you know?"

Again, Frank's face lost its color and Graham knew things were bad for the man. When he put everything together—the rush to hire him, the hiding of the decision from Tess and the haunted look on the man's face—he could see the writing on the wall. Frank Ullo was a very sick and scared man.

"Goodbye, Graham. Thank you for coming," Frank said, once again grabbing the reins and becoming the man who didn't bend.

Graham made his way to the car Frank had sent him, eyeing the big Easter basket sitting on the back floorboard beneath the new booster seat he'd bought for Emily. He hoped the bunny hadn't melted and that his daughter would consent to riding in the seat she still needed, according to the state laws he'd looked up a few days ago.

Daughters were indeed hard to manage, swerving around feelings, tip-toeing around their dreams, hot-stepping out of arguments a father couldn't win, but Graham wouldn't trade his Emily for a billion dollars.

And he knew Frank felt the same.

Graham just wished things were different between himself and Tess, wished he could have a second shot with her. Even now, as hard as it was between them, he wanted her. Wanted to trace the curve of her stubborn jaw, kiss the corner of her delicious mouth and gather all her sweet, hot wonderfulness against him.

But Graham had learned long ago he didn't always get what he wanted, so he would shelve the desire for Tess and try and focus on what he'd come to New Orleans to do—be a better father to his daughter and kick ass as the CEO at Frank Ullo.

Those things he could do.

He hoped.

TESS EYED HER reflection critically in the bathroom mirror. She'd twisted her hair into a messy knot—a look *Cosmo* said was professional but also revealed her playful side. Swiping a creamy nude lipstick across her lips and clasping a cool Norman cross necklace she'd bought during the French Quarter Festival around her neck, Tess blew herself a kiss and left the bathroom.

Her first job interview and her stomach had filled with jumpy frogs.

After leaving her parents' house, she'd dropped by Cuppa Joe's for a frappé and checked her messages. To her surprise, she had two: one from Joe Rizollo who ran Mardi Gras Creations and one from Monique Dryden. Against a small niggle of doubt she'd smothered with the justification she'd been screwed by her father and Graham, Tess had followed through and sent her resume to Upstart and a few other of her father's competitors. She'd half hoped no one would call so she didn't have to step across to the other side. But when the bitterness edged in on her, when the hurt of Graham not calling and then taking over what she'd loved for so long surfaced, she didn't feel so bad about interviewing for a position at Upstart.

She carefully placed the files of her best past designs inside the attaché case her mother had given her when she'd graduated from college. Fortuitously she'd re-created many of the designs with software because many of the hard copies were filed at the Ullo warehouse. Dave wouldn't mind forwarding some to her, but she hadn't wanted to ask.

Half an hour later she pushed through the door of Upstart Float Design and Rental with the crowing rooster emblem centered in the glass. A man with a loud silk shirt and cargo pants sat kicked back at the desk. He snapped to attention when Tess approached.

"Hey, you must be the Ullo chick," he said with a shy smile.

Ullo chick?

"Yes, I'm Tess Ullo," she said with a businesslike nod.

"Yeah, I actually met you once at one of the balls. Endymion? I don't remember. Anyway, Monique's on a call right now. Negotiation's her deal. Have a seat over there. Can I grab you a coffee? Water?"

Tess walked over to the small reception area and sat in one of the folding chairs, pressing her hands over her navy pencil skirt. "No, thank you."

"Oh, I'm Josh, by the way. I'm Monique's partner and husband." He gave her another smile. Josh's face looked lean and hungry, like a stray dog. He had an earring that dangled, a soul patch on his chin and wore a newsboy tweed hat to complement his New Orleans artist look.

She might be biased but if Monique was stupid enough to trade Graham in for this guy, she might not want to work for the woman. Josh wasn't unattractive by any means, but Graham made Josh look like the Shaggy to his buff Fred.

Some girls liked a Shaggy, but Mr. Uptight Naquin who performed magic with his mouth and had a butt she could bounce quarters off was definitely more Tess's type. To each her own.

The office door opened and Monique swept into the reception area like a queen greeting her subject.

"Ah, Tess Ullo. You actually showed up," she said in a melodious voice.

Monique wore a tight pair of leggings beneath a bright sweater that dropped to midthigh. Her dark wavy hair brushed thin shoulders revealed by the wide boatneck. Her flawless skin was enhanced by subtle makeup and large diamonds winking in her ears. Blood-red polish tipped her elegant fingers. She made Tess feel like an over-dressed heifer.

"Yes, and I appreciate your replying to my inquiry."

Monique gave a secret little smile. "You're Frank Ullo's daughter, and I'm thinking you're a pissed off Frank Ullo's daughter, so of course I'm interested, darling."

Tess raised her eyebrows, struggling to her feet in the serviceable pumps, wishing she hadn't dressed so formally. Fish out of water.

"Come on in. Josh, get us some coffees around the corner."

"Aye-aye, Captain," Josh joked with a salute.

In that instant Tess totally understood why Graham hadn't lasted with Monique. Tess waited to see if the woman would mutter "good boy" before following her into the office.

Seconds later Tess sank into the armchair situated in front of Monique's massive modern steel desk. Monique landed on her bright red office chair as gracefully as a butterfly and popped a pair of glasses on her nose. Extending her hand she blinked at Tess.

Tess stared at her.

"I'm waiting to see your designs," Monique said. She might as well have added "dumb ass."

"Oh, sorry," Tess said, opening the attaché and pulling out a folder before placing it in Monique's hand.

Monique waffled through the designs, her eyes

narrowing, occasionally turning the paper this way or that. "These are good."

"Thank you," Tess murmured.

"But let me be honest," Monique said, tossing the copies onto her immaculate desk. "I'm not looking for an art designer so much as I'm looking for someone who can bring in new business. That's why I left you a message yesterday."

Tess didn't know what to say to that. She'd wanted to do design work only. Felt less Benedict Arnold.

Monique smiled. "You intrigue me. Even more than having considerable experience in the float decorating business, I like what you're doing—a little revenge, if I'm not mistaken. Your old man pissed you off by hiring Graham, and you want him to pay. I love that kind of emotion. It burns holes in things. It makes things happen. Know what I mean?"

"You're saying you want to hire me because one, I'm an Ullo, two, I'm pissed at my father and three, you love the idea of stealing from your ex-husband."

"Not my ex-husband. I was smart enough not to marry Graham. That would have been disastrous." Monique snorted and it was cute. When Tess snorted it wasn't cute. More like a sinus infection.

"But—"

"Yes, we have a child together. But that's all. Graham and I are water under a bridge with a fast current."

Tess relaxed a little. She didn't really know what

to think about Monique. Part of her didn't like the relish showed at one-upping not only her competition but her ex-lover. Like a predator, Monique smelled blood on the trail. Yet part of Tess warmed to the same idea—she wanted to make her father pay for his mistake…and Graham, too. Nothing wrong with that, right?

Still, Monique put her on edge. There was something untamed about the woman and Tess knew she wasn't one to trust.

So who went to work for someone like Monique?

Someone reckless. Someone fueled by emotion and not thinking clearly. Someone who needed to prove herself.

Someone exactly like Tess.

"I can put you on as co-director of art and design and I will pay you well, but I want something in return."

Tess raised her eyebrows.

"Some of Frank Ullo's business."

Tess's gut heaved at the thought of tearing clients away from the company she'd helped build over the last few years. Her name was attached to that business. Tess couldn't take from the company that had given her so much. She set her feet on the floor, intending to leave, but then that same inner voice that had prodded her to contact Monique Dryden whispered to her now.

Didn't seem to matter to your father, did it? Daddy doesn't think you're vital to his business.

He thinks Graham can do better. Prove him wrong, Tess. Tell her yes.

Tess tossed her hair, her confidence returning. "My plan was for design work—"

"If that is all you have to offer, I'm not interested," Monique said, crossing her arms. "I have a designer and I oversee all proposals. It would be overkill. But I'm willing to pay for your 'experience' with the krewes."

Tess stared at the hot pink stapler sitting on the desk, realizing Monique desired what Joe Rizzolo and every other company would desire—her ability to snag business. This wasn't about her talent. "Well, I have the keys to the kingdom. As point woman for the krewes we did business with, I have a list of contacts a mile long and a good relationship with each captain and art director."

"Which is why I'm happy to pay you handsomely," Monique said, her mouth stretching into a grin over white teeth. Passing Tess several papers, Monique sank back into her chair. "This is my offer along with contract terms."

So formal. Tess allowed her gaze to flicker over the salary which was more than fair. So final.

If she signed on with Upstart, she'd be betraying all she'd been. An Ullo working for the competition? Tess could hardly fathom the thought, but she needed a job. Her father might have covered tuition and helped finance her loft, but Tess paid her own way. She had two months' rent in her savings, but that was it. She needed a job sooner rather than later and once she signed on, her designs would convince Monique she was an asset in more than one way. "Can I have until Wednesday? I need to have my attorney review these."

"Of course, but no longer. Your service to Upstart is valuable right now. We have a month or so to pin down these krewes and set our contracts for 2016. I still need some floats rented for 2015."

Rising, Tess extended her hand. "I'll be in touch. Thank you for taking this meeting and for the offer."

Monique ignored Tess's hand and instead picked up the drawings, shoved them in a folder and handed them to Tess. "I know what you're thinking. I'm too ambitious. Maybe even bloodthirsty. Does that scare you?"

Tess shook her head.

Monique laughed. "It's okay. I *am* ambitious. I want to succeed. This business has been a good ol' boy network for too long. I bet you did a lot of your father's work, but the krewes wanted to deal with Daddy, didn't they?"

"Yeah, but that's the way it is down here."

"Maybe so, but I'm tired of being marginalized and I think we can do great things together, Tess. Take that anger at being thought of as less and channel it into something new and challenging. Come be a part of a company that refuses to be shoved aside because a woman runs it. Time to prove to the world that Tess Ullo can stand on her own two feet." Monique moved around the corner of her desk and glanced down at Tess's shoes.

Tess frowned. "Yeah, I know. I thought they looked like interview shoes."

Monique smiled, this time looking younger and not so apt to eat her young. "A little tame, but you can buy something fierce with your first paycheck. You'll need something fabulous to wear to schmooze with the clients. In the business world, a gal has to be willing to use every advantage she has."

"Even her legs?" Tess joked.

"Especially her legs," Monique said, assessing Tess again. "You're pretty, and with the right clothes and makeup, you'd be devastating."

"Thanks, I think," Tess said inching toward the door, shoving both the contract and the folder in her case. "I'll be in touch."

Josh bumbled in with a tray holding three cups of coffee.

"I'll be waiting for good news," Monique said, reaching out for her cup, nodding at Josh to give Tess hers.

Tess refused the cup and instead pushed out the door into the cloudy Monday. The day reflected her emotions—gray.

Or maybe not so gray. After all, she'd just gotten a job offer.

One she really didn't want.

But this is what she'd set into motion when she'd

mailed her resume last week. She'd have to deal with it.

Her phone buzzed in her purse, and hope sprang inside her. Maybe it was her father calling to say this was all a bad nightmare. Or maybe it was Graham calling to say…what?

There was nothing left to say between them.

They were over before they'd even gotten out the gate. Okay, they'd gotten out the gate several pleasurable times, but the race had already been run. Both she and Graham were losers.

It was Gigi.

"Hey," Tess said into the phone.

"Come meet me for lunch. I got a scoop."

"On what?" Tess pressed the button on her key fob and unlocked her car.

"Your man, that's who."

Tess blew out a breath. "Gigi, I don't have a man."

"Nick has dumped Miss Slutfest and is out and about. He told Shari Grabel he missed you." Gigi made a low noise in her throat.

"Well, I don't miss him. If you like Nick so much, why don't you date him?"

"Maybe I will." Gigi laughed. "Is he good in bed?"

"Lord, Gigi," Tess complained, pulling her seatbelt on. "I'll meet you because I've got a scoop… and a contract for you to review."

"You got the job at Upstart?" Gigi crowed, before lowering her voice. "I would be happy to review that contract for you at a time of your convenience, Ms. Ullo."

Tess rolled her eyes. "See you in a few."

Tossing her phone on the seat, Tess pulled away from the Upstart office, nestled next to the den they'd built from an abandoned grain storehouse in the 9th Ward. Her life had been turned entirely upside down. But she might as well go to lunch with Gigi. She hoped wherever they went had ice cream. Suddenly, she felt like she needed a double scoop with chocolate sauce.

CHAPTER TEN

GRAHAM HAD SPENT all of Monday and Tuesday in meetings with the team at Ullo and in impromptu lunches or cocktails with board members and captains of various krewes. Tess's leaving had stunned the team at Ullo and many of the major players who wrote the checks for the krewes were nervous about a new person taking charge of one of the oldest float builders and decorators in the Crescent City. Graham had smiled so much his face hurt.

Frank had given him an empty office that had been used for storing files and supplies. His new assistant, Billie, had grabbed one of the full-time painters and had him clear out the boxes and bring in an unused large wood table and chair. The rest had been left to Graham, but much like his new apartment, the space remained Spartan.

He'd just sunk into his chair when a knock sounded at the door. "Come in."

Frank stormed in like he owned the place...which Graham supposed he technically did. "I'm going to kill her."

"Who?"

"Tess. She went to work for your old company."

"Wait! What? Tess is working for Upstart?" Something heavy dropped in his stomach. Tess had gone to work for Monique? "Why?"

"To punish me, of course." Frank leaned across the desk and knocked his knuckles against the calendar blotter that was still pristine. "To punish you."

"Shit."

"You can say that again."

"Shit."

Frank rubbed a weary hand over his face and stepped back. "Already got a call from Edward Mendez's office. Tess has her claws in him and has subbed a bid for outfitting and renting most of Pan's floats. She knows what we charge and she's going to undercut us. She's also friends with Edward's daughter-in-law. This ain't good. The Krewe of Pan is a big account."

Graham straightened. "We can deal with it. We have your reputation and I have inside knowledge of how Upstart works."

"We gotta take a meeting with Ed. Whatever he wants, he gets. Understand? We gotta make sure we keep the super krewes before even considering harvesting some of the smaller krewes around the metro area. We have the talent and workforce here. Gotta move and shake."

"What about you?"

Frank sighed and sank gingerly into the folding chair. His face fell as if he just grasped the ramifications of his former VP and daughter working for the competition. "I won't be here much."

Graham sighed before he could catch himself.

"I know. I had hoped to have Tess to ease you into this, to be your guide, but with things the way they are in my personal life…"

"Can you clarify for me?"

"I know you know something is wrong, and you're a perceptive man." Frank looked at the closed door, his thoughts obviously drifting away. Graham gave him space and sat quietly as the older man gathered his words. "Thing is, I have pancreatic cancer."

"Jesus," Graham breathed, reeling back so that his chair butted into the wall. He'd known something was up with Frank's health, but pancreatic cancer was almost always a death sentence. "What is… How…"

How did you ask a man something like how long you got?

"Three to six months, depending on the success of the chemo. I actually start this week over at Oschner. It's gonna make me sick and I won't be able to do much other than puke my guts up for the next few weeks."

Graham had no words. How could he?

Frank stared down at his clasped hands. "Everything's pretty much screwed. This whole thing with Tess. I don't know what to do. I never thought she'd be this mad. Never thought she'd turn her back on family and quit the business."

"But you knew she'd be hurt," Graham noted.

"Sure. She's like her mother. She don't like when she has no say so I knew she'd be ticked, but I thought eventually she'd see things my way. This," he waved a hand in the air, "ain't a one-person job. You gotta have someone to be your right hand."

Graham wondered if he could make things easier for Frank. He couldn't. Nothing would be easy for this man. He faced dying and a daughter who was angry enough to take her talents and knowledge to the competition. "It will be okay."

Frank looked up. "No, it won't."

"So we will make it okay. You have a viable, reputable business that has always put forth outstanding product, and now you have me. Fate led us to one another. You can trust me. I, too, have contacts. And experience. We needed Tess, but we won't let that stand in our way."

Frank looked down at his hands, looking older than he had when Graham had first met him. For a few moments the man didn't speak. "My whole life I've always known what to do. Always. But I've lost a grip on this."

"The truth usually works, Frank. I'm assuming neither Tess nor your sons know about your illness?"

"Joe knows. He's the one who set me up with an oncologist, but he can't tell anyone on account of a confidentiality clause. He's upset I haven't told everyone yet, but I wanted to do it—"

"On your terms," Graham finished the statement for him.

"No, that's not what I was going to say. I didn't want to do it at Easter is all."

"You're facing a tough battle, Frank. Not here at Ullo—that's why you hired me. I'm going to take care of things here." Even as he spoke the words, he said a small prayer that it would be true. That he could rally the troops that had been lackluster at best, keep the accounts they had and give Frank some peace of mind. "But you've got to help yourself as you prepare to fight cancer. You need your team, and Maggie needs support and help. Tell your family and allow them to do what they need to do for you."

For a second Frank bristled and Graham prepared to argue, but then it was as if the air leaked out of him. "How do I tell them? How do I destroy all they've known about me?"

"I've only known you for a short time, Frank, but I sense your biggest flaw is your desire to handle every aspect of not only your life, but your kids'. You don't like to be weak, and I get that—it's in our makeup as men. But fact is, you're not merely man, but human. Which means you are vulnerable. Don't allow pride to stand in your way of admitting you were wrong or of asking for help."

Frank rolled Graham's words around in his

mind—Graham could see the battle within the man who stepped down yesterday at the CEO, officially handing the reins of the company to Graham with little fanfare. All the employees had seemed confused…unsettled at the news their leader stepped down so casually.

Finally, Frank nodded. "You're a smart man."

"Not always. It's easier to see what someone else needs to do than to apply the same logic in one's own life. I've made a lot of mistakes, and I'll make a ton more. It's the human condition. We can't control the world around us, and at times, we can't control our own responses. I do a lot of backpedaling. In fact, I need to do some with your daughter myself."

Frank searched Graham's face for an answer to his admission, but Graham would give the man nothing more than the suggestion he'd also wronged Tess. Frank had matters to settle with Tess, and Graham had ones of his own. Both men had handled Tess badly.

Rising, Frank set his hands on his hips and squared himself like a puffer fish ready to fight. "I'll handle my life. You handle this company. I trust the man you are, Graham. Don't make me regret it."

Graham nodded, hoping like hell he could do all Frank needed him to do. It would start with procuring the contract with the Krewe of Pan. Time to schmooze and dazzle. Time to show the world he'd left behind he wasn't a one-trick pony. Applying his vast knowledge of materials and construction, Graham knew he could revolutionize Frank Ullo Float Builders. Graham was back doing what he'd loved, doing what he'd started before the wheels had fallen off at Upstart, before he and Monique became more enemies than lovers. The task before him was large, but not impossible. He needed time to win over his new employees. He needed time to heal Tess.

Problem was, time wasn't exactly something he could control any more than Frank could.

ALMOST TWO WEEKS after signing a contract at Upstart, Tess had the first twinge of doubt. Oh, hell. Who was she kidding? She'd felt close to vomiting when she'd signed the Upstart contract and followed Monique to her new cubicle. Making the decision about joining arms with the competition hadn't been easy, but the more Tess lay in bed, beneath the sheets she and Graham had tangled themselves in, thinking about her father and how he'd created a path for her that she'd followed like a stupid cow, never looking to the left or right, only ahead to what she thought her destiny, the more pissed she'd grown…at her father and herself. She'd never allowed herself to consider any other world but her father's, and he'd never demanded much from her. To say Tess had been stretched and put through the paces was such an underwhelming statement it was almost a lie.

Going to work would piss off her father—and Graham—and that thought pleased Tess. Neither had valued her.

Of course, Gigi had been smart, insisting on a provisional three-month period to protect both Monique and Tess in case the job didn't work out, but Tess was thrilled by the blank slate spread before her. Here was a chance to make her mark in a whole different way.

The first few weeks hadn't been easy. Outside of avoiding her family like the plague, Tess had spent much of the time navigating the torrents of Monique's complex ego. Monique demanded she have the final say in each design and had changed a few of Tess's visions. Tess had bitten her tongue over a few, choosing to bend rather than break.

But the biggest challenge came when she faced Cecily Webb, the head of design for Upstart. The fifty-year-old artist, who'd been with Monique since Graham had left the business, resented Tess and obviously wasn't going to play fair, if her cold treatment was any evidence. Not to mention, the woman seemed to have hoodwinked the staff by giving counter directives on several float designs, making Tess look wishy-washy. Monique seemed to look on with amused tolerance, as if she thought it best for Tess to handle Cecily herself.

At Ullo Tess had had final say in design work…

even when it came to her father. And she'd never had to deal with fellow employees who didn't love her.

"Hey, new girl." One of the papier-mâché guys who worked on a sculpture of a pig flying motioned her over.

"Yeah?" Tess asked, walking over to the man wearing overalls and a fedora—artists were wonderfully weird.

"You told Halle to make this part larger, but I think it distorts the face."

Tess studied the sculpture critically. "I think the larger body will have more punch. The face will be forward but this prop is on the back of the float, so the effect is in the wings and body. Let's do it that way."

The man frowned and studied the shape in front of him for a few seconds. "Cecily trusts my judgment."

"I trust the design. Nothing to do with you, Ben."

"Whatever you want."

Tess closed her eyes and sucked in a short breath. "I'm open to suggestions for the poster board props along the sides. What do you think?"

"Bacon?"

Okay, so Ben was a master of sarcasm. "Hmm… actually I like that idea. Let's go with bacon."

"Seriously?" He made a face, but after a few seconds he laughed. "It *would* be ironic."

"And I love ironic. Let me check with the captain

before we go to too much trouble, but I think the effect will be almost iconic. Good call."

Ben smiled turning back to the large foam pigs torn down to basic concept.

Score one for the new girl.

She strolled over to where Upstart's head sculptor showed Monique the start of the huge image of the governor that would be affixed to the float for the Krewe D'Tat's royalty float. Never easy to win the trust of a group of artists. By definition, artists had their own ideas about what worked, and at a Mardi Gras float company they were often free to interpret many props in their own way, but Tess wanted this lead float for the satirical krewe to be spot on. She'd promised Mark Curtis it would have the proper "wow" factor the acerbic krewe demanded.

"Let's build the nose bigger," Monique said studying the work-in-progress. "It needs over-emphasis to give the right effect."

"I agree," Tess said with a nod, sweeping her hand over the entire sculpture. "Makes it more comical…like the guy on *Mad* Magazine."

Monique tossed her a smile. "Exactly."

Score two for the new girl.

Yesterday Monique had asked Tess to attend a meeting with the Krewe of Cleopatra and they had contracted five of the company's thirty rental floats. Tess had worked on some designs for the company that would meet their theme of "Take it to the Dance Floor" but also be versatile for several other krewes that would be looking to rent. As of yesterday, Monique hadn't altered the sketches.

Maybe Monique would trust Tess's visions soon…rather than merely tugging her along for liquid lunches with krewe fat cats.

"Mommy!" the shriek came from their left.

Graham's daughter. Tess had seen her once from afar and hadn't engaged her yet, hoping she could forget every aspect about the man.

Tess watched as a rounded little body collided with Monique, causing her to stumble in the too-high-for-the-warehouse stilettos.

"Emily," Monique admonished, trying to gain her footing. Louie, the head sculptor who'd been passing by, pressed a hand against the woman's back and kept her from falling.

"A spider!" the child cried, burying her head against her mother's thighs.

"A spider?" Monique asked, prying the little girl off her. "All this over a little spider? Emily, Momma is working, honey."

The little girl kept her eyes shut and refused to let go of her mother's leg. In fact, she re-strengthened her grip and held on for dear life. "It was really big and mean-looking. It had hair on its legs like a tarantula. I'm not going back in there."

"Emily, let go. I'm going to fall," Monique said, pushing against the little girl's shoulder.

"It's probably just a wood spider," Tess said, rather unhelpfully.

Emily's eyes opened and they were the exact bright blue of her father's. Damn.

"Who are you?" she asked.

Tess managed a smile, wishing the child didn't look so much like her father. "I'm Tess. I'm new here."

Loosening her hold, Emily tilted her head like an inquisitive puppy. "I like your watch."

"Thanks," Tess said, looking down at the Cookie Monster watch Gigi had bought her as a joke. Turns out, it was the watch she chose most often over the Rolex her father had given her last Christmas. "I'm a big fan of cookies."

"Me, too." The little girl smiled, finally unwinding from her mother's leg, seemingly forgetting about the child-eating spider in the next room.

Monique ignored them both, choosing to tap on her phone.

Graham's daughter wore her light brown hair in a ponytail with streaming green ribbons. Her cotton dress was wrinkled and she looked as if she'd been eating cheese puffs because her lips were ringed in orange. Her cheeks were adorably chubby as was her middle. She looked nothing like her sophisticated mother, and for a moment, Tess felt absolutely sorry for the poor baby, as if she could see Monique disliked this about her own daughter. Wasn't fair of Tess to allow this immediate thought to pop up, but there it was all the same.

"Mom, can I have some Girl Scout cookies? I can share with Tess."

Meanwhile Monique had turned to Louie. "Make those adjustments and I'll take a look before the mâché goes on."

"Mom?" Emily intoned in that whiny voice invoked by almost every child on the planet.

"Whatever you want, Emily. Just don't ruin your lunch. Your father will be angry." Monique moved toward another painting bay, the click of her heels accompanying her dismissal of her child.

Emily's expression dissolved into bitter disappointment. Tess felt her own heart flinch in response.

"Know what? I'm about to take a break and go to Magglio's for a slushie. You want to come with me?" Tess asked, having no such intention but feeling like she needed to do something more than stand there watching Emily hunger for a crumb of her mother's affection.

Emily's blue eyes lit. "Yes, please." Then she yelled across the wide aisle, "Mom, can I go?"

Monique tossed her inky hair over her shoulder and looked at Tess. "You're already taking a break?"

"Actually I've been working on sketches for Eddie all morning and I need something more than coffee. Saturdays were made for strawberry slushes, don't you think?"

"Yay." Emily clapped.

"Sure," Monique said before turning back to another painter to inquire about a shade of brown that didn't match on one part of a prop.

Tess motioned Emily toward the exit. The little girl skipped ahead, pushing the exit bar, struggling against the heavy steel door. Tess shoved it open, allowing sunshine to tumble inside the dusty building.

Outside, the world was in weekend mode...or maybe it merely felt that way. Tess usually didn't come in to work on the weekend, but Monique had demanded she drop by and show her the preliminary sketches for Edward Mendez's krewe. The woman salivated over the chance to earn some of the krewes' business. So Tess had tugged on old jeans and a too tight T-shirt because she hadn't had time to do laundry and hustled down to Upstart to show Monique her sketches.

Needless to say, Tess had spent the last two hours making the adjustments Monique wanted. Tess had liked them the way they were and her father never would have nickel-and-dimed her lines or colors, but she now accepted she wasn't in charge.

Monique was...and her controlling nature was very evident.

Something she'd run into when it came to the sketches for Oedipus. Tess had worked personally with krewe captain Miles Barrow for years, but Monique and Cecily had already completed designs for the floats. Tess all but insisted she be given the chance to design something for the krewe's silver anniversary, a kernel of an idea she'd been playing around with for months. Tess hoped a superior design might dazzle Monique enough to give her the account. Monique relented, telling Tess she could work on the Oedipus design on her own time, but she would decide which designs were subbed to Miles based on cost, ease and design.

"I like Coca-Cola slushes," Emily said, jarring Tess from her contemplation. The child looked up at Tess as they waited to cross the intersection. "You like strawberry best?"

"I'm a strawberry-mixed-with-Coca-Cola girl. I like peach, too."

"Yuck," Emily wrinkled her nose, sticking out her hand so Tess could lead her across the street.

"Well, I like it." Tess laughed, looking down at Graham's daughter. Emily wasn't a beautiful child, but Tess had a sneaking suspicion she'd grow into quite a looker. She had long legs, thick wavy hair and a sparkle of good humor in her eyes…and Graham had gifted her with the most beautiful eyes.

Minutes later after snitching a brownie made by Alva Magglio herself—a treat since Alva had contracted rheumatoid arthritis and shifted the baking over to her daughter-in-law who didn't have the touch—Tess and Emily made their way back to Upstart's den. Sitting outside in his shiny silver car was the man Tess had tried like the devil to forget…and failed, of course.

"Daddy!" Emily screamed, trying to run across the street without looking.

Tess grabbed her, yanking her back and causing Emily to drop her slushie. "Emily, you can't cross without looking."

"My slushie," the little girl groaned looking down at the mess on the edge of the street.

"I'll get you another, but it's more important you don't end up as roadkill."

"What's roadkill?"

Graham jogged over, scooped up the busted cup and narrowed his eyes at Emily. "Young lady, you are not to cross the street without an adult. You nearly got hit by that truck."

Lip edging out, Emily dropped her head. "Sorry."

Graham tossed the crushed cup in the garbage can outside Magglio's. He wore a pair of khaki shorts, a plain T-shirt and running shoes. Tess had never seen anything sexier on a man. Well, except his suit. Graham had looked hot in his buttoned up suit and power tie. And, well, he was smokin' without clothes. So maybe he looked sexy-level eight on a ten-point scale, but it was enough to do funny things to Tess's resolve to hate him.

Okay, not hate him. Maybe just an eight on her dislike scale. Or a seven.

"Hey," he said to Tess, his smile wary. "Why are you with Em?"

"Well, we *were* having a slushie." Tess held up her own cup.

"Mine got smushed. Can I have another?" Emily asked.

Graham reached down, scooping Emily up into a hug. "Gotta have my sugar first." Dropping a kiss on Emily's nose, he jerked his head back toward the corner store.

"Yay," Emily said, dropping her own kiss on Graham's nose.

Tess's heart expanded at the pure beauty of a daddy and his girl. And then when she thought about her own father, it split open. Tess had always been daddy's girl. What was she now that they had no words for each other? It had been almost three weeks since she'd quit Ullo, and a layer of ice had built between them. Still, she could see no way to go back to where she'd been.

"You know, I think I'll have one, too." Graham set Emily down.

"Well, I should get back," Tess said.

"No," Emily said, tugging on Tess's shirttail. "Stay with us. Daddy's nice. I promise. And we're going to the park today. I can swing myself."

"Really?" Tess offered her hand up for a high five.

Slapping her hand against Tess's, Emily spun toward the door of the store, pressing her nose against the glass. Alva must have waved her in because she pushed through, nodding her head and laughing.

Tess and Graham were left alone on the corner.

"Gotta say I was surprised to hear you went to work for Monique. Came out of left field," Graham said, toeing a cigarette butt.

"Why? I needed a job and I know this business."

Graham's gaze rose to hers. "I get it."

"Do you?"

"Yeah," he said, not offering anything more on the subject.

"Are things going well?"

Tess didn't answer. Merely looked at him with a "what the hell do you think?" look.

"Yeah." Graham's eyes dropped slightly as he studied her lips, then they dropped even lower to where her breasts strained at her too tight T-shirt advertising Big Mouth Sam's Blues bar. The suggestive slogan "Open Wide" didn't help, either.

Her mind tripped toward the way she'd run her fingers under his T-shirt, the way she'd licked that little place at the base of his throat, the way he'd tasted, the way he'd felt moving inside her.

Sweet Bessie, Tess. Stop reliving those moments. You can't allow yourself to go there. You can't allow your resolve to fade.

"I gotta go," she said, spinning away, wanting to stretch the tight T-shirt away from her chest, not merely so he'd stop dropping his gaze to her breasts but because she needed to breathe.

"Wait," he said, his hand closing around her bicep. His touch was warm. *He* was warm and she wanted to wrap herself in him in spite of hurt that clung to her much like that T-shirt. "Don't go on account of me."

"I have to go on account of you. Don't you get it? I can't—" She snapped her mouth closed and tried to pin down the reason she couldn't stay right where she was. Because he'd been a jerk? Because her father had chosen him over her? Because she didn't want to like him, didn't want to let go of her hurt? She wanted to nurse it, obsess over it like Gollum and his precious ring, because it felt like that was her right.

He dropped his hand. "How about we strike a truce?"

Tess started shaking her head.

"For Emily's sake?"

"I just met your daughter this morning. Presumptive to think I'd do anything for her sake."

"Then for me. For you. For being grown-up people in a bad situation."

She wanted to step away and tell him to go to hell. She wanted to lean against him and close her eyes. But she did neither. Instead Tess stood there and looked confused.

Maybe because she was confused.

She wanted to hate him…but she didn't.

"Fine," she said, stretching out a hand. "We'll agree to be polite to one another. That's all I got."

Graham looked at her hand. "Just polite? Seems cold."

"Really?" Tess said, dropping her hand. "What

do you expect? We work for rival companies and our 'relationship' lasted for all of twelve hours."

"Thirteen," he said, reaching forward and picking up the hand she'd dropped.

Oh, she knew exactly how long they'd spent together that night nearly two months ago—thirteen hours, eight minutes. Something about his knowing, too, plinked a few heartstrings.

Graham studied her hand clasped between his. "I'm sorry, Tess. I don't know how much more I can say it to you. I guess I can't. I'll see you around." He released her hand and turned toward the store where Emily stood inside waving, a huge, loving smile on her face.

Tess waved back to the child and headed back to Upstart, her step heavy as her heart. She wanted the heaviness to leave. She wanted to be happy again.

But life wasn't always happy, was it? Life held as many tears and as much loneliness as it did hugs and belonging. Tess had just skidded into that other 50 percent for maybe the first time in her life…and it pretty much sucked.

Monique met her at the front door, carrying a pink duffel bag. "Where's Emily?"

"With her father. Her drink spilled and he went to get her another."

"Uh, he's been spoiling her."

"That's what daddies do," Tess said, sliding past the woman and reentering the warehouse.

"Tess?" Monique called, turning toward her. "I hope you're happy here. I'm glad you're here at Upstart."

Unexpected words delivered by a tough-as-nails woman. Tess still couldn't read Monique—they'd only spent two weeks together. Still, the words did what they were intended to do. "It's been hard for me, but I'm determined to carve my niche here."

"Good. We want you happy. Happy Tess means happy Upstart."

Tess wouldn't go as far to say "happy" but she nodded anyway. "I'm going to run by Edward Mendez's offices and drop off the corrected sketches, and hopefully I'll have my vision for Oedipus ready by Monday."

"Good. And don't forget we have drinks with the Rivera brothers on Monday afternoon. The Prometheus account isn't as big as the others, but they've been with me for several years. I want them to meet you."

Right. Dog-and-pony show. The Ullo name hard at work again. Well, at least Monique hadn't lied to her about her reasons for hiring her...or done anything behind her back like Tess's father had. If Tess hadn't been an Ullo and hadn't the connections she had with the krewes, she wouldn't be working for Monique right now.

Sometimes honesty sucked. Maybe she'd rather have smoke blown up her skirt and be told how great she was at designing floats. Or maybe she'd have to earn that designation.

Carving a niche wasn't as easy as Tess had hoped.

CHAPTER ELEVEN

FRANK ULLO LOOKED down the table at his family. It had been three weeks since Easter Sunday. Two and a half weeks since he started the experimental drugs that had ravaged his body. He'd lost nearly ten pounds and looked like something the dog had barfed up.

"Dad, you don't look good at all," Frankie Jr. said, not bothering to stop shoveling Maggie's lasagna into his mouth. His wife, Laurie, wasn't much of a cook, so every Sunday Frankie approached lunch like a man who'd spent twenty years in a third-world prison.

"Hush, now," Maggie said, sliding her eyes to Frank and giving him a small nod.

Frank looked down at where Tess sat studying the food on her plate. They hadn't spoken since she'd left that Easter day, and frankly, he was so angry at her for quitting Ullo and working for Upstart, he didn't want to talk to her...especially since he felt so damn weak and helpless. His daughter should be ashamed to even sit at the table, eating the food Frank Ullo bought.

Graham had said a lot of things about making peace with Tess, but Frank wasn't ready to do that just yet. Tess had purposely poked a stick at him... and the damn thing was sharp. He wasn't saying anything to her. He didn't care what anyone else thought.

Maggie kept staring at him. She wanted him to tell them all about why he looked like death. Something other than the "I'm a bit under the weather" he'd been using with everyone he saw over the past week.

"Your father has something he wants to tell all of you," Maggie said, setting down her fork and giving him a final "get on with it" look.

"Let everyone finish their food, woman."

"Don't you 'woman' me, Frank Clyde Ullo," Maggie said, anger shooting from her eyes.

"Meh," Frank said, shoving his food to the side. His stomach rebelled and he rose. "Pardon me."

His family looked up at him, concern etched on their faces.

"What's going on with Pop?" Michael asked his mother.

Maggie shook her head as Frank left the table. He needed to make it to the lavatory so he could puke his guts out. No big deal, right? He hadn't been able to hold down anything but applesauce for the past few days. He hated applesauce now.

Minutes later, he emerged from the restroom, shaky on his feet, but determined to return to the table. He'd already spent much of his time in bed, and he wasn't giving up his Sunday lunch with his boys and Tess…even if she and he weren't talking.

"Pop?" Michael said, rising and coming to his aid. Taking his elbow, his youngest son steered him to his place at the head of the table. "You okay? Can I get you anything?"

Frank patted his son's arm as he sank into the chair. Such a good boy. Always had been. Ran a bit wild in school, but always so caring, nursing felled baby birds, teaching children how to play hopscotch and sitting for hours in the yard contemplating God's world. "I'm good."

Joseph raised his eyebrows, as if to encourage Frank to let the cat out of the bag. But this cat would scratch and create havoc in his family.

Maggie had tears in her eyes. His boys sat, eyebrows gathered in concern. And his Tess still stared at her plate, taciturn, an unfeeling statue.

"What your momma wants me to say is that I got cancer and I'm dying," Frank blurted, slapping a hand on the table. "There, Maggie, I told them."

A collective sucking in of breaths met his ears.

"Oh, my God," Laurie cried, clasping a hand over her mouth and turning to her husband. Frankie Jr. sat still as dawn, his mouth open, his brown eyes growing angry. His oldest never liked surprises.

Joseph exhaled with a groan. "Dad…"

"What? Your mother wants you all to know. So there. Now you do."

"Frank," Maggie yelled, tossing her napkin on the table, her face crumpling even as her eyes blazed outrage. "What on God's green earth is wrong with you?"

"It's the truth. You been nipping at my heels like a dog wanting me to tell them," Frank said, trying for a nonchalant shrug even as he was wound as tight as a Swiss clock inside. It was out there for all to know—he was dying.

"Not like that," Maggie cried before heading at a fast clip toward the kitchen. Laurie and Beth came to the same unspoken conclusion, rose and followed.

Frankie Jr. leaned back in his chair. "Christ, Dad."

"Hey," Michael admonished, holding up a hand, his black cassock and white collar stark against his shocked face. His youngest son cast a worried look at Tess who still sat frozen in place. Her eyes were wide and because she'd refused to even glance his way, Frank hadn't a clue what she thought or felt. "Let's all take a deep breath and a moment to think before we speak."

The scrape of Tess's chair against the floor was the only response to Michael's plea. His daughter flew toward the living room, not bothering to utter a word.

"Well, that's getting to be a regular thing," Frank said, his heart sinking at the sight of Tess running. He'd thought her being forced to talk to him a silver lining in his delivering such terrible news. The slam of the front door told him there was no silver lining. There were just stormy, pain-filled clouds hovering over all of them. Maybe Tess more than anyone else. The hurt between them prevented even an umbrella to shield her from the onslaught of the rain that would fall.

And it would fall. Joseph, the oncologist and Maggie could talk all they wanted of his beating this, but Frank knew his chances were slim to none. He'd ignored the symptoms for too long. He'd started feeling weird before Christmas and because Mardi Gras was breathing down his neck, he'd ignored it, telling himself he was just older, more stressed with the business he'd lost that year. But it wasn't age or stress. And his casual dismissal had repercussions.

"I can't believe this is how you told us." Frankie Jr. shoved his empty plate toward the crystal saltshakers Frank's mother had given Frank when he'd gotten married to Maggie. She'd said they'd been made in the old country as if that was the most special of things. The shakers worked and that's all that had mattered to Frank, but now he wondered if he'd missed too much in life, wondered if he'd been too dismissive of what mattered most. Took dying to appreciate living. "Very shitty, old man."

"What? There's a better way? You can't put lipstick on a pig. Ain't no good way," Frank said, his stomach cramping and his vision a bit spotty. He really wanted to lie down, but couldn't leave things this way.

"Joseph, you want to explain this? Then someone should go check on Tess." Frankie Jr. assumed the role of firstborn, his gaze not quite so angry as resolute. Frankie Jr. always met problems head-on. That particular trait made him a fine trial attorney and a fine older brother to his siblings.

Joseph launched into a complicated description of his stage of cancer (not good) and the experimental drugs (not guaranteed) as Frank listened in objectively. Easier to do so than to think about what was happening within his body…though feeling the effects of the cancer and drugs wasn't an option. Couldn't wish those away. Joseph finished explaining the diagnosis, the symptoms of the chemo and the likely outcome (neither good nor guaranteed) as Maggie came back and sat down, reaching for his hand. Tears still in her eyes, she nodded at him. Frank's heart swelled at the love in her eyes. God had blessed him his entire life. How could he complain when he'd been given so much?

"This is why you asked us to not bring the kids. This is why Granny B isn't here," Frankie Jr. said, his expression no longer shocked. Just sad.

"We thought it would be better for you to tell your children yourself. Obviously your father has no tact when it comes to relaying delicate information," Maggie said. "Your father will tell Granny Bella this evening. We're taking her leftovers and a napoleon from La Madeleine's. She's been bugging us for one, says they're better than Gambinos or the ones I make from scratch. Maybe that will help somehow."

Michael rolled his eyes and gave a harsh laugh. "That's *so* going to make telling her easier."

"Where's Tess?" Maggie asked, staring at the empty seat.

"She bolted," Michael said, rising from the table, craning his neck toward the living room. "I'll go see about her."

"No, give her a little time. Things have been hard on her lately." Frank knew his daughter. She needed time to process. Time to figure out how to react. Tess was much more complex than most thought. On the surface she'd always been quick to smile and quick to action, but beneath her positive exterior beat a discerning woman…a woman who needed time.

Michael hesitated. "What about her, Dad? I sort of humored you in hiring that Graham guy. He seems okay. Capable. But now we're talking about…"

His youngest left off, shifting his gaze to his brothers who occupied the right side of the table.

"We're not sure what the results will be," Joseph intoned.

"No, he's right," Frank said, waving a hand, fighting against the sheer exhaustion knocking at his door. He'd need to leave the table soon, but first he had to finish what he'd started. "Graham is part of this. I needed someone to run Ullo."

Michael lifted his eyebrows. "But not Tess."

"Not alone," Frank said, shaking his head. "I never meant for her to see it the way she did. I merely looked for someone to come in and do what I do so she could keep doing what she did. I wanted to find her a partner. Didn't want to stress her with the undue burden of running Ullo alone. Graham was to be the new me."

"Why didn't you tell her that from the beginning?" Frankie Jr. asked in a very lawyerly way.

"I don't need to be cross-examined. I just puked my guts up," Frank said, rising on shaking legs. "Tess needs to see things for herself. She's young and thinks she can handle everything tossed her way. She's arrogant and spoiled. I did her a disservice and I'm paying for it."

"Tess isn't wrong here, Dad," Michael insisted.

Frank held up a finger. "But she's not right, either. Leave her alone for a bit and let her find her way. She needs that right now. She needs to feel a bit of the bite life gives."

After a moment, Michael nodded, his dark eyes meeting Frank's. In that gaze, Frank saw his boy understood. Michael had a way of seeing into the future and getting the big picture.

"Okay, we'll give Tess space. But you have to think about things with her," Frankie Jr. said, rising to take Frank's elbow and assist him from the room. "And you gotta fight, Dad. We're all here with you through this."

Frank patted his son's hand and then reached out and clasped Joseph's shoulder. "I got a son to pray for me, a son to heal me and a son to get my affairs in order in case the first two don't work. I'm set."

Passing by Michael, Frank reached out and roped the boy into him, kissing him on the head.

"What's Tess for?"

"Reminding me who I was and who I am."

With that, he slowly crawled toward the open door, hooking toward the stairs.

THE SOUND OF her soles slapping the pavement was little comfort, but the rhythm gave Tess something to cling to.

Her father was dying.

Slap, slap, slap.

He'd known this when he hired Graham.

Slap, slap, slap.

He'd refused to apologize to her, knowing he was sick.

Slap…slap…slap.

Tess stopped and bent over, her lungs burning, her eyes aching from unshed tears. Sucking in breaths, she held on to her knees and tried to pretend like everything that had happened in her life within the past few months was a nightmare.

That's it.

Pinch yourself and wake up, princess. This isn't real.

"Ma'am?" The words came from behind her.

Tess shut her eyes.

"You okay?" A young female voice.

Tess stood up, placed her hands on her hips and tried to still her ragged breathing. She knew tears leaked from the corner of her eyes…or was it sweat? She looked over her shoulder to find a girl of about thirteen or fourteen studying her with concern. "I'm okay. Thanks."

"You sure? I mean…" The teen glanced down at what Tess wore.

Right. She had on jeans and a pair of ballet flats. Not exactly running gear. "Yeah."

Not like she'd planned for a run through Old Metairie. Kinda happened when a gal found out the father who she supposedly hated was dying. Guilt and grief had crashed down on her. All she could think to do was run. Out the door. Down the street. All the way to…Bonnabel Avenue?

"Thanks," she called out to the girl with a wave. Unusual for a teenager to check on someone like that.

Tess pushed the sweat-dampened hair from her face and sucked in the humid air as she turned back the way she had come. Around her the quaint, expensive neighborhood hummed with children laughing, the sound of a lawn mower and the swoosh of cars down Metairie Road, which was strung with businesses, some open, others not. She'd run a decent way for a chick in ballet flats.

The phone in her front pocket vibrated and she pulled it out.

Michael.

She wasn't ready to talk to her brother about her father. Too close to home and the sadness would sheet off of Michael—the man felt everything so deeply. Tess didn't want to feel anything at the moment. She wanted to hide. To avoid. To pretend. For at least fifteen minutes. Maybe an hour. Or maybe she could hide from the entire afternoon.

Pressing the button to bring up her contacts, she hit Gigi's number. Several rings and a voicemail later, she hung up. A ding sounded. Text message from Gigi.

Found a date to the wedding. I'm trying him on right now. Catch up with you tomorrow. This might take a while ;)

No Gigi.

Tess wondered if she should call Nick. He'd been calling lately. Probably because he was lonely. But Nick was a dead end. At one time she'd hoped they could end up as more than what they were, which was a sometimes convenience. No sense opening that can of worms.

The phone vibrated again. Michael was a persistent devil...for a priest.

"Hey," she said into the phone. "I'm not ready to deal with Dad and this shit, okay? I can't—"

"Tess?"

She pulled the phone from her ear, looked at it and then tugged it back again. "Graham?"

"Yeah."

"What—why are you calling me?" Tess asked as she looked both ways and crossed the street that led to her parents' house.

"I don't know. Well, I do. There are a couple of good reasons, I guess, but mostly I wanted to check on you."

He knew about her father...knew Frank would tell them today. "You know about Dad's cancer?"

Duh. Of course he knew. Graham was her father's new golden boy, his trusted right-hand man, and she was, yeah, just his daughter. Resentment burned in her gut before she batted it down. She couldn't handle any more negative feelings. She could barely deal with what was squeezing the breath out of her. So Graham knew her father was dying. Big deal. The important fact was *her father was dying*.

She stifled a sob, catching it with her hand.

"Actually I guessed something was wrong," Graham said with a sigh. "Last week when your father came in to tell me you went to work for Upstart, he finally told me the truth. Shocked me to realize if he weren't facing what he's facing, I wouldn't be here in New Orleans…or at least not at Ullo. And I would never have met you."

Tess swallowed at a different emotion burgeoning within the grief swelling within her gut. The only reason she and Graham had happened in the first place was because her father had gotten sick. Bittersweet emotion coasted on crippling regret.

"What do you want me to say?" she said, stopping, realizing she'd rather walk all the way home than go back to that dining room table and her mother's tears. She just couldn't do it. She wasn't strong enough. Not yet.

"Nothing," he said, his voice weary. "I just worried about you."

His words hit her between the eyes. Graham cared. She already knew this, even if his initial actions after they'd slept together proved differently. But in the light of the afternoon, his slight felt very, very small compared to learning her father was dying.

"What are you doing right now?" she asked.

"I'm driving back from Monique's. Emily spent the night with me last night. Headed toward the grocery."

"What area? What street?"

"Uh, West Esplanade and Transcontinental." He sounded confused.

So was she. "Can you come get me?"

A surprised pause. "Where are you?"

"On the corner of Old Metairie and Sycamore," she said wondering what in the hell she was doing asking him to come get her. In her mind, hell, in everyone's mind, Graham was the enemy. She was supposed to hate him for what he'd done, not ask him to rescue her from the tidal wave of grief threatening to wash her away.

"I'm on my way," he said.

Clicking the phone off, Tess sank down on the curb and set her head against her knees. Her body ached to cry, to release all the bitterness she'd held within. She needed something. Maybe a cocktail. Or maybe she needed therapy. Could a shrink help her figure out her life? Inside, Tess felt like a ripped sail on a forgotten boat, fluttering in the gale with no hope of repair.

In the past her family had always reeled her in and stitched her up, assuring her all would be right again. But her father couldn't fix this. Nor could her mother or brothers. No one could.

A car turned onto the street, slowing down. But it was a red convertible Mercedes with a thin blonde at the wheel. The over-sized sunglasses blocked the woman's eyes, but somehow Tess knew she looked concerned.

Tess raised her hand and waved.

The woman waved back and sped off.

And people thought some New Orleanians weren't friendly. Two strangers in the space of twenty minutes checking on her.

Eight minutes later Graham pulled up, rolling down the window. "Tess?"

She lifted her head and suppressed the sob rising within her. Why Graham? Why the man who'd stolen her dream? Why was he the one she wanted on the day she found out her daddy was dying?

Because he felt like someone to watch over her as much as he felt like someone who could move her forward. Any other lifetime, and Graham Naquin would be the perfect man.

But not in this life…. Graham could never be her Mr. Right because he'd already stepped into the shoes of Mr. Wrong.

"Hey," she said, reaching for the door. Climbing inside the cool exterior, she tried not to give in to the tears, but her heart didn't get the memo her brain sent out.

"Sorry, sorry," she choked on the sobs, wrapping her arms around herself, rocking slightly. "I don't know why—"

His hand on her back felt so good and it only made her cry harder. The car moved, but only a swerve to the curb before he put it in Park.

"Tess," he said, his voice soothing like a velvet night skimming over her.

"I can't stop. I can't—"

"Hey," he said, sliding his hand up to push her hair back, "Just get it out. Just let it all out, Tess."

So she did. For a good five minutes she sobbed against the dashboard of the car her father had brought her one-time lover and present rival. The entire time she cried, Graham rubbed her back, comforting her.

Finally, Tess sat back, wiping her face with her hands.

"Here," Graham said, pulling a travel package of tissues from the compartment that separated their seats. "Use this."

Tess took the tissue and wiped her face, before grabbing another to blow her nose.

A few seconds ticked silently by. The world outside the car moved—a man on a lawn mower, an older lady walking a fluffy dog and squirrels scampering up and down the graceful oaks. All going about their business on a Sunday afternoon.

"I'm pathetic," Tess said finally, tearing her gaze from a bed of tulips dancing in the breeze to his. "I don't know why I called you."

His smile tipped the corners of his mouth. "How is it pathetic? Besides, I called you."

"Oh, yeah. But I shouldn't have asked you to come."

"Why?"

"Because."

He issued a soft laugh. "Things are weird between us, but that doesn't mean I don't care about you, Tess."

"I know," she said exhaling, looking back down at the tissue wadded in her hand.

"I'm very sorry about your father," he said.

Tess's heart squeezed and she pressed her fingers to her temples where a dull headache throbbed. "It feels surreal. All of this."

Graham draped his hands over the steering wheel and stared at the sunshine filtering through the leaves. For a long while he didn't speak, and somehow the stretch of quiet comforted her more than empty platitudes. Eventually he turned back toward her.

"You want to go somewhere?"

Tess nodded. "I can't go back yet. My thoughts are too mixed up, and I don't know what to say to my dad yet."

"He'll understand," Graham said, turning the key, bringing the car to life. Pulling away from the curb, he hooked a quick left and backed around so they were headed back toward Metairie Road. "Coffee?"

Tess shook her head. Her rolling gut couldn't handle the acrid brew or the shot of caffeine.

"Something stronger?"

"No."

Graham said nothing more. Merely drove toward New Orleans, bypassing the on-ramp and going under I-10, passing Delgado and the cemetery with the raised tombs sitting vigil over the city. As he drove, radio on a soft rock station, Tess tried to gather up her shredded pride and erect the defenses she'd put in place weeks ago. She didn't want to open the door to Graham again.

So why'd you ask him to come get you?
She didn't have the answer.

Turning off the boulevard, he looped around and entered City Park. Pulling into a parking lot, he shut off the engine. "Let's walk."

Without waiting for her answer, he climbed out and shut the door. Her door opened and Graham leaned in, extending his hand.

Tess looked at it. She didn't want to touch him. Didn't want him to crawl inside the walls she'd so carefully put back into place.

"You don't want to walk?"

"I don't want to do anything. I don't want to feel anything. I don't—"

"Get out," he said, not unkindly, but with a firmness that told her he was used to stubborn women… or stubborn seven-year-old girls. "You need to process. You need to walk."

"I already walked." She looked up at him.

He arched one eyebrow, looking quite dashing in the bright afternoon light, wearing a pair of shorts and a long-sleeved T-shirt pushed up his forearms.

Tess sighed. "Fine."

He locked the car behind her and started down the nearest path. Around them kids shrieked, adults jogged and a group of twenty-somethings played Frisbee golf. Unlike the lush privacy of Audubon Park, City Park was more open, with a golf course, several playgrounds, tennis courts and even a small amusement park. And there were lots and lots of paths to pound while examining the ups and downs a gal's life took.

For a long time they walked, side by side, footfalls falling soft.

"How am I supposed to be angry at him?" Tess said finally.

"Good question."

"You're not much help, you know."

"I've pretty much screwed up every relationship in my life, Tess. I'm not here to give you advice."

She stopped. "What are you here for?"

He shrugged. "I'm not sure. To be your friend?"

"To be my friend?"

"We can be friends, can't we?"

"I don't know. For two people who don't really know each other, we sure have a lot between us." She fell in step beside him again.

For several more minutes they walked without talking. Arriving at a small pond, Tess veered off the path and sank down onto a bench. Graham settled beside her and they both contemplated the water buzzing with dragonflies, lined with lanky irises.

"I feel empty. Numb," Tess said.

Graham sat down, clasped his hands and said nothing.

"You sort of suck as someone to talk to."

At that, he laughed. "I told you. No good with advice."

"Why didn't you call me?"

"I did call you. I'd been thinking about you all morning. The whole time I was with Emily, I kept thinking about how much I love her and want to protect her. And then I thought about Frank and you."

"I don't mean today. I meant after our night together."

"Oh, that," he said, staring down at his clasped hands. "It's hard to answer. I can say a lot of things about why I didn't, but I suppose I'm embarrassed by the real reason." He looked out at the pond and said nothing more.

"I shouldn't have asked. Don't know why I keep bringing it up. Guess it seems so unlike you. Jeez, the thing is I don't know you well enough to even say that," Tess said, shaking her head. "I've got way more important things to think about, don't I? A new job and my father dying. Yeah, my plate's sorta full right now."

"Come back to Ullo."

Tess stiffened. "What…what do you mean?"

"You need to be there. It's where you belong."

"You'll step down?"

Graham made a face. "I can't step down—I need the job." He glanced away from her, hiding from her any vulnerability.

"My father doesn't need me at Ullo. If he did, he would have appointed me the CEO. He would have given me what I have worked so hard for. In case you didn't get the memo—I'm not wanted."

She might as well have added "and you didn't want me, either," but she had to let that hurt go, had to stop clinging to the sucking wound in her pride...to the idea she wasn't worth the effort. Why did she hold her fist so tight around Graham's rejection? Did she really think love had blossomed between them?

Stupid.

And now because she couldn't let the offense go, she came off as pathetic. This was now her issue, not his. He'd apologized.

Graham brushed his knee against hers, jarring her out of her reverie. "So much would be solved if you would just change your mind and come back."

"For you," she said quietly. "But not for me. Falling back into who I was, forgetting the total dismissal my father gave me, would be taking the easy way. But it wouldn't be the right way. Not for me."

"So you're going to teach the old man a lesson, huh? And in doing so, make my task harder? Hurt the company you loved?"

"I'm not being spiteful. I'm doing what is right for me.... My father manipulated me again today. He knew what his announcement would do to me, but he tossed that ace onto the table." She wondered if her father had used the cancer card to manipulate her. Otherwise, why hadn't he told her and her brothers when he'd been diagnosed? Why hadn't he told her before going to a headhunter and hiring someone to run the company? She didn't understand him any more than she understood the reason she sat beside Graham in the dying light of the day.

"So you're going to keep this wall between you. You're going to work for Monique…work on stealing the very accounts you helped bring to Ullo? That's your plan?"

"You make me sound like a bad person. I'm not. I'm just not giving in to my father's wishes. I'm not accepting his vision for my future. He wants me to fall in line and do what he expects, but I'm not going to do that. I'm devastated about the cancer, but that doesn't change anything."

She stood and stepped away. She didn't want to talk about her father anymore. No more allowing the love she felt for him to mold her intent. Nothing had changed her goal: to prove herself to everyone. To prove to herself she could make her own future without her father's name, without her father giving her all she had. This was business. Wasn't that what her father had said?

It's not personal….

But it felt that way.

"Tess," his voice followed her, pricking at her resolve. It was business between her and Graham, too. She shouldn't have asked him back into her world, shouldn't have showed weakness in front of him.

"We should head back to the car," she said, moving in the direction they'd trod minutes before, not bothering to look over her shoulder.

He spun her around. She jerked her arm away, but he didn't release his grasp. "Tess."

Armor in place she looked up at him, at the softness in his blue eyes. "What?

"What's wrong with you?"

"You know what's wrong with me. The same thing that has been wrong with me since the day I walked into an ambush in my father's office. Life has been bitch-slapping me, serving me up shit sandwich after shit sandwich. I'm pretty full on what life's been giving me. Look, you were nice to come and get me, to play the knight on a white horse, but I shouldn't have asked it of you."

He dropped his hand. "So nothing between us has changed?"

"How can it? You're still you. I'm still me. And between us is a gap full of hurt, anger and betrayal. Nothing has changed."

Graham's mouth formed a line and gone was the softness he'd lent her when she'd needed it. "I'll take you back."

"I'd appreciate it."

GRAHAM LOOKED DOWN at Tess as she stood in front of him, chest heaving with emotion, green eyes resolute, and his heart ached.

He should take her home and be done with her. After all, she'd made everything so damn difficult in his life. Things were supposed to be good—he had a decent job and a steady paycheck. Emily had fallen back into the same easy relationship they'd shared that summer. Monique had taken the high road…for a little while at least. Life smelled like a summer rose.

Yet Tess was the thorn pricking him.

He thought about her constantly. The way her skin felt beneath his fingertips, the scent of her hair, the way she'd made love to him, fierce and tender at the same time. He wanted her desperately. Wanted to sink inside her, brand her, make her his.

But he was so far away from having Tess in his bed, he might as well be standing on the other side of the world.

And her leaving Ullo had made his workplace a living hell. Not only was he juggling more than what he'd signed on for, but the staff resented the hell out of him. The coffee Billie brought him was old, papers were misplaced and a cold shoulder would have been welcome compared to the icy reception he'd received. It was a wonder he didn't have frostbite.

Everything would be so good if Tess would come back.

Damn her stubborn pride.

"Don't shut the door, Tess," he said, giving a last-ditch effort to bring her to him…even if it was begrudging.

"The door is already shut." Her delicious lips pressed into a line and she crossed her arms.

"No, it's not," he murmured, brushing her hair back from her face.

She batted his hand, even as something hummed between them. He felt the buzz of desire and knew she felt it, too. "I can't, Graham. Things are too complicated. We made our beds, and now we'll lie in them whether they're lumpy or not."

"Somehow I don't think lumps would bother me a bit as long as you were in that bed with me. I still think about you tangled in those soft sheets."

"That's all we can ever be—a memory," she said, her glance dropping to his mouth before shooting back up to his eyes. "We can't go backward."

"You can tell yourself all kinds of things, Tess, but convincing yourself you don't feel something and actually feeling something... Those are two different things, baby." He clasped her elbows and brought her to him.

Tess let him.

More than anything he wanted to kiss her, but after the afternoon she'd had, he knew it would be manipulating her emotions for his gain, so he merely wrapped his arms around her and held her with tender resolve.

Tess was angry and hurt, but she needed him. This he knew. For a few seconds she held herself stiff, refusing to relax, but suddenly, as if someone had cut an invisible string, she sagged against him, wrapping her arms around him, her face tucked against his chest.

For a full minute, he held her, dropping the occasional kiss atop her head, begging his body to remember this wasn't about sex. It was about proving to Tess there was a connection beyond their bodies.

She inhaled deeply and then exhaled.

"You do what you need to do, Tess, but remember this," he murmured, loosening his grasp and looking down at her. "We have something between us. It's not going to go away because either of us *want* it to."

Her green eyes, soft as the grass lining the path, lifted to his, and in that moment he saw the truth. Her lips were parted and he couldn't resist the invitation.

Lowering his head, he kissed her softly, tasting the sweetness briefly before stepping away. "I'll take you home now."

Wiping her lips, Tess straightened and turned from him. Like a soldier she marched forward, spine straight. Part of him withered, but another part deep inside knew her. Knew she'd thrown up defenses, protecting herself because she needed to survive the day.

In his bones, in his very gut, Graham knew he and Tess belonged together…or at least deserved the chance to see if they did.

But how?

It was the question he'd mulled over night after lonely night. He'd tried to tell himself he didn't want her. He'd convinced himself things were *too complicated.* But still his mind and heart nudged him away from being logical toward the one thing he'd always clung to—hope.

Where there's a will…

Tess disappeared around a curve before ducking back. "You know the way back, don't you?"

Graham smiled. "Put one foot in front of the other."

She made a face. "I'll meet you at the car." And then she spun and disappeared again.

Graham stood a second longer and started after her, the hope inside him uncurling and stretching in the small crack she'd opened in her resolve.

CHAPTER TWELVE

FRANK WATCHED AS the nurse slid the needle into the vein in his arm. A quick sting and it was over. A turn of a ring and the liquid started flowing into his body into his bloodstream.

Go forth and conquer, he silently beseeched the drug.

Leaning back in the hospital bed, Frank closed his eyes and wished for the umpteenth time that day that he was mulling over figures at the office, calling James to tell him to order more primer, arguing with Tess over using paper too expensive for the floats.

"Frank?" Maggie's voice worried him.

He cracked open an eye. "Still breathing."

"Stop making those jokes." Maggie, with her hair in a topknot and the cut of her jacket, looked as if she'd skidded back in time to when he'd first met her. 1962. Pretty as a magnolia, sitting on an iron bench in the Quarter, eating an ice cream with one of her coworkers from Henry's department store. She didn't look all that different to him now. The years had been kind to his Maggie.

"You tell Jack Baumgartner to keep his hands off your can, Mags. I've seen the way he looks at you."

"What?"

"He's always had his eye on you, and he'll move in before I'm cold in the ground."

"I can't believe you," she said, rising, crossing her arms and giving him her best evil Maggie glare. "As if I would even consider going out with Jack Baumgartner. Maybe Perry Underhill, but never Jack."

"Perry? Meh, he probably has herpes or something. He's slept with half your bridge club." Frank eyed Maggie, trying to see if she was serious or not. He didn't like Perry with his overly white smile, golfer's tan and cheap shoes. The man acted as if he were the George Clooney of the country club, swilling around the card room, plying the ladies with vodka collinses and a thick layer of charm.

"Lydia Babin said he was totally clean. She made him present her with a clean bill of health before she would climb on for a ride," Maggie said, smooth as velvet…even though a wicked smile hovered at her lips.

The nurse writing down crap on a little clipboard snickered.

"Lydia slept with Perry? What? She hard up or something?"

Maggie laughed. "Well, yeah, she was married to a man who raised crickets and sold them for bait for five years…a man who had sex with her only twenty-four times. She's so hard up she'd likely sleep with Jack Baumgartner, too."

"The woman only had sex twenty-four times?" the nurse said, spinning around and looking horrified.

"She kept a journal," Maggie said gravely. "Very little sex because her husband had erectile dysfunction. The woman is due some fun."

Frank snorted as the nurse saluted. "Okay, Mr. Ullo, I'll be back in a bit. Try to rest." She winked at him and shot Maggie an encouraging smile. Nothing about chemo was much fun, but the employees in the cancer center worked hard to make the environment as welcoming as possible.

Silence descended like a cold blanket. Maggie looked down at her nail, pushing at a cuticle, trying to pretend everything was normal.

"You talk to Tess?" he asked.

"Yeah, she came back while you were asleep. Oddly enough Graham dropped her off. Couldn't get a word out of her about that, though."

"Graham?"

"You know, the man you hired over her."

"I didn't hire him over her. I hired him for her."

Maggie frowned. "That makes no sense and you know it. But I can't figure out how she came to be with him that afternoon. After your ill-timed announcement, she disappeared for hours. Her car stayed, so she had to have run into him or something."

Frank nodded, not quite understanding how his

daughter had ended up with Graham, but understanding why. Something had happened between
Graham and Tess—he'd seen that firsthand in his
office. They'd both been shocked to see the other…
and then there was guilt and anger. He wasn't the
sharpest tool in the shed, but he could put one and
one together to get a solution. Tess and Graham had
something going on long before Frank had hired
Graham. "I don't know why Graham brought her
home. I don't even feel like I know Tess anymore."

Maggie harrumphed.

"What?"

"Who's to blame for that? You've handled things
wrong at every turn, Frank. I tried to tell Tess you
didn't mean to make her feel unappreciated, but
she's like a damn billy goat. Won't be budged."

Frank said nothing. Part of him harbored deep
anger at his daughter for being so irrational, for
putting Frank Ullo Float Builders in jeopardy. But
another part of him admired her courage and conviction. His daughter refused to be a victim, refused to take the easy way. She *was* his daughter.
"She has that right."

"How can you say that? You're sick. Everything
has changed, Frank. She's being intentionally stubborn."

"Only because she believes in herself. I like that
about our girl."

"She's hurting. You're hurting. And both of you
are too bullheaded to make it right. Doesn't make

sense at a time like this to be so set against each other. You need her, and she needs to be there for you."

"It makes sense to me, Maggie. I know Tess loves me, but I also know she's had me wrapped around her little finger ever since she gave me that first gummy smile. I've given her the world—the best schools, a new car on her 16th birthday, a job after she finished that expensive college. We made our boys walk a tougher road than Tess."

Maggie frowned. "So you're trying to teach her to stand on her own two feet now?"

"It's not the best time, and I never intended it to be this way. But when I saw how she reacted to not being given control of the company, I knew I'd made a mistake in raising her. I'm not saying she ain't a good girl, Mags. But she's never been tested. Tess has leaped and now she must deal with where she's landed. We all have to deal with where she's landed."

His wife of forty-nine years shook her head. "I don't understand you."

He gave her his boyish crooked smile, the one he'd used to get in her pants all those years ago. "Yeah, you do. Deep down you know Tess needs space and some growing room."

"But you don't have much tim—" Maggie clamped her mouth closed and blinked away sudden tears.

"Come here," he said, motioning her to him.

She moved toward him, reaching out to clasp the fingers he wiggled her way. Her touch warmed him, comforting him, giving him strength the way it always had. "Oh, Frank, this is terrible."

He nodded because she was right—it was. Clasping her hand, he tugged her to him, around the confounded machines. Maggie bent down and pressed her lips to his. "I love you, Maggie, my Irish lass."

Her fingers lightly caressed the side of his face, which was scruffy because he hadn't bothered to shave that morning. "I love you, too."

"Say it," he begged, grinning up at her.

"My Italian stallion." She laughed and his heart lightened.

"Hell, yeah." He gave a fist pump with his free hand. "I'll give you a ride, too, princess. Just as soon as I stop vomiting every hour."

She sighed and rested her forehead against his, smelling like spring and spearmint. She favored mint gum and expensive perfume, and she smelled like home.

"I'll take you up on it, Frank, but until then, I'll focus on your being sick meaning the medicine is doing its job."

Frank closed his eyes and prayed her words were true. Please let it be true.

TESS WATCHED AS Emily bounced on a scrap piece of metal, the thwump, thwump, thwump of the assault echoing in the large warehouse. The child was dressed in a pair of athletic shorts and a too small T-shirt that hugged her little tummy. Long red-and-black polka-dotted socks covered her legs and a pair of new cleats contributed to the incessant noise.

Monique was nowhere to be seen.

"Hey, Emily," Tess said, shouldering her new messenger bag containing the drawings she needed to tweak by hand that evening. It had been a long Tuesday of meetings with potential and long-standing Upstart clients—all after a Monday evening meeting with the captain of Prometheus and his partner. And two nights of crying over her father and the argument she'd had with her mother. All Tess wanted was an hour at the gym, a protein shake and the comfort of her bed. She didn't want to think. Didn't want to feel. Just wanted to pretend everything was peachy keen. But she wasn't going to ignore the chubby seven-year-old bouncing and thwunking her way along the tin.

Emily's face lit up. "Hey, Tess!"

"What are you doing out here? You could get hurt on that."

The child hopped off the scrap metal. "I'm waiting on Mom to take me to guess where?"

"Where?"

"Soccer! I'm going to play this summer. Isn't that so cool?"

"The coolest."

The clack of Monique's high heels drew both their attention. The woman advanced like a field general…if a field general wore Jimmy Choo shoes and Chanel. "Let's go, honey."

"I'm ready, Mom," Emily said, scrambling over to a pink gym bag and backpack that sat on a stack of wood. "I'm wearing my ladybug socks, see?"

Monique made a face. "Oh, baby, I'm sorry, but I don't have time to take you to soccer today. Mommy has a thing tonight. You can go tomorrow."

Emily's eyes widened. "No, practice is today. It's the first one. I have to go."

"Sorry, honey. I absolutely can't take you today. We can try and phone your father, but otherwise, I'm dropping you at Grandy Pete's and then I have to scoot over to Mr. B's Bistro for an important meeting." Monique shifted her attention to Tess. "It's with Miles Barrow. Nothing I need you for."

If Tess didn't know how much in love Miles was with his wife, she might think Monique was using some creative bargaining to get the captain of Oedipus's signature on the dotted line, using those assets she was so proud of. Oedipus had always contracted with Ullo for the super krewe's float building needs, but Monique seemed to think next year would be different. Tess had been working on some really good stuff for the krewe, hoping Monique might present her designs over the ones she'd done herself.

But Monique could do what she wished—it was her company. The boss lady had already informed Tess she was expected at the krewe's annual May

Madcaps and Cocktails social on Saturday night, so maybe Tess could get an answer from Monique by then.

Up until this point, Tess had done what Monique had asked for when she hired her—bring in new accounts. The men and women of the krewes had been impressed to find Upstart employing an Ullo, even as the question sat in each of their eyes as they pulled out their pens to sign on the dotted lines of the contracts pulled out at the ready.

Still, something felt shady about the "thing" Monique had that evening.

Emily stomped her foot, bringing Tess's attention back to the seven-year-old with a stormy face.

"Mom, I have to go. Have to. Dad signed me up and that's like a promise," Emily said.

"I didn't say you couldn't play. Just not today."

"It's supposed to be good for me. Dad said." Emily crossed her arms, face taking on an expression that teetered between mulish and distraught.

"Emily, I said no. Your father should have checked my schedule."

"He did. You said yes. Remember?" Emily persisted, edging closer, looking as if she neared fit-pitching stage. "So take me. You promised."

"Hush," Monique said, jabbing a finger at her daughter.

"I can take her," Tess said.

Crap. Why had she just volunteered? Jeeza Louisa. She needed to go to the gym and pound out her frustrations, run the pain of her father's diagnosis away, sweat out the longing for the kid's father. She hadn't been sleeping well. Stress ate away at her, souring her appetite, making her stomach ache. She'd lost a few pounds and had baggage under her eyes so big they needed luggage tags.

Emily tackled her with a hug. "Thank you, Tess. Thank you."

Tess gave the kid an awkward pat. "I know how much fun soccer is. It was my sport."

Monique cocked a perfect eyebrow at her. "You don't have to do this. Emily can go next time."

"No problem," Tess lied. Because taking a seven-year-old to soccer practice, no doubt across town, meant she'd likely be skipping the gym. "Where do I drop her off?"

"I'll have to look at the flyer her father gave me. He said he'd be there to register her or something like that, and he'll take her home."

Great. The last person she wanted to see. Actually he *was* a person she wanted to see and that was the problem. She didn't want to think about him, about the way she'd sobbed like a baby in front of him, about the way she'd so easily said, "Come rescue me." Made her feel weak.

But obviously when it came to Graham, she was weak.

"Okay, I'll make sure Graham is there before I go."

Monique nodded. "Good. Let me get you his number just in case."

"I have it," Tess said.

Monique lifted her gaze from her phone. "Why would you have Graham's number?"

Busted.

"Ah, I think my father gave me all his contact information when I left, you know, so if I needed access to anything I'd left behind..." Lamest excuse ever.

"I thought you weren't talking to your father," Monique said, sliding her phone back into her designer purse.

"It was in an email. My contacts synced up automatically." Tess tried to sound like it was no big deal. Like she'd never wrapped her legs around Graham and shattered against him during the best sex she'd had in forever.

"Oh, well, I'll see you tomorrow. Wish me luck," Monique said with a shrug before giving Emily the eagle eye. "Be good."

"I'm always good," Emily said with a grin that looked far from angelic. "Let's go, Tess."

"Good luck, Monique," Tess said, relieved the woman hadn't pressed the issue over Graham's phone number.

Emily grinned up at her with an excited gap-toothed smile. "I don't want to be late for my first practice. We're the Lake End Ladybugs. See my socks?"

"Cool," Tess said, allowing Emily to pull her toward the door. "Uh, do I need your car seat?"

"I don't sit in a car seat. I'm not a baby," Emily said, rolling her eyes.

Tess almost laughed. "Never thought you were, ladybug."

"Well, Dad makes me ride in a booster seat. He looked up rules on the internet and says I'm still not big enough to sit regular, but I'm in second grade. My dad just doesn't get it."

Or maybe he did. Something about Graham taking the time to look up rules regarding booster seats and signing his slightly overweight daughter up for soccer made Tess like him even more…something she didn't want to do. But there it was. Graham Naquin was a decent guy even if he'd stolen her place at Ullo and dropped her like a bad habit…for whatever unstated reason.

Wait. She was supposed to forget about that. Let it go.

Twenty minutes later, Tess pulled into the sports complex in Metairie. The afternoon had softened into evening and the emerging green field in front of her was a sea of activity.

"I wonder what field you're supposed to meet on," Tess remarked as Emily opened the car door. Emily's cleats were untied, so Tess sat the girl back on the backseat and bent to double-tie them.

"Daddy!" Emily screamed in her ear. Tess jerked up and conked her head on the top of the door frame.

"Ow," she said rubbing her head and turning toward Graham, who wore a pair of khaki pants and a mint-green broadcloth button-down. Tess tried to look like she hadn't just broken into a sweat merely looking at him.

"Hey, where's your mother?" Graham asked, scooping up the child who'd launched herself at him.

"She hadda go to a meeting. Like always," Emily said, grinning at her father. "Look at my socks. Mom got them for me."

Graham peered down at the child's legs. "Looks like a ladybug to me." He lifted his eyes to Tess and her heart sped.

Stupid heart.

"I'm just the chauffeur. Since you're here now, I'll go," Tess said pushing the car door closed.

"No," Emily yelled, wiggling out of Graham's arms. He dropped her to the ground and she bolted toward Tess, grabbing her hand. "You gotta watch me, Tess. You said you like soccer."

"But your dad is here," Tess said.

"Pleeeease." Emily made puppy dog eyes at Tess.

Damn it. Tess had never been able to resist puppy dog eyes. She sighed. "I'll watch for a little while."

"Yippee!" Emily whirled around like only a seven-year-old could do.

Graham eyed Tess. "How did you get suckered into this?"

Emily overheard and said, "Mom said I couldn't

come, but then Tess said she'd take me. Tess plays soccer, too."

"I only play a few Saturdays a year. I sub," Tess muttered, hoping he didn't think she had volunteered merely so she could see him. She'd done this for Emily. Because it was crappy that her mother had chosen business over her daughter. Upstart seemed to be Monique's primary focus in life, and though Tess could attest to her father seeing business as important, he'd never put it over her or her brothers. He'd made almost all of her soccer games even during Mardi Gras season.

Graham gave her a smile that made her stomach flop over.

Stupid stomach.

She shrugged off her reaction to his charm. "So where are we heading? Uh, for soccer practice," Tess clarified.

Graham turned to study the fields. "The guy said it was the field in the back left."

Minutes later they stood in a gaggle of kids, a couple of moms and one older man struggling to balance on crutches. The man sat his clipboard on the collapsible bleachers and turned toward where they all stood. Emily stood close to Graham, looking uncertain.

"Hey, everyone. I'm Jim Thisbe and I'm the coach of the Lake End Ladybugs. As you can see, it's going to be a bit difficult for me to coach this season, but I'm hoping to have a few of you assist me. Anyone have any experience coaching soccer?" Jim eyed Graham, his eyebrows raised in a hopeful manner.

Graham gave a quick shake of his head. "Sorry, dude."

Emily pointed a finger at Tess. "She plays soccer."

Jim smiled at Tess. "Very good. Love having a female coach. Always a great role model for these young girls."

Little heads with swinging ponytails turned her way.

Tess felt like the kid in school who got called on and didn't know the answer. "Uh, I'm not a parent. I'm a friend."

"That's okay," Jim said, with a panicked smile. He looked like he might latch on to her leg if she took off running. Of course, she'd have the advantage since he was gimped up. "Friends are just as good as parents."

Not really, but she was sure Jim was convinced of its truth. "You don't understand. I'm not really available." Tess gave him an apologetic smile.

"Oh." Jim looked at the other parents assembled. "Anyone else know how to play soccer? Anyone?"

Blank looks all around.

One woman held up a hand. "I have a cousin who played. I can ask him if he'll be willing to help."

Jim snapped his fingers. "Good. That will work."

"Are we going to play today?" one of the other

girls asked, bouncing a pink-and-black soccer ball.
"I got a new ball."

"Uh, sure," Jim said, unclipping forms from his
clipboard while balancing on one foot. One of the
mothers had pity on him and helped to pass out
the paperwork. "If you will fill these out, make the
check payable to the organization, and then I'll turn
all the registrations in at one time to the league."

He then turned and blew his whistle. Tess sank
onto the bleacher feeling both guilt and relief.
Graham and the other parents set about filling out
forms. Jim hobbled around and tried to instruct the
kids. Good-natured? Check. Determined? Check.
Good coach? Uh, not a chance.

Tess stood. The least she could do was teach him
a couple of warm-up drills that would focus the
frolicking kidlets and work on their eye-foot co-
ordination.

"Hey, Jim," she called, approaching the area
where the kids basically wrestled with each other
in line. "I'll give you a little help today."

The man literally looked as if he would hug her.
"Thank you…"

"Tess," she supplied for him, waving the kids
over to form a circle around her. "I've played soccer for as long as I can remember, so I've got a lot
of great warm-ups you can use."

Tess kicked off her ballet flats, the cool grass
heavenly beneath her toes, and split the group into

teams, showing them a simple relay drill that would keep them all busy.

Graham jogged over. "You got roped into bringing Emily. You shouldn't have to do this."

Tess gestured to Jim who had sunk onto the bleachers, gathering the paperwork. "He can't do this."

Graham looked over at Jim. "No, he can't, so you'll have to show me these drills and I'll sign on as the assistant coach. I can't have the team fall apart. I need Emily out here in the fresh air, running, kicking and participating in something besides Playhouse Disney."

Tess looked around at the other girls smiling and laughing as they worked the balls around the cones. She remembered that feeling of working together as a team, sweat rolling down her back, eyes on the goal at the end of the field. She'd always had good coaches—men and women who'd sacrificed their personal time to help kids learn the sport. Maybe this was an opportunity for her to give back…and spend more time with the new sexy assistant coach.

Strike that, moron. It's for the kids.

"Tell Jim I'll help out. It's the least I can do to insure these girls get to play and learn the sport the right way," Tess said before she could talk herself out of it.

"Really?" Graham looked over at her, his expression slightly guarded, slightly hopeful. Damn, the way that man looked at her made her shivery.

"Sure. I've never coached, but it can't be too hard."

An hour later, Tess wanted to eat those words. She'd never worked with a group of seven-year-olds, and it was, well, challenging. They squabbled, they dawdled, they tripped, they cried and they had to be soothed with overly kind words. But still, even with all those challenges, Tess enjoyed teaching the fundamentals to the girls. Coaching them felt like the right thing to do, especially when at the end of practice Emily wrapped her arms around Tess's legs and hugged her.

"Thank you, Tess. You're the bestest coach ever."

Tess patted the child's back. "I'm not sure about that, but you're welcome."

Emily looked up, her eyes bright, her chubby little cheeks flushed from the last running drill. "You'll come on Thursday won't you?"

Tess looked up and caught Graham's eye, and in that moment, Tess knew there was no other place she'd rather be on Thursday afternoon. Except maybe Disney World. She had a thing for the Mouse and the rock-n-roller coaster. Or maybe Tahiti. Those beaches looked heavenly. "Of course. I'm going to help Coach Jim this season."

"Yay!" Emily crowed.

Jim walked over and extended his hand, but since it caused him to lurch sideways, Tess waved it away.

"Did I just hear right? Are you going to come back and help out?"

"I'll see you Thursday," she said with a smile. "You need help, and though I've never planned on being a soccer coach, the job found me."

Jim cracked a huge smile. The man was in his early fifties with thinning hair, a trim physique and a nice smile. "Best news I've heard in a while. I signed up to coach because Harv Turner, who runs the league, was short on coaches. That was before I hit an infamous New Orleans pothole on a recent bike ride and learned what it feels like to tear an ACL." He looked down at his booted foot and grimaced.

"Ouch," Tess said, looking down at the cast before glancing back up. "I'll try my best."

After getting the details on practice times and game schedules, Tess and Graham headed toward the parking lot. Emily skipped between them, smiling, rambling on about school and someone named Jillian who got in trouble for chewing gum and bringing in her iPhone. The intimacy of the moment struck Tess and she felt odd being a part of something that was very much "family" in nature, but at the same time, she liked being part of Graham and Emily.

Scary.

When they reached her car, Graham took her elbow and turned her to him. "Thank you, Tess."

The warmth of his hand on her arm, the way

his gaze caressed her made her body warm. Unconsciously she leaned toward him. Or maybe she was conscious of wanting to be closer to him. "Uh, you're welcome. I wanted to do it for Emily."

The corner of his mouth twitched. "Just for Emily, huh?"

And for you. So I can be close to you if only for an hour.

But she didn't say that. The awareness pulsed between them—it always did. Tess wanted Graham. She needed to feel his arms around her again. She craved him with a "what the hell" abandonment the way she craved chocolate when she had PMS. Maybe one kiss?

And in his eyes she saw he wanted the same thing—his lips, her lips, hot, wet, fulfilling.

"Tess," he breathed, lifting his hand, reaching for her jaw.

"No," she said, finding her resolve and stepping back. "We can't."

"Why?"

"Because we're in a parking lot…with your daughter."

Graham shook his head. "Jesus, I think about you all the time. I'm starting to think you're a disease."

"Just what every woman wants to be called," Tess murmured, trying to pretend his words didn't swat at the resolve she'd shoved in front of raw desire seconds ago.

"You know what I mean," he said.

"We said all that needed to be said Sunday." *Way to remind him how much you needed him a few days ago.*

"I'm not giving up," he said, shifted his gaze over to where Emily balanced on a low bar in the jogging park workout area.

"It can't work. Things are too complicated—I can barely tread water right now, barely stay afloat. No way in hell can I fight against the waves for something we can never go back and capture." She closed her eyes briefly, trying to convince herself as much as Graham. "We're a missed opportunity. It's not going to work no matter how much we wish differently. I just—"

"Why? Because of Monique and Upstart? Because I didn't call? Or is it because your father thought I would be a good fit to run Ullo?"

She jerked because his words were a slap of reality.

"Actually, that's it exactly. There's too much between us." She scooted back, bumping into her car. "It's best we remain exactly what we are."

"Which is?"

"I can't even begin to put a name to it." She unlocked her car, gave Emily a wave and slid into her car. Like a frightened bunny, she scurried away from the want, the hunger—the fact she wanted her words to be a lie.

But they weren't.

Graham didn't make sense.

She caught sight of Emily holding his hand as they made their way toward his car, and her heart shattered into small pieces.

As she pulled out onto the highway, her phone rang.

Caller ID showed it was her ex-boyfriend Nick.

Maybe that's what she needed—a distraction. Nick had always been her favorite distraction. Handsome, wealthy, spoiled and always ready for a good time, he was the perfect someone to occupy her time, to pull her away from all thoughts of Graham. Picking up the phone, she pressed the answer button. "What's up, Nicky?"

CHAPTER THIRTEEN

THE DAY AFTER soccer practice, Graham trudged into the office, cursing the key that always stuck in his office door. He flipped on the lights, glad he was the first one at the office. Somehow the stillness of the warehouse comforted him. In the small quiet of the morning he felt he could accomplish anything.

He surveyed his domain as he set down his briefcase. Finally all the old files had been removed and the office was in workable shape. Plans for the upcoming season, some drawn by Tess, others by Dave Wegmann, the designer, littered the table, ready for Graham to review and stamp with his seal of approval. He'd had to rely on skills he hadn't used in years to tweak a few plans, and that very day he had meetings scheduled with two krewe captains looking to rent at least twelve floats. Their themes had been turned in weeks ago, but the work had gone unfinished because Tess had left. Graham had divided them between him and Dave. Though Graham had never been talented creatively, he'd managed to get some ideas on paper for a series of Egyptian-themed floats.

He needed to hire somebody else in design, but had left the position open for several weeks more because he'd hoped Tess's anger would grow cold and she'd come back to Ullo and resume the work she'd left behind.

Damn stubborn woman.

A sound outside the door had him spinning in his chair.

Dave peeked inside.

"Oh, hey. You're here early." The man was clasping a folder in hands that looked too large to wield a drafting pencil skillfully. Dave looked nervous.

"Have to get here early—we have a lot to do," Graham said, motioning him inside.

Dave grunted and came in, setting the folder on the worktable. "Here are the sketches for Caesar's Muse floats. I think it's going to work nicely. Maybe have to have the carpenters do some adjustments on the ship. Wasn't sure if it would come in under the height maximum. We gotta clear the Causeway Bridge."

Graham leafed through the drawings and specifications. "Looks good. Are we going to have room for the waves on the back of the float?"

Dave shrugged. "Dunno. Maybe."

Graham lifted his eyebrows. "Dunno?"

"Look, I wanted to talk to you anyhow. I've been thinking about making a change."

"A change?"

"Yeah, I've been here a long time, you know?"

Graham felt something sink in his stomach. He'd wanted to talk to Dave later today about stepping up to fill Tess's position and then maybe hiring a grad student from Delgado's art program to train as a designer. He had to do something to fill the gap Tess left, but the words coming out of Dave's mouth made him long for the Pepto-Bismol he had hidden in his drawer. "Don't tell me you're leaving?"

"Sorry. I have an offer from Toledano Bros. It's closer to my house and with Tess gone and Frank sick, I feel like it's a good time to leave."

"I'll give you Tess's job."

"You should have weeks ago," Dave said, crossing his arms and trying to look angry. The man didn't seem to have much ire in him, so it was akin to a toddler refusing a vegetable.

"I had hoped to talk Tess into coming back—that's the only reason I didn't ask you to step into her shoes."

"Yeah, well." Dave shrugged and looked away. "I've been here forever, but I ain't good with change and I ain't good working with them asshole krewe captains, so I really don't want Tess's old job. Figure if everyone else is changing things, it's a good time to make this one for myself. Here's my letter."

Graham sighed, wishing he could slam his fist on the desk instead. "There's no way I can talk you into staying? Ullo needs you. I need you."

"I'm sorry, Mr. Naquin. I've made my mind up." The large man stepped back, ducking his head. "I'll stay for the next two weeks, give you time to find someone else."

Mild panic knocked at the door to Graham's soul. Sliding into the CEO's position at a stable, reputable company was supposed to be easy. But Frank Ullo Float Builders was no longer stable. Mere weeks into the job and everything had started unraveling at an alarming rate. "What about Frank?"

Dave stopped in flight. "That's who I feel the worst about, Mr. Naquin. Frank's been like a father to me."

"Then why abandon him when he's down?"

The man's head shot up. "I'm not—"

"Yeah, you are. This company is in transition and we need stability. We need men like you." He stopped short of begging, but thought if he had to drop to his knees, he might.

"I already told Mack I'd come over to Toledano. Rita wants me to work there, too. Gas is high as a cat's back and I ain't exactly getting younger."

"Just through this season. With a raise. And then we can see how you feel."

Dave cast his eyes toward the table with all the plans spread out, labeled by krewe and float number. Several seconds ticked by as the man grappled with the offer...with thoughts of doing what was right for the company he'd help build into prominence. "I suppose I owe Frank that much."

Graham stopped a huge sigh of relief. He didn't want Dave to know how scared he was to lose him.

Or maybe he did. Appealing to Dave's sense of decency worked. "Thank you, Dave. I appreciate that on Frank's behalf. It will be a comfort to him during this hard time."

Dave nodded. "Okay, I gotta go call Rita. She's going to be pissed, but maybe the raise will help. How much will I get?"

"Whatever Tess made."

"I was already making what Tess made. Her old man didn't give her more just because she was his daughter."

"Okay, I'll look at the numbers. This was off-the-cuff, man. Honestly, I'm going to have to look at—"

"In good time, Mr. Naquin," Dave said, a slight smile around his mouth. "Maybe you need to call a meeting. You know, announce Frank's illness officially and tell everyone you need help. They don't know you, but they love Frank, and nothing makes a person feel like helping out more than knowing they're needed."

Graham paused in sifting through the images and looked up at Dave. "First, please call me Graham. And second, thank you. Not just for staying, but for realizing I need help. You're right. I need to stop trying to spin plates and build a team."

Dave nodded. "No one knows you yet. Everyone's on pins and needles, scared about stuff, about Frank, about Tess, about losing business. But we'll all feel better if you are more accessible. This ain't about being a CEO or a COO or whatever you're calling it. It's about leading a team. You can't lead what you don't know. That's what made Frank and Tess good. They knew us, loved us. That's what works in this business."

"You're absolutely right. Guess I've had my head up my ass." Graham walked over to Dave and extended his hand. "You came in to quit, but you just may have ended up saving Frank Ullo Float Builders. Thank you, Dave."

The man took his hand. "This is gonna sound nuts, but I actually feel relieved. I really didn't want to leave—just wanted to feel like I was valued. How about we have pizza at that meeting? And you might want to invite some of the seasonal people, too. Let everyone in on your plan for continuing Frank Ullo's success."

A plan? He'd had one, but problems had started flying at him. He'd wanted to meet with each head—carpenters, sculptors and painters—to talk about new materials, better construction, efficiency. Keeping up with Tess and Upstart had started wearing on him. But Dave was right. Before he could go out and reconquer the Mardi Gras world, he had get his foundation secure. That meant getting the employees of Frank Ullo on board with a vision. He needed them to feel good about where and who they worked for.

"Pizza sounds perfect," Graham said, eyeing the high metal desk sitting just inside the office area. Billie wasn't here yet, but he'd take Dave's approach—tell the woman how much he needed her. How much Frank needed her.

Maybe hearing an appeal for help would soften the woman.... Maybe he'd get fresh coffee without having to make it himself.

As that thought hit him, Billie walked into the office area, carrying a box of Krispy Kreme Donuts and a frown. "Frickin' traffic is absurd. I nearly got sideswiped by some idiot on the bridge."

"Morning, Buttercup," Dave crowed.

Billie gave him the finger. Dave's laugh echoed in the lobby.

Maybe it wasn't such a good idea to talk to Billie right now. Her mood wasn't bad...it was putrid.

But then she smiled, obviously enjoying the ragging she gave Dave. Then she zeroed in on Graham and her expression changed.

"Good morning, Billie," he said.

"What's good about it?" she asked, her expression dead serious.

"You're alive and have donuts?"

She stared at him for a few seconds. "Okay, there's that."

"When you have a second, I want to talk to you about having a staff meeting for everyone here at Ullo."

She raised her eyebrows. "You want to call a meeting in the warehouse?"

"I think we need one, don't you?" Graham

said, shooting a glance to Dave who nodded his agreement.

"About Frank?" Billie asked setting down the donuts and switching on her computer.

"And Tess and the situation we're facing in securing the same business we've had for the past few decades. We need everyone to channel their energies and offer up solutions. Basically, we need to have a come-to-Jesus meeting."

Billie looked thoughtful. "Okay. I can shoot a memo to all the departments to make it official, but the easiest way will be to call all the heads of the departments. When you want it?"

"Sooner rather than later," Dave interrupted.

"I thought you were quitting?" Billie asked Dave.

"Graham talked me out of it."

She turned to Graham. "Really? This guy talked you out of going to Toledano?"

Graham smiled. "I do have talents."

"I never thought you didn't."

"Well, I'm not sure it was talent. I'm pretty sure a grown man near to tears helped bring him around. I fell just short of hitting my knees and begging."

Dave laughed. "It wasn't that bad."

"Thankfully, I didn't have to do either of those things, but I was prepared. I need you, Dave." And then he looked at Billie. "I need you, too. I've been trying so hard to hold things together, to give everyone the impression I have everything under control."

Billie straightened. "Well, then. I think we need

that meeting and we need some pizza for lunch. Those guys will do anything if you set a pie in front of them."

Graham smiled. "Dave said the same thing. Order whatever pizza you want and set it for tomorrow. We've got to get back on track. For Frank's sake."

Billie lifted her coffee mug. "For Frank's sake."

Dave nodded. "Damn straight."

FRANK LOOKED AT the phone as if it were defective before setting it back on his bedside table.

He felt like shit. The doctors hadn't lied when they said the cancer-killing meds surging through his bloodstream would rob him of his energy. No, not just his energy, but his flippin' manhood. He'd tried to put on a game face for Maggie, but he knew she knew. It was a game they played. A game all married couples played.

"Did you get in touch with her?" Maggie asked, entering their bedroom with a cup of tea. She'd gone to a health food store and come back with all kinds of disgusting tasting teas and several packages of nasty gum that were supposed to beat back the nausea.

"She don't answer," he said, making a face at the steaming cup that smelled like the backside of a troll...or what he imagined a troll's backside to smell like. "She ain't ready to talk to me yet."

"Tess is stubborn. Like Bella."

Frank sighed. When he'd tenderly taken his mother's hand and revealed his diagnosis, she'd uttered words he'd never heard her use before…right before telling him to get the hell out of her house. Then she'd called him a liar and accused him of playing with her emotions. She'd even thrown a bottle of menthol rub at him.

Frank hadn't known how to handle the diminutive woman who'd called him a selfish son-of-a-bitch, and he damned sure wasn't going to point out her insult actually doubled back on her. He'd merely picked up the—thankfully plastic—bottle of menthol rub, set it on the chest Bella had imported from the old country and shut the door softly behind him.

The heavy wood didn't block out the sound of his mother crying.

God, there was no way a man could prepare himself for hearing his mother sob her heart out, especially when it was something he'd never heard before. Not even during those hard years of covering her bruised face with pancake makeup and losing a baby at the hands of the bastard Frank had never called father had Bella lost control of her emotions.

Maggie rubbed his shoulder, drawing his thoughts back to Tess and the reason she wouldn't respond to his call. "Time is all she needs."

"Who? Mom or Tess?"

"Both of them?"

"My mother is in her nineties, Mags. And there is that time thing."

Maggie arched an eyebrow but didn't say what they were both thinking. Time wasn't exactly overflowing from his pockets.

"Well, I've had about all I can stand of her stubbornness—Tess not Bella—and if our daughter doesn't call you before Sunday, she and I are going to have a little heart-to-heart."

"Don't, Maggie. Let her alone. She'll come around."

"Yeah, she will, even if I have to plant my foot on her rump." Maggie held out the tea. "Now have a bit of this to help with the ickies."

"I don't want it, Mags."

"Come on, Frank. You'll feel better."

"Have you tasted that crap?" he asked, pushing the cup back toward her.

"No," Maggie said, trying again to get the cup in his hands. "I don't need it, but you do. It will help you feel less nauseous so you can eat. You need to eat something, sweetheart."

"I tell you what. I'll drink it if you will."

Maggie stared down at him, frowning for several seconds. Setting the cup down on the bedside table, she huffed, "Fine. Be right back."

Frank smiled as she stalked toward the door, her fanny swaying, her brownish-red hair bouncing at her shoulders. If he didn't feel like barfing up the dry toast he'd struggled to get down earlier, he'd pull her into bed and remind her what she did to him every time she entered...and exited...a room.

Minutes later she returned with another steaming cup in hand. "I have mine, so let's have tea, my fine gentleman."

"Bah, you know I ain't no gentleman. That's why you married me."

Maggie smiled as she lifted the tea to her lips. "So I'm not into stuffy old boring by-the-book guys. You got me pegged."

And then she took a sip.

Before spitting it right back into her cup.

"Dear God, that's terrible," she said, coughing and setting the cup beside his on the bedside table.

Frank laughed and opened the drawer beneath the two cups. "In that case, can I interest you in a piece of chewing gum?"

Maggie laughed and that was all he needed to feel better. In fact, he should suggest it to the doc the next time he went in for the chemo—Maggie's laughter in a bottle.

Cures whatever ails you.

Now if he could just get his daughter to talk to him...and get his mother to realize he wasn't a liar.

TESS JOGGED TOWARD the sideline of the soccer field, the whistle from her refereeing days slapping a rhythm against her sternum. They'd wrapped up practice early...not because they'd accomplished much, but because the attention span of a seven-year-old resembled that of a dog. She might as well have yelled "Squirrel!" every five seconds.

"Okay, Ladybugs, huddle up," she shouted, beckoning the frolicking seven-year-olds toward where she stood. They tumbled over one another, giant bows bobbing as they skidded to a halt around her.

"We're so good we're going to beat everyone," one little girl said with a fist pump.

"Yeah, the other teams are gonna eat our dust," another one said.

"Yay!" Emily squealed, hopping around, making all the other little girls do the same thing. They looked like popcorn on acid.

Tess blew the whistle. "Okay, settle down. We still have work to do before we can take on any challengers. And, first thing first, we have to work on a team cheer."

Ten blinking eyes met her gaze.

"We gotta have a cheer?" one asked.

"Well, sure. It's how we show unity. The other teams will know exactly who they are playing when we do our Ladybug cheer. So I'm giving you a homework assignment," Tess said with a smile.

"Awww," several groaned.

"Well, this is a fun homework assignment," Tess conceded, putting her arms around the nearest girls and drawing them into a huddle. "I want all of you to go home and work on a fun little chant. Something about being red, black and not afraid of anyone."

"Are ladybugs mean?" Emily asked, her expression growing concerned.

"Of course not, but they're tough just like we are. Can everyone do that?"

Heads nodded, bows bobbed and smiles met hers.

"You're the best coach ever," one girl said. Tess thought her name was Piper. She needed to go over the roster and put names with faces.

"And you're the best team," Tess said, deciding she'd missed her calling. Who cared about Mardi Gras floats when there was kids' soccer to coach? "Now everyone put your hand in. I'm going to count to three, and then we're all going to yell 'ladybugs,' okay?"

More head bobbing.

"1-2-3—"

"Ladybugs!" they all screamed.

The team broke and scampered toward their parents sitting in the collapsible stands, and Tess walked to where Graham stood cleaning up the paper cups around the cooler he'd brought.

"Good practice," he said looking up. He wore athletic shorts and a T-shirt that skimmed his toned stomach. He was totally drool-worthy, but Tess pretended he had a wart on his nose and hair growing out of his ears. No noticing his thighs with the sprinkling of hair. No ogling the smooth tanned nape of his neck. No thinking about licking those abs.

Nope.

Not at all.

"Yes, they did better today."

"You're really good with them," he said, squinting against the sun. "I'm glad you volunteered to help."

A warmth blossomed inside her. She shrugged it off. "I'm not the best, but I'm better than poor Jim."

The both turned and looked at Jim who waved at them from the top of the bleachers. He had his leg propped up and looked relaxed in his new job of team manager.

"Seriously, Tess, thanks for doing this."

"Surprisingly, I like it."

Emily came galloping over. "Guess what?"

"What?" Both she and Graham said in unison.

"Kathryn is inviting me to her birthday party. We're going to ride ponies!"

"Cool," Tess said, offering the child a high five.

Out of the corner of her eye, Tess spotted Monique charging across the field in her wrap dress and metallic strappy sandals. Her oversize sunglasses covered most of her face, but she smiled at Emily as she approached them.

"Mom!" Emily shouted, kicking it into high gear to reach her mother. Monique caught Emily's shoulders before she bulldozed her over. "You came to practice…but it's already over. You shoulda seen me. I kicked the ball good today. I'm pretty awesome at this soccer stuff."

"Good, sweetie," Monique said, heading toward

where Tess stood with Graham. Tess couldn't see her boss's eyes, but she had the feeling they carefully studied her and Graham, weighing, measuring…perhaps even suspecting. Especially after Tess admitted having his cell phone number. "Tess, what are you doing here, and why are you wearing a whistle? Are you coaching the team?"

"I told you I volunteered to help Jim. I brought Emily to practice, remember?" Hmm…what was Monique's game? Or maybe she had ADD and hadn't really listened when Tess had told her.

"Oh, of course," Monique said, propping her glasses on her head and glancing at Graham. It wasn't a possessive glance though it was familiar. "And you're helping, too?"

Graham nodded. "Jim needed it."

Monique looked over at Jim before shifting her attention back on her ex. "I'm sure it's nice for Emily to have her father so involved in her everyday life. Finally."

Monique's words should have been complimentary, but they sounded anything but. A sudden wave of dislike flooded Tess. The woman liked making Graham feel guilty for the years he'd been in Houston, and that seemed such a petty thing to do in front of their daughter. In front of Tess.

"Yeah," he said, smiling at his daughter, who came and nestled herself against his side. He wound an arm about her shoulders, squeezing her to him.

"I'm happy to help the Lake End Ladybugs get ready to win the championship."

Emily giggled.

"You shouldn't get her hopes up," Monique said.

"Why not shoot for the stars? Right, Em?" Graham patted his daughter's back and gave Monique a sharp look.

"Yeah, you should have seen us practice. We're good," Emily said, nodding at Tess. Tess smiled back, affirming the girl, though she wasn't so sure they could win a game, much less the championship.

"Time to go, Emily. Tell your father bye. Tess, too," Monique said, suspicion tight around her mouth. Maybe she didn't suspect a physical thing with Graham as much as she suspected he might try to mine tidbits about Upstart. Tess hadn't thought how it might look from a business standpoint to be coaching soccer with Graham…Upstart's rival.

Jeez. They were a Maury Povich show waiting to happen.

Emily gave each of them a hug and even jogged over to Jim and bestowed one on him. Seemed like Graham was right—a little fresh air and exercise brought out the best in his daughter.

Seconds later, Tess stood with Graham, watching Emily and Monique stride ahead of Jim who hobbled behind them toward the parking lot.

Graham lifted the cooler off the bleacher and tucked it under his arm, looping the plastic garbage bag over his arm. "Sorry about Monique. She's good at popping bubbles. I'm trying to get her to look at the bright side with Emily, let the kid dream a little."

"You don't have to apologize for Monique," Tess said, picking up her clipboard, falling into step beside him.

He cocked his head. "You're right. I'm sure you've learned quickly who she is."

Yeah, she had. Tess respected Monique's drive and business smarts, but she would have likely never been friends with the woman. There was something hard about Monique, something that told Tess when push came to shove she couldn't rely on her boss to have her back. Very different from the way she'd felt at Ullo. Of course, maybe that's because her daddy was her boss and she'd always known she was safe. She didn't want to talk about Monique with Graham, so she changed the subject. "Are you going to the Oedipus thing tomorrow night?"

He slid blue eyes over to hers. "Of course. They're one of our biggest accounts."

Tess lifted her eyebrows. "Oh, you sure about that?"

"As sure as it gets."

"Mmm," came Tess's response.

Graham stopped. "You love this, don't you?"

"What?" she asked turning around. "I'm making conversation. It's what friends do."

"No, you're protecting yourself by playing a little game between Ullo and Upstart. Keeps you from feeling anything, keeps you from wanting me."

"Why, you egotistical—" Tess whipped her head around to find him grinning at her. "I'm not playing games, Graham, merely giving you a heads-up in regards to Miles. Monique had drinks with him Tuesday night—that's why I brought Emily to soccer. So don't accuse me of games when I'm being more than nice to warn you."

"And why would you do that?" His face grew serious.

"Huh?"

"Warn me?"

Tess stopped midstride. She spun toward him, mouth open. But…she didn't know what to say. Why was she warning him? She had no business saying anything about Upstart's plans for Oedipus, or the fact Monique had pulled out all the stops to tear the lucrative account from the hands of the new Ullo CEO. Was he right? Was she needling him to keep herself from falling prey to the attraction between them, or did she subconsciously want to help the company she'd loved for so long? Or maybe she felt like she should rub his nose in Upstart's success, proving she was loyal to Monique. Her actions and emotions mystified her. It was as if she were in a house of mirrors, her image stretched and distorted at every turn.

Graham studied her, his expression not what she

was accustomed to. No soft blue eyes full of sympathy or alight with passion. Instead he looked intrigued. It was a good look on him—made him intense and somehow even more desirable. This man who had hurt her now stood ready to protect her father and the company he'd built with sweat and tears. It should have pissed her off, but instead, something inside stilled at the thought.

"Just wanted you to know what you're up against," she muttered, moving toward her Prius, wanting to escape Graham examining her every motive.

"I thought at first this was about inserting something between us so you didn't jump my bones and have your wicked way with me in the parking lot," Graham said, trailing behind her, seemingly unwilling to let the conversation die.

She wrinkled her nose. "As if."

"But that's not it. You can't help it, can you?"

"Help what?" She faced him, chin up. No way she backed down, even if she longed to get in her car and escape…just the way she had two nights ago. Sticking her head in the sand had become a strategy. Ask her father. She couldn't seem to dial the number and return his two phone calls. Not like she hadn't tried. She just didn't know what to say to him yet.

She needed time, but that had been her excuse all along. Time. Maybe it would run out before she was ready.

"You left your heart at Ullo."

No shit, Sherlock. Of course she had left her heart at Ullo, but that didn't mean she hadn't tried to move on. She'd spent the past weeks since she'd signed the contract with Monique putting her all into designing brilliant floats for Upstart. She had stuff that was going to blow Miles Barrow's mind for the Oedipus floats…if Monique submitted it. Anger and hurt tied to her pride were good motivators and she'd created some of her best work over the past few weeks.

And it should have been for the company that carries your name.

At that thought, anger flooded her. He didn't have to be so smug, questioning her loyalty to her new job…even if it was partly true. "My allegiance is to the person writing my paycheck. When Upstart does well, I do well. Tomorrow night I'll prove to Miles and Oedipus that Upstart can and will build their floats in 2016. And they will be the most stunning, beautiful and cost-effective floats in the history of parading."

"So you think Upstart will replace Ullo as their go-to floatmaker?" Graham said, his eyes flashing beneath the parking lot light blinking on. No more smiles. Game on.

"Every dog has its day. Upstart has been whittling away Ullo's business for the past two years. I've already brought in the captain of Thor, and Stacy Reynolds just gave us all of the floats for

Rhea. We're almost too busy…but not for Oedipus, of course. That parade would be icing on the very large cake we'll be serving." Tess turned and unlocked her car, the beep-beep punctuating her declaration.

And then Graham smiled at her. Not the sexy smile he'd used that beautiful night under the stars, or the sad one he'd given her in the park last Sunday. No, this one was sharky and slightly amused. Like he toyed with her. "Well, do your damnedest, sweetheart."

She bristled. "Oh, you can bet I will."

His smile got larger. "And why don't you warn your boss—tell Monique she'll stay a small potato. I don't care if she went down on Miles under the table at Brigstons, she's not getting that account."

"You sexist pig," Tess growled, disappointment flooding her at his presumption of how Monique… or any woman did business. "You think women earn business by getting on their knees? We don't have to give sexual favors to get accounts. Our work speaks for itself. How dare you imply such a thing?"

His expression shuttered. "That's not what I meant and you know it."

"You used the words."

"Don't slant the intent. I wasn't implying Monique offered sexual favors for Oedipus's business. My point was no matter how good the offer from Upstart, you aren't getting the account. Period. I'll do whatever it takes, but the long-standing agreement between Ullo and Oedipus will stand. I'll bet my job on it."

Tess lifted her eyebrows. "We'll see. And it might literally be your job on the line. You forget how well I know my father. He won't suffer you to lose Miles's business. Paired with the other losses…" She trailed off with a shrug, feeling a little ugly, but a lot powerful.

But she didn't want to see Ullo lose business, even if she herself was making moves toward accomplishing just that. Why did Graham *and* Ullo have to lose in order for Tess to win?

"I'll see you tomorrow night, Tess," Graham said, his tone detached. A pang of regret flickered inside her at his coldness. This was what she wanted, right? They were on the opposite sides of a river with no bridge in sight. It was Ullo versus Upstart. Graham versus Tess. With no real winners.

She nodded and lowered herself into her car. "Yeah, I'll see you."

Graham walked away and Tess told herself she was glad. But she wasn't. Her heart hurt for what had been between them…and what would never be again.

The other side, a place where hope lay, felt very far away.

CHAPTER FOURTEEN

TESS WALKED INTO the Oedipus May Madcap Mixer with Nick on her arm…or rather she was on Nick's arm. Either way, she'd conceded to a date with her ex and had selfishly used this annual fete hosted by the Oedipus Social Club as the one-more-shot merely so she wouldn't have to attend alone.

It had nothing to do with Graham and everything to do with looking confident and successful.

And for all of ten minutes she'd convinced herself Nick deserved another chance…until he'd shown up all tanned from a week of golf on the Gulf Coast, dressed in an Armani suit, smelling like new money, and she'd felt zero attraction. In fact, seeing him so loose, smiling and making flirty jokes made her somewhat disdainful. He kept trying with little brushes of his arm and casting meaningful glances, but the effect fell flat.

Graham had ruined her for all men…or maybe what little she and Nick had once had together had dried up like Granny B's estrogen.

"Get you something to drink, babe?" Nick said, wrapping an arm around her waist. She waited to feel warmth, some flicker of something at Nick's touch, but there was nothing.

Pulling away, she smiled. "I'll take my usual."

Nick brushed back his golden hair. "Aye-aye, Captain."

"Hey, I'm the captain around these here parts," Miles Barrow said from behind her.

Tess spun with a grin—how could she not? The man was hard to dislike. "Miles."

"Ah, Tess of the Ullos," the captain of Oedipus joked, kissing her cheek and giving her a brief squeeze. "You're looking ravishing, as usual."

"You flatterer," she murmured with a smile. Miles Barrow had been the captain and art director for Oedipus for as long as she could remember. Flamboyant, loud and slightly annoying, he loved his position of power within the super krewe, but there was something decidedly lovable about the overweight man with a gray-streaked beard.

"Of course I am, but I ain't no liar, neither, darlin'," he said, his New Orleans East accent thick as gumbo.

Nick stuck out his hand. "Miles."

"How ya been, friend?"

"Good. I'm here with Tess, aren't I?"

Miles nodded. "Damn straight. Go get you some food. We got everythin' you want. Have a ball."

Nick slipped away and headed to the bar. Tess nodded at Miles, knowing Monique expected her to help bring in his business. But he wouldn't be easy to pull away from Ullo because he was the kind of guy who respected tradition. Frank Ullo had been a friend as much as he'd been the guy building spectacular, elaborate floats with all the intricate posterboard flowers the krewe was known for. "I want to talk to you about the 2016 floats… after I snag some of those smoked oysters and do the wobble with Margaret Ann."

Miles's guffaw filled the foyer. "Ah, damn, chérie. My wife's been practicin' that dumb thing all week. You go dance with her. Will tickle her fancy, for sure. Business can wait." He waved at someone across the room and was gone in a blink just as Nick returned with a vodka tonic with a wedge of lime and offered it to her, clinking it with his own scotch and soda.

"I'm glad to be here with you, babe," he said, brushing a lock of hair off her shoulder. "It's been too long since I spent time with my Tess. I can't even remember what we fought over."

She lifted her eyebrows. "Really?"

Nick played dumb which unfortunately suited him. "Naw. What was it over? A silly Christmas present? Drinking too much at the Ullo holiday bash?"

"Merrill Wynn?"

"Merri?"

"You took her home and screwed her right after giving me that bracelet and talking about forever. Remember?" Tess said.

"Oh, yeah. I forgot. But you know she didn't mean anything. I was drunk and she was all over me."

"You don't really believe that."

"So I screwed up. I know that now. I'm ready to be the man you need." He looked down at her, so earnest, so sincere, so…freaking lying between his teeth.

"We're here as friends, Nick. That's it."

Nick smiled. "Sure. We're totally friends. And if we hook up, we hook up."

She pulled his hand from her waist and surveyed the room, wishing now she'd just come solo. Monique had urged her to bring a date, even going so far as to suggest a double date, but for some reason Tess held her off, declaring she had an appointment earlier that day. She hated lying but the thought of sitting at a table with her boss and Nick made her feel itchy.

Monique and Josh should be here by now.

Graham, too.

Her stomach did a loop-the-loop. She'd taken extra care with her appearance that evening, donning a short gold cocktail dress that clung to her hips and showed off her toned legs. The blousey crepe top showed her equally toned arms by gathering at her shoulders and dipping low to show the tops of her breasts. She wore diamond hoop earrings and her hair pulled back soft against the nape of her neck. Killer high-heeled sandals completed her look.

She'd told herself the outfit had nothing to do with Graham and everything to do with feeling confident and together—the same reason she'd brought Nick. But she lied to herself. Rubbing the satiny lotion over her body and sliding into her lacy underwear, her thoughts had been of Graham. Of the way he'd loved her, made her feel like forever was something within her grasp.

Damn it. Why couldn't she have all she wanted, including Graham? Why was everything so hard now?

"Tess, you look lovely," Monique said, sweeping alongside her.

"Oh." Tess jumped at the unexpected greeting, sloshing her drink on her hand. "And you look gorgeous as always, Monique."

Monique, clad in something short, slithery and magenta, smiled. "I see you've brought a date. Your taste is exquisite as always."

Tess made introductions for her "friend" Nick, who applied his charm with a light hand. Tess's earlier reminder about his indiscretion must have taken the wind from his sails. Wouldn't last long. Nick was anything if not impervious to "no."

Josh bumbled up, carrying two glasses of champagne. He handed one to his wife and turned a goofy smile on Tess. "You clean up good, girl."

Josh wore a jaunty hat that should have looked

ridiculous but somehow went perfectly with his atypically dark, somber suit. Monique rolled her eyes at her husband's trademark joviality and got down to her trademark sharkiness. "Graham will be here looking to get chummy with Miles. I think I've got him in our corner, but I want you to do a little hustling. I sent him our sketches a few days ago."

Tess smiled. "So you liked the sketches?"

Something in Monique's eyes glittered. "I sent him the best sketches. You did well, Tess."

Pleasure bloomed inside Tess at her boss's vote of confidence. She'd had to work to earn the Oedipus account and obviously it had paid off. "Float sketches are like Christmas morning to Miles. He'll get back to us soon."

"But as added insurance, don't be afraid to kiss his ass a little bit. Where is Miles, by the way?" Monique perused the room like a pro. Tess did the same and that's when she caught sight of Graham.

Her heart leaped so hard in her rib cage she pressed a hand to her chest. He looked so damn good she wanted to run and throw herself on him, maybe dropping various pieces of clothing along the way.

Tall, dark and so good-looking it should have been against the law, Graham had heads turning. The sudden feminine interest caught Monique's attention too, and she spun toward the entrance.

"Ah, the wonder boy himself. Speeding up heartbeats," Monique said under her breath.

Josh peered around Tess and gave a shrug. "Don't know why you think he would change now."

Monique patted Josh's hand as if she worried about his insecurity. "Now, Josh, being devastatingly handsome is not all it's cracked up to be."

"Bite your tongue, woman," Nick piped up, finally, turning to his good side and giving Monique one of his charming grins. Yeah, he was over the "just friends" speed bump.

Graham caught sight of them and moved their way. His stride was purposeful and naturally elegant. The same navy suit he'd worn for his interview—that had lain in her polka-dotted chair—stretched the breadth of his torso, the same classic tie lay against snowy pressed white. Same wing tips, same icy blue eyes, same response inside Tess. Shivers.

"Evening," he said, with a nod to Monique, his eye snagging on Nick who still grinned like a jackanapes. "How is Upstart this fine evening?"

Monique looked nonchalant. "We're just dandy, Mr. Naquin."

"I'm not dandy," Josh said, with a secret smile. "I'm thirsty. Grab you a beer, Graham?"

"Sure."

"I know what you like." Josh headed to the bar, looking relieved to escape.

Graham held out a hand to Nick. "I'm Graham Naquin."

Nick took his hand, a flicker of a frown marring his all-American good looks. "Nick Ashley."

And then silence so uncomfortable it might have been improved by a dog licking itself…or a kid picking his nose…or Nick saying, "I'm Tess's boyfriend."

"What?" Graham and Tess asked at the same time.

Monique raised her eyebrows.

"No, he's not," Tess clarified, smiling as if it were a joke. "He's kidding around."

"Okay, I *used* to be Tess's boyfriend," Nick said, winding his arm around Tess's waist again and tugging her against him.

Mood had gone from uncomfortable to knife-in-the-eye excruciating. Like a hound sizing up the competition over a bone, Graham eyed Nick. In fact, he looked as if he might rip Nick's arm off and beat him with it at any minute.

Aww…Graham was jealous. Warmth washed over Tess and she removed Nick's hand from her waist.

Monique studied the three of them, narrowing her eyes. "How interesting."

"Yes, but we haven't been together since last year," Tess said, searching for some other way to lighten the moment. Or maybe she should just run. "I think I'll find Josh and trade in this cocktail for something stronger."

Nick looked down at the untouched cocktail in her hand. "You haven't even taken a sip."

Tess raised the drink to her lips and took a gulp,

smacking as she backed away. "Definitely not strong enough."

Graham suddenly looked—dare she think it?—hurt.

"Wait a sec." Monique clutched Tess's elbow, making her drink slosh yet again on her wrist. All three looked at the small woman who had a knowing gleam in her eye. "Did you sleep with Graham?"

IF GRAHAM HAD been a lesser man, he might have gotten embarrassed at Monique's query...or cussed like a cabdriver....but he prided himself on keeping his composure. Tess, however, wasn't as composed.

"What?" she squealed, the glass in her hand slipping to shatter on the marble floor of the Yacht Club foyer. It was a scene from a bad movie. Or a soap opera.

Several people mimicked Tess's shriek, stepping away as the liquid spread. Tess dropped and tried to pick up the shattered glass, but a waiter moved quickly toward her with a towel and tray, brushing her hands away, as he made quick work of the mess.

Monique shot a knowing smile at Graham—the kind he'd always hated. "How did I miss this? You two have something going on and it's more than just business."

Graham gave her a quelling look. "Not now, Monique."

"Suddenly things are so clear."

"There's nothing clear in any situation with you,

Monique. You've never been uncomplicated, and in my limited experience with your new art designer, neither is she."

Tess looked up from where she squatted, her expression something between tortured and angry. "Stop talking about me as if I'm not here. And, frankly, who I sleep with—" she glanced over to Nick "—or who I *don't* sleep with, is no one's damn business."

Monique gave a choked laugh. "Oh, dear Lord, this is so effed up it's crazy. You never change, Gray. Always find a way to needle me. Sleeping with one of my employees…really classy."

Nick, who'd stood looking slightly confused, clued in. "Wait. You're with this guy, Tess?"

Shaking her head. "I'm definitely not with him."

Tess's quiet words sank into him. He didn't want them to be true. He wanted to be with her in every way. If only…

"But you're not with me, either." Shooting Tess a look of outrage, Nick stalked off. Graham understood. Nothing like getting smacked in the face with that kind of news along with a pointed message about the night ending with a cursory "goodnight" rather than an invitation to come up for coffee.

"I know how he feels," Monique said.

"That's enough, Monique," Graham warned, giving her the hardest look he could manage.

Monique inhaled and exhaled with great show. "Please tell me this happened before you took a job with her father's company? Please tell me you didn't sleep your way into daddy's good graces because that would be low even for someone like you."

"Someone like me?" He tried to keep anger from his voice.

"A man who likes to grind his heel on everyone who stands in his way. A man who would go to work for the competition just to rub my nose in it. A man who would seduce Frank Ullo's daughter… all so he could get ahead."

"Don't you dare go there," he said, gritting his teeth, wishing Monique would shut the hell up. Things were already tenuous between him and Tess. He didn't need his ex making it look like he'd spent that night with Tess for any other reason than that she'd taken hold of him.

And it felt like she'd never let go…even during those weeks he'd convinced himself it had been a fleeting moment and nothing more. But he'd known even then that Tess was special. That she was a forever kind of girl.

"You love to hurt me." Monique jutted her sharp chin, her eyes crackling.

"I still have that power? Somehow I doubt it."

"You don't," she sniped.

Graham sighed. "Why do you always think everything is about you? What happened between me and Tess has nothing to do with Upstart or Ullo. Never had anything to do with business."

Tess edged a shoulder between him and Monique.

Pointing a finger at each of them, she hissed, "Both of you, zip it. People are staring…and listening."

Monique snapped her mouth shut and glared at both of them.

He took several steps back, tossing an apologetic look at Tess. "I'm sorry, Tess. I came to say hello, not create drama."

Tess looked unconvinced. "Drama has become my stalker. I should start walking backward."

Graham gave her a tight smile. Hell, even annoyed, Tess looked spectacular. Her dress fit her to perfection, and she'd carefully applied makeup that highlighted her expressive green eyes and pouty lips. Her toned legs looked amazing in the short skirt and strappy sandals, and underlying her sultry scent was the fresh scent of apples. He wanted to whisk her away from the fake laughter and clinking glasses, wanted to go back in time to that rain-soaked night. He wanted to peel the dress from her body, kiss his way along her collarbone and make her shatter against him again and again.

What he didn't want was her standing there frowning at him. Maybe even setting more bricks in the wall they had between them.

"I'll say goodnight," he said, ducking his head in farewell.

Monique nodded. "Yeah, you should say goodnight."

Tess said nothing in his defense, so there was little left to do than walk away.

So he did.

And ran right into the main reason he'd buffed his dress shoes—Miles Barrow.

"Hey, Graham Naquin, new man about town, I've been looking for you," Miles said, extending his hand. "Gotta tell you, you've got competition with those gals over there. When we meet, I'm going to need to be dazzled."

Graham took the proffered hand. "You think Ullo isn't prepared to do that? Frank and I have worked up a deal you won't be able to refuse, but we shouldn't discuss it now. I'd love to have drinks with you this week or maybe drop by your offices. The sooner, the better."

"Call my office Monday morning and tell Jules to schedule us a liquid lunch." Miles grinned, slapping Graham on the back.

Out of the corner of his eye, Graham saw Monique and Tess watching them. The two women looked mildly concerned and he liked that. Graham wasn't going to let Monique get her stiletto in the Oedipus door...even if she had the magical Tess on her team. After the exchange with Tess on Thursday night at the soccer field, he'd dropped by to see a bedridden Frank, seeking his approval on a three-year contract with Oedipus. He knew that as CEO he didn't need Frank's permission, but it felt like the right thing to do.

Frank had been weak, but in good spirits...except when Graham had mentioned Tess. A prickly

yawn still gaped between the father and daughter.
But overall, he saw gratitude in Frank's eyes as they
hammered out a proposal that would give the super
krewe early priority in the building schedule, locked
in prices and a hefty discount on tractor rental. It
was a to-the-bone contract, of little benefit to Ullo,
but he'd be damned if he lost this account. Oedipus, with its overindulgent floats and eye-popping
fiber optics, had always been a showcase for Ullo
Float Builders. Making calculated risks was part
of the business, and Graham felt in his gut it would
be a good gamble.

"I'll call Monday morning. Go ahead and get a
bucket of ice ready for the champagne. We'll have
a lot to celebrate," Graham said.

"I like your confidence, Naquin. Can't wait to
see what Ullo wants to do for Oedipus next season. Now go have a good time and meet some of
the other members of the krewe. They're good
people who love a good time. No more business
tonight—too much wine to drink and pretty girls
to dance with," Miles said before melting into the
crowd.

Graham couldn't resist looking back at Tess, not
because he wanted to one-up her, but because he'd
hated the way he'd left things between them…hated
Monique's ugly words. Nothing about the way he
felt about Tess had to do with Mardi Gras, floats
or getting a leg up in business.

No, it had everything to do with something he'd believed couldn't exist for him.

But Tess was no longer standing in the foyer.

She was gone.

CHAPTER FIFTEEN

TESS PRESSED HERSELF into a small shadow on the balcony of the Yacht Club and wished herself away to anywhere other than where she now stood. Stock-still and breathing shallow, she wondered if she stood motionless long enough she'd turn into a statue.

God, she wished she were a statue. Then no one would expect anything of her. Wasn't there a play or something about a girl who turned into a statue... or was that about a girl who had been a statue and then fell in love with her creator?

Falling in love.

Every little girl's fairy tale. She'd cherished the wonder of that moment, imagining it as she lay on her down comforter, staring at the soccer posters on the wall of her childhood bedroom. She'd look sophisticated, holding a glass of champagne. And he would be handsome (looking like David Beckham), swooping in, kissing her hand and taking her in his arms. And she would know. Somehow she'd know this was the man for her. Love would slam into her, and happily ever after would be sitting right behind her smiling prince.

That was the way it was supposed to be.

Easy.

But nothing about what she felt for Graham was easy. She hated him. She loved him. Wanted to punch him. Wanted to kiss him. Falling in love wasn't supposed to be this confusing. Usually, she wasn't the kind of girl who looked at the glass half empty. But this particular glass from the tales of Tess Ullo's life looked cracked. No, shattered…just like the one she'd dropped minutes ago, making her look incredibly stupid in front of everyone.

Someone stepped onto the balcony and walked to the edge overlooking Lake Pontchartrain, a stark figure against the light of the full moon.

Graham.

Her flippin' prince.

Shame, embarrassment, guilt and longing throbbed inside her. The sight of Graham did nothing to relieve it. She didn't want to deal with him again so she scooted even farther into the shadows, craving some time alone before she attempted to carry out Monique's directives given mere seconds ago—mix, mingle and nail Miles down to the floor. Monique didn't seem all that affected that her newest employee had slept with her ex and rival. For Monique, it was always about the business.

But Tess needed a few minutes to compose herself.

Her furtive movement drew attention, and Graham turned, presenting her his profile.

Shit.

"Tess?" His voice was soft as the night spread before them.

No sense in playing statue anymore. She stepped forward. "How did you know it was me?"

"You're wearing gold and it catches in the moonlight," he said, moving so close she caught the scent of his cologne. The fragrance wound itself around her just like this man who had enraptured her that night long ago.

"I knew I should have worn the black dress my mother bought me on sale last spring. It was practically made for subterfuge," she cracked dryly. Wasn't like she could hop over the railing and disappear into the depths of the lake. She wore her only pair of Manolo Blahnik heels.

"You look spectacular in the one you're wearing," he said, a smile flickering at his delicious mouth. Oh, damn it all. Why was his mouth so delicious?

"You're just in suck-up mode and can't turn it off. I saw you with Miles. You both looked very chummy.... Makes me wonder what you're working up for him. Should have kept my big, fat mouth shut."

"Yeah, but I like your mouth open," he said, his eyes deepening. This man's words were silk against her skin, making her yield.

She didn't want this. Couldn't handle moonlight and seduction...not when so much was at stake. "Do you? Well, then you won't mind when I open it and tell you you're grasping at straws with Miles. He prefers quality above all else. My sketches give him that. Paired with Monique's offer, he can't resist. So save your pandering."

"Tess, I'm just doing my job."

"Which should have been my job," she muttered and immediately wished she hadn't. It was moot. Indulgent. A freaking dead horse. Her inner toddler may shout "It's not fair!" but the reality was life wasn't fair.

Suck it up, Tess, and stop dragging that hurt out into the light.

"Touché," he said, staring out at the boats anchored in the marina, bobbing in the gentle waves. He probably wondered how many times he'd have to hear about something that wasn't his fault. "I wish things were different for you, Tess. I wish I could make it better."

Something pinged inside her and made her aware of her constant harping on being usurped. "I have to move past what happened. I have to let it go."

He didn't say anything. Just stared out into the inky darkness as if he could find the answers for her there. After a minute or so, he turned. "About what Monique said. You know that's not true. That night wasn't—"

"I know. That night belongs to us. No one else. It's our memory, Graham, and I know you didn't know I was Frank Ullo's daughter."

"Monique likes to paint me as the bad guy."

Tess gulped back a laugh. "You *are* the bad guy."

He moved closer still. "Is that what you really think?"

She didn't answer. He knew she didn't think he was bad. He knew she wanted him...maybe even knew she admired the way he loved Emily, the way he stood up for Ullo.

Graham cupped her chin, raising her face to his. The moonlight cast a soft glow on his face, making his eyes soft and mystical. "I'm the bad guy? I used you?"

Still she said nothing.

"Tess?"

Swallowing hard, she closed her eyes. "No."

"No?"

She opened her eyes. "You're not a bad guy, Graham."

He lifted another hand and brushed back a tendril of her hair. "I want to be your good guy. I want things you can't imagine."

"I know you do," she whispered, longing rising within her. How did he always manage to do this? "I thought you were the right guy that night, but everything went so wrong. How could it have gone so wrong, Graham?"

Her words brought him to her. It was as if he could see she hadn't fully closed the door to him. She wanted him. She couldn't keep him out.

Wrapping an arm around her waist, Graham maneuvered them both even farther into the shadows.

The touch of his body brushing against hers ignited a torrent of desire. She couldn't resist him…. She didn't even want to stop him.

Maybe just a little taste.

Couldn't hurt to have one secret moment on the balcony, maybe then she could let him go. Maybe one kiss would be enough, maybe it would be average and not at all as special as she remembered.

She lifted her face to him…and then his mouth was on hers, hungry, almost punishing.

But she didn't care. She welcomed the nip of his teeth, the tightness of his grip, the tug of her hair as he tipped her head back so he could deepen the kiss. Like a pirate in tales of old framed against the moon on the water, Graham plundered and she surrendered.

There was no other recourse.

"Tess," he groaned against her mouth, his hands sliding down to her ass, bringing her hard against his body, against his erection. Like a match dropped onto lighter fluid, lust exploded in her. Nothing average about this kiss.

"I need you, Tess. I want to—" He kissed her again…and again.

Tess anchored his head with her hands as the world fell away. There was only Graham—his hard body and hot mouth moving her to a place where nothing else mattered but a man, a woman and a deep pulsating need.

"Just one more time," she said as his head dropped and his lips moved against the pulse beating strong in her neck. She dropped her head back, brushing the weathered paint behind her, giving him what he wanted. Threading her hands in his hair, she held him to her, thrilling as his hands wandered over the backs of her thighs, rising to cup her bottom beneath the short skirt.

"Come with me," he breathed against the valley between her breasts as his fingers brushed the dampening heat gathered between her legs. One finger slid along the soft lace of her panties, drawing a half sigh, half groan. "I need you. Just once, Tess. Just one more time so I can remember forever."

His words did more than even his magic fingers, his hot mouth on her skin. She wanted that, too.

"Your car?" she panted, lifting her leg to give him room. Her body was a slave to him. She could no more stop herself than a moth could ignore a flame.

And then his mouth was back on hers, nearly frantic. "Yes, somewhere. Hurry."

Stepping back, he looked down at her, his breathing ragged, something so intense in his eyes. Tess had never seen anything so compelling. He stood in that buttoned-up suit, looking as if he might lose control. In that moment, she was certain nothing could keep him from her—she'd do anything for him. Rob a bank. Run away to Vegas. Have his babies. Whatever he wanted. Because there was nothing between them but an uncontrollable need she had to quench one more time.

Then she'd let him go.

He reached in his pocket for his keys, withdrawing them, looking around for an exit even as his other hand slid over her back and bottom.

Tess felt drugged and knew at that moment what an addict felt. She was hooked on Graham.

And that's when Tess heard Nick.

"Tess is out here somewhere. I saw her slip out when I went to the bar," Nick was saying to someone.

"I haven't seen her in forever," came the responding trill, which sounded really flirty and really drunk. "But if we don't find her, we can always find something else to do."

Nick laughed and then there was a girly squeal.

"Oh, you bad boy. I love it." She giggled.

The effect was like cold water down her back.

Good Lord. What was she doing? How easily she'd tossed all her convictions for one more time in Graham's arms.

Who had she become that she'd consider running out on her date? She'd come with Nick, and though he was a jerk, she still owed him some semblance of decency. She couldn't sneak off with another man, no matter how damn good Graham looked standing slightly rumpled, his silvery blue eyes moving over her with a hot hunger. It was, well, wrong. Even if it looked like Nick would rebound just fine with his new friend.

"Stop, Graham," she whispered. "I can't do this. It's wrong."

"Are you serious? This isn't wrong, Tess. Nothing about this is wrong," he said, drawing her back to him.

She pushed against his chest. "I'm here with Nick. I can't."

"He doesn't sound too worried about it."

"Maybe not, but I'm not that kind of girl. I'm not sneaking off with you just because I have a hard time resisting you."

He stopped stroking her, dropping his hands from a body shaking in need.

Stepping back, he gave a beleaguered sigh. "Still fighting it, huh?"

"I have to. I'll admit I want you. It's obvious you trip my control switch, but if things are complicated now, what will they be if we do this?"

"The same, but we'll feel a hell of a lot better. Jesus, Tess, I need you." The longing in his voice nearly unraveled her last shred of control.

"I—I want you, Graham. That's not the problem. It's all the other stuff."

Eyes narrowed, he said. "Because we're 'against' one another?" He made the quote marks with his fingers…his beautiful, masculine fingers…the ones she wanted on her body doing delicious things.

Tess swallowed the need clawing to get out. "Yes. Exactly."

"So because we're both hustling Miles Barrow for a contract and because you're working for my ex and because I took over the operation of your family business and because you're here with Nick—" Graham tilted his head, his mouth sardonic even as a twinkle of amusement sparked in his eye "—those little things are keeping you from leaping the locked gate over there and getting it on in the parking lot with me?"

And in that moment, Tess's heart gave a lurch in her chest. He'd unlocked an escape hatch with a large dose of absurd humor. Tess covered her mouth to keep from almost hysterical laughter, but she sent him a thank-you with her eye. "And I'm wearing a dress and heels. Hard to scale a gate in this getup."

He held up his hands. "Hey, you can't blame me for trying. I've never been a saint, and you are pretty much the perfect girl for me…outside all of those other things."

Before she could stop herself, she snorted.

"No, it's true. You're highly uncomplicated and without any baggage. How can I resist?" More teasing, more lightness, more squeezing of her heart. He was being more than decent. He was living up to being her prince…even when she wanted him to be the pirate. To scoop her up, toss her over his shoulder and then have his wicked way with her despite her protests.

"If that's what you're looking for, then yeah, I'm your girl," she said, still wanting to kick off her heels and scale the iron gate, but glad Graham had not pressed the issue. It was not the right time or right place.

Might well never be the right time or place.

And that made her heart ache.

She moved toward the rail and Graham trailed behind her, looking casual and not so "I'm about to rip this chick's clothes off in the middle of a business mixer."

"Hey, there you are, Tess," Nick said, spotting her as she emerged from the shadows, the sequins of her dress no doubt catching in the light of the glowing orb hunkered over the gentle lake waves. "Look who I found."

Riley Ann Richard waved and spread her hands into a big hug. "Tess."

"Hey, Riley," Tess said as she was enveloped in a cloud of Vera Wang perfume. Her old teammate squeezed her hard and brushed her cheek with a kiss.

"I haven't seen you since we graduated. Isn't that crazy?" Riley said, stepping back into her towering platform shoes. The dress Riley wore was a bit too small but had gorgeous lace detail across the bodice. Her friend had blond curly hair piled on her head, bright blue eyes and a salon tan. She

looked stunning as always which made Tess want
to kick her.

"It is. How are you?" Tess asked.

"Good. I'm a buyer for Saks now. I'm in for Leo's
wedding. Mom and Dad are over the moon to have
me here for two weeks." Riley eyed Graham, who
stood just over Tess's shoulder.

Tess moved back and made introductions…which
seemed to make Riley's night. Her eyes ate Graham up and she cooed, flirted and basically did
everything short of handing him a room key. Jeal-
ousy, like a cur catching scent of meat, raised its
head inside Tess. She'd never felt that before, and
she didn't like it. Had no reason to own that emotion when it came to Graham. If he wanted to take
Riley up on her offer, it was none of her business.

Of course, Tess might have to rip her friend's
throat out if he did. Dear Lord, she not only was
jealous, she was feral.

"It's been nice meeting you, Riley," Graham said,
smiling congenially, "but I need to talk to Miles
before I slip out."

"Oh, I'll walk with you. I haven't seen him in forever," Riley said, shooting Tess and Nick a smile
and linking her arm with Graham's. "Who knew
I'd find such a handsome escort when I showed
up tonight. I didn't even want to come but Daddy
begged me."

Riley gave a little ta-ta wave and dragged Graham off.

Graham glanced back and in the depths of his eyes she saw resignation. He was stuck. And she wasn't going to rescue him the way she had that night at Two-Legged Pete's. Nick gave a heavy sigh as he saw his only chance for a random hookup striding away on Graham's arm.

"That dude is ballin' with the chicks, huh?" he said, his expression hangdog.

"Really?" Tess said, shooting him an incredulous look. "An hour ago you were telling me you've changed. Don't think I didn't see you putting the moves on Riley."

Nick blinked. "I was not."

"Oh, don't give me that, Nick. I know you. That last statement was you bemoaning the fact you're not getting underneath Riley's too tight dress."

"Well, I'm not getting underneath yours, that's for sure."

Tess snapped her fingers. "You got that right, buster."

And then she stalked away, heading for the exit. Monique could kiss her ass. She cared about her job, but she had to get out of the May Madcap Mixer. Like, pronto. Like, yesterday. Like, at that second.

Before she punched Nick, ripped Riley away from Graham and had a nervous breakdown in the middle of a primo Mardi Gras krewes shindig.

Tess Ullo was finally cracking up.

And there was nothing funny about it.

GRAHAM PRIED TESS'S friend's hands off his ass for the second time that evening. Seemed the woman was a veritable octopus.

"I'm feeling a little drunk," Riley trilled, grinning at him as they danced on the small dance floor set in front of a New Orleans funk band. "And you know what that means…."

"You're going to bed early?" he cracked.

"Oh, yeah. With you." She wiggled her eyebrows and grabbed his hands, moving them down to her ass.

Graham had to admit that any other time in his life, Riley would have gotten that early night. She was extremely pretty and obviously very available. But this wasn't the old Graham.

Coming to New Orleans had been about starting over, and he wasn't going back to the man who'd walked on the edge, wondering if any day he might drop down into the same pit his own father fell into. No. Conviction had grown inside him—the conviction to be a respectable businessman, an available father and a good person. No letting his goal slip through his fingers, which meant no more sleeping around with pretty, half-drunk girls.

Except when it came to a stubborn dishwater blonde with a perfect mouth, spectacular breasts and a laugh that made angels jealous. That's how you started, dude. Picking up a half-drunk girl in a bar...and falling in love with her.

Tess was the one.

Even though a gulf stretched between them, he knew deep down inside in places he pretended didn't exist that he'd fallen for Tess.

"Riley, you're a beautiful woman, but I'm not available in that way," he said as she slightly ground her pelvis into his.

A furrow gathered between her pretty eyes. She studied him for a moment before raising her eyebrows. "Ohhhh. Yeah, that's unfortunate. Uh, for me."

What did that mean?

"The good ones are always gay," she muttered, jerking his hand back up to her waist.

Graham almost laughed but controlled himself. "Yeah, we are. Sorry about that."

"That's okay. You can salvage this evening by telling me what you think about Armani's new collection. I'm a buyer for Saks and all my other gay friends are so conflicted about the new cut on the jacket. What do you think?"

"You think all gay men know fashion?" Graham asked.

"Most the ones I hang with do, but then again, I'm in the fashion industry. So give it to me from a layman's point of view," she said, looping an arm around his neck and studying him intently.

"What do you think about Armani's newest line? Or Tom Ford's?"

Graham opened his mouth but couldn't figure out how to get out of this one. "Riley, I have no clue."

She studied him, this time a little longer. "You're not really gay, are you?"

"No."

"So you're unavailable because you're with someone?"

"Sort of."

She sank against him. "Well, then, do me a favor. For the next few minutes pretend like she's watching and show her what she's missing not dancing with you."

But she wasn't watching. Graham had seen Tess leave, looking as if a pack of wildebeest chased her. And he knew some of it had to do with Riley, some of it had to do with Nick but most of it had to do with what had passed between the two of them— the passion neither of them could control.

Thing was, Graham no longer wanted to control it.

He just couldn't figure out how to get from Point A to Point B. Usually that was his greatest talent. That was his freaking job. But this whole situation he and Tess had blundered into was like tiptoeing through a minefield. One wrong step and…

"Just hold me a little closer, please," Riley said, her eyes not so much drunk as…sad?

"Sure," he said, gathering her up tight against him.

"Thank you." She sighed against his lapel. "I recently split with my boyfriend of two years. It's been pretty hellacious. I shouldn't have drank so much and propositioned you that way. Thought it might help stop the freaking bleeding inside, you know?"

"It's fine, Riley," he murmured against her hair. And then he did what she suggested. He danced with the broken-hearted Riley like he meant it, holding her tight, treating her like she was the center of his world, sliding his hands against her back, even giving her a little twirl.

When the music died, he gently brushed a kiss against her cheek. "Be happy, Riley."

She looked up and smiled, still a little shaky on her feet. "Yeah, I wish I could. Things would be a whole lot easier if he wasn't already married."

"Sometimes the things that stand between two people in love are insurmountable. And sometimes we can knock down those walls…or bridge those waters."

"Yeah, but not in my case. His wife is pregnant." Riley lifted herself on her tiptoes and kissed his cheek. "Good luck with Tess, Graham."

He stood alone on the dance floor as Riley faded into the other dancers.

The woman had known him for all of half an hour and had known he was in love with Tess. That's how obvious his feelings were. But what could he do about it? How could he break down the enormous wall between them?

It would already have been there if he'd come back and she wasn't an Ullo. He'd have had to grovel, admit to her his weakness, his greatest fear of being a failure like his father. But add in the fact he'd taken the job she'd expected to get, her father's terminal illness, and the fact they were rivals scrabbling for the same accounts and that wall felt never ending. His own personal Great Wall of China.

But walls could be torn down. And he would have to figure out a way to reach the woman he wanted on the other side.

Like a knight of old, he needed a plan to breach the castle. If he wanted Tess Ullo, he'd have to do more than mope and complain.

He had to be a man of action.

CHAPTER SIXTEEN

SUNDAY DAWNED HOT for early May. Tess had struggled from bed, forced herself to go for a run, showered and journeyed to her parents early as requested by her mother.

She had thought about faking a migraine because the idea of bed and a never-ending series of Lifetime movies seemed to suit how she felt today. But duty called and she found herself entering her parents' house via the backdoor.

"Hello there, my Tess," her mother said, from her position behind the mammoth stove. "You look pretty this morning, hon. I like the way you're wearing your hair."

She'd braided it down the side. "Thanks."

"And you've lost a little weight."

Not sure if that was good or bad. Her mother was always trying to fatten her up with Italian pastries and calorie-laden pastas. "Stress takes it off me. You know that."

Her mother lifted the spoon from the red sauce, tasted it, tossed in some salt and turned to her. "Time to talk turkey, missy."

"You wanted me to come early to talk about poultry?" Of course, Tess knew this wasn't about anything as inane as food. This was about her father. Neither she nor Frank had figured out how to traverse the gulf between them, so Maggie had built the raft. Tess had dreaded this moment as much as she had craved it. She needed to be moved and her mother was the woman to kick her ass in gear.

"Turkey is fowl," her mother intoned, tossing the spoon into the sink and untying her apron. "Let's go out back."

"It's hot, Ma."

"So is the kitchen," Maggie said, grabbing a sweating glass of lemonade and shoving another one that had obviously been waiting on Tess. "Here. Follow me."

Tess had no recourse but to do as directed. Her mother wasn't a woman to be questioned—people just did whatever the diminutive drill sergeant said. Yep, Maggie had missed her calling in life. Tess sighed. "Fine."

They walked to the flagstone patio sitting near the waterfall her mother had insisted they build to cover the noise of the nearby highway. The oaks gracefully bowed, magnanimously sharing the cover of their leaves, casting pure shadow on the outdoor living room her mother had created. With the tumbling verbena and vibrant canna lilies clustered with the blooming irises, the patio looked like the cover of a gardening magazine.

"Sit down," her mother said with a gracious wave of her hand, reminding Tess of the spider opening her parlor to the fly. Suddenly Tess felt twitchy. She so should have faked a migraine.

"What's up? I'm looking for the coals you're about to rake me over but I don't see any." Tess set her glass down, plopped onto an overstuffed chair and crossed her arms. Realizing she probably looked like a sullen teenager, she uncrossed them, hooking one on the back of her chair.

"Oh, honey, you know I don't have to tell you what is up. You know what's up," Maggie said, taking a careful sip of her lemonade before setting it beside Tess's on the stone coffee table.

Tess sucked in a deep breath and tried one last-ditch effort to prevent the talk they were about to have. "Dad told everyone this is between him and me."

"Oh, no, honey. It's not." Maggie leveled her with the "mom look" she'd used on Tess her whole life. Tess refrained from doing the requisite squirm.

"I can't—"

"Oh, yes, you can. I understand your disappointment with his decision regarding the company, but he *is* your father."

Silence fell hard and the tinkling of the waterfall fountain thing might as well have been fingernails on a chalkboard. Tess already knew that. What she didn't know was how to forgive him so she could deal with his illness.

"Let me say that again, Tess. He is your *father*."

"But he didn't remember he was my father when it came time to choose his replacement. I'm his *daughter*."

"So you are," Maggie said with a sigh. "But have you ever paused to wonder if you were the one who was wrong?"

She jerked her gaze up to Maggie's. "What?"

"Have you ever examined the notion you truly aren't ready to run the company?"

Her mother's question might as well have been a bucket of cold water in the face. *Not ready?* "How can you even suggest that?"

"How can I not?"

Tess looked away, grappling with the thought her own mother didn't think she was able to run Ullo. Tess *was* capable of running the company. Sure, there would be a learning curve, just like at Upstart. But Tess knew she could do it, and that her own mother doubted her felt like a razor blade swiped across her heart.

Maggie waited.

Tess raised her gaze to the woman who'd always believed her daughter could do anything she set her mind to. "You don't think I can."

Maggie hesitated for a few minutes, seemingly looking for the right words. "I'm not sure. You know the answer to that, but you've clung to the belief it was your birthright for so long, you never stopped to consider whether it was the right place for you. I don't work for Ullo. My job is to love the man who built the company…and my job is to love you."

Tess sank back on the cushion. "I can run Ullo."

"Maybe the question is not whether you can run Ullo, but if you are ready to run it at this moment."

"Yes," Tess said, even though a flicker of doubt grew stronger within her. She'd never stopped to really think about her father's motivation for hiring Graham. Maybe it wasn't that he hadn't thought Tess capable of being the head honcho, but rather that she wasn't prepared for the task at present. Or maybe she would have never been ready to step into her father's shoes. Maybe she'd already found the shoes that fit her…and she hadn't wanted to let go of her intention. "This is what I'd been working toward. I followed in Dad's footsteps because my brothers didn't. I did this for him. For Ullo."

"Is that the right answer?" her mother asked, her expression thoughtful. Annoyingly thoughtful.

Tess wanted to slap her mother for making her think—no, doubt—all she had believed. "I've always thought it was the right answer."

"Maybe it is, but your father never made any of you feel as if you had to work for Ullo. He made sure each of his children knew they were free to find their own path and follow it. He's always been proud you chose to work in the world he loves, but he never said he'd give you the key to the company one day, did he?"

"No," Tess said, feeling a lump in her throat. Those words hurt. God, they hurt almost as much as the day her father had said them from the chair in which Graham now sat. "I always thought that's what he intended. That he had faith in me. He's never questioned my abilities."

"He does have faith in you, and he's been amazingly patient while you've figured things out," Maggie said, clasping her hands and leaning forward. "Don't you get it, sweetheart?"

Tess stared at her mother, the woman she'd expected to be on her side, the woman that she expected to cajole her to reconcile with her father... not make her doubt herself. Not make her examine herself. Tess shook her head and blinked the tears away.

Maggie gave her a small smile. "Your father wasn't slighting you or saying he didn't trust you—"

"Then why didn't he tell me about Graham to begin with?" Gone was the hurt of her mother siding with Frank, and in its stead reared aggravation. "Dad never had the conversation he should have had with me. He allowed me to think this, Mom."

"Frank never wants to hurt you," Maggie said.

"Really? 'Cause he did, Mom. He should have respected me enough to tell me I wasn't good enough."

"I'm not saying he handled this well."

"Finally, something we agree on." Tess folded her arms, feeling justified ...petulant. No matter what her father believed, he should have been honest. Tess deserved as much.

"There is no black and white in this situation, Tess."

"No shit," Tess muttered.

Maggie briefly narrowed her eyes before sucking in a deep breath. "I can admit Frank made mistakes, but his frame of mind was to protect you. He's a man who has spent his entire life working hard to take care of us all, and he found out he has pancreatic cancer. Can you imagine what he felt?"

"Of course I can't imagine, but you can't use his cancer as justification for tricking me."

"Shut up," Maggie said, her eyes crackling. "Just put your outrage on hold and listen to me for a minute."

"Fine." Tess pressed her lips together.

"All our dreams of retirement are—poof—up in smoke. And it's not just about the family he leaves behind. It's about the company with its fifty-plus employees. All of that places an enormous burden on your father. Have you thought about that?"

"You said 'leave behind,'" Tess said, her heart trembling at the thought of what might happen. No. What would likely happen. Up until this point her mother had been super positive, refusing to even think Frank could leave anyone or anything behind. The possibility of Frank not beating this cancer had never been uttered.

Maggie's eyes sheened and she looked away,

blinking rapidly. "Look, I'm *not* giving up on your father, but you and I both know the percentage of people who have beaten this kind of cancer is not good. My point is, your father has a lot he's worrying about and all of this has been very tough on him. Maybe he couldn't face telling you one-on-one that he didn't think you capable of running Ullo yet. You aren't the easiest of people, Tess."

"What do you mean by that? You make me sound like I'm some kind of unreasonable diva. I'm not."

"No." Maggie paused for several seconds before turning her gaze back to Tess. "You've never taken no for an answer. It's a great quality…sometimes."

Not easy? Never take no for an answer? Her mother made her sound…spoiled. So maybe she was a little manipulative when it came to getting her way, but she wasn't a total pill. "I take no for an answer."

"But only after you've exhausted every angle. You don't make it easy."

Tess stared at her mother, disbelief gathering inside.

Maggie spread her hands. "Remember when you wanted your ears pierced? Or how about when you wanted your soccer team to wear bright green cleats? Or when you wanted the VW Bug? Or when it came to picking colleges? Or the paint color in your condo? From sleepovers to cereal choices, you wheedled and wore us down until you got what you wanted. You're not a diva, but you are a master manipulator."

"No, I'm discriminating. That doesn't mean I'm irrational or illogical…or can't accept not getting my way."

Her mother's blank stare said it all.

And Tess didn't want to admit she was right, but… "Okay, I'm slightly difficult."

"Well, your father is overloaded with difficult things at present. Maybe he was cowardly and dishonest, but he's not perfect, and neither are you."

"So you're saying it's okay to lie to me and sneak behind my back to hire a new CEO," Tess intoned, still aggravated by her mother's calling a spade a spade.

"I'm telling you your father loves you, didn't want to hurt you and has never been good at telling you no. If he'd have told you what he planned, you would have talked him out of it. You would have made him make you CEO, which in his emotional state of mind might not have been a wise decision. So he went around you."

Her mother's words found their mark, and again, pierced her. But she knew those words were true.

From early on, Tess had always been able to talk her father into anything she wanted. Case in point, he'd bought her diamond earrings when she was seven, donated lime green cleats to her eighth grade soccer team and a bright red convertible VW Bug had tooled her around the campus of the college she insisted on. Tess was accustomed to getting what she wanted…mostly because Frank Ullo had seen she got it. "You make me sound like a bad person."

Anger flashed in her mother's eyes. "Don't put words in my mouth, Tess. You know that's not what I'm doing. You are a very good person, but your father spoiled you. Quite frankly, I think he realized it when the doctor gave him the diagnosis and he had to think hard about what direction to go with his company."

Tess stood and walked to the edge of the patio. She'd held on to her anger at her father for weeks, and then when she'd found out he was gravely sick, the guilt and confusion over what she felt had blanketed her, smothering the rage she'd felt over the slight she'd perceived her father to give her. She'd never looked at it from his point of view, never wanted to even entertain the idea she couldn't slip right into the old man's shoes and run the company without a hitch.

Turning away from the beauty of the emerging cannas along the fence line, she looked at her mother. Maggie had always seemed eternally youthful, but in that moment, Tess noted how tired she looked. Her roots showed gray, and her face seemed more lined than ever. Worrying about her husband had taken its toll on her. "My emotions are so mixed up, Mom. I don't know what to do."

Maggie came to Tess and wound an arm about her waist. "You'll find a way. You always do."

"I'm still hurt, and there's no way to fix what I've done. I work for Upstart. It's like I'm not even an Ullo anymore." Emotion welled in her, choking her at the thought of what she'd done for pride's sake. What she'd given up because she couldn't accept the fact her father might have been right.

"Ah, Tess, that will never be true. You're an Ullo to your core. Your father is proud of you no matter who you work for." Maggie smiled at her. "And I am, too."

Tess had tried so hard not to cry, but tears came anyway. "This has all been so terrible, Mama. Everything in my life feels so off-kilter. How can I change that?"

Maggie wrapped her arms around Tess, and the emotion unleashed. Just like in Graham's car, grief, hurt and anger swamped Tess, rending her control, sloughing away any power she had against the feeling. For several seconds she allowed herself to cling to her mother's strength.

Finally, Maggie eased Tess away from her. "I can't fix things for you, baby. You should have learned that long ago. Or…maybe I learned it."

"That was before. When my life was golden."

"Life can't be golden every day. Having dark days makes the golden ones precious. Believe me, I've learned to bask in the light and hold tight to the memories of the sun on my shoulders during times I can't see. Nothing's perfect, Tess. You just never learned to accept that sometimes good and bad must exist together."

"I haven't had much bad in my life until recently. Now everything's turned to shit." Tess rubbed her eyes.

Maggie sighed. "Yeah, it is kind of shitty, but we'll survive as best we can, enjoying the golden moments that crop up."

For a moment, they stood quietly, each wrapped in their own thoughts.

"Mama?"

"Yeah?"

"I can't talk to Daddy yet. I need more time."

Maggie turned and measured her with astute green eyes before giving a curt nod. "Okay, you think about the words we exchanged today, but…"

Tess looked up, expecting more words of wisdom.

"…don't take too long thinking about forgiveness. Imagine a world without your father. Imagine a world in which you never break through your anger at him. Your life has always been better because your father was in it."

And then something hit Tess. A sort of understanding, heavy and dark, slammed into her. There were no words for what it was. Or maybe there were, but Tess couldn't have found them.

And it hurt like a knife stuck into her soul.

"Mom, don't say that. Don't act like he won't make it," Tess said, her voice cracking.

Her mother shook her head, waving off the tears, waving off falling apart as she'd done for all of Tess's life. "Don't. Don't make me cry."

Tess sank back against the cushions and fell silent while her mother reclaimed herself. Finally, Maggie tugged her tunic shirt down, breathed deeply and gave a small smile. "I have to get back to lunch. If I burn the sauce, your grandmother will tell everyone in Golden Oaks. Last time, I got recipe cards from three of the women there."

Tess tried to smile but the effort fell flat. "I'll be up in a minute."

Maggie nodded and walked up the stone pavers toward the grand patio sweeping across the back of the house. Well-maintained flower beds spilled beautiful blooms onto the manicured lawn. Everything was picture-perfect, the absolute best available, marred only by the cancer growing inside the walls her mother entered.

The irony soured Tess's stomach.

She closed her eyes as if doing so allowed her to close out the world she didn't want to face.

But that was the problem.

She'd stuck her head in the sand and hoped things like dealing with her father and dealing with what she felt for Graham would go away. Thing was… they hadn't.

Can't run from the world, Tess.

She'd have to face her demons, putting one foot

in front of the other. The first hurdle she'd face would be her father.

The fact he'd lied to her, even by omission, still hurt. Then fresh pain tumbled in at knowing he'd tried to protect her from her own ego. He'd tried to fix her mistakes before she'd even made them, planning from his grave to take care of Tess. Something about that thought was comforting, and the other half was maddening. He hadn't had faith in her.

But maybe she'd had too much faith in herself.

She'd never considered her father might be right. So certain she could handle every situation that came up at Ullo, Tess hadn't accepted any weaknesses in her skill set. But she'd learned very quickly at the smaller Upstart, she had little experience with hammering out contracts, crunching the numbers, dealing with insurance and codes and reviewing the legalities. At Ullo, she'd always handed that stuff over to someone else. Working hard to prove herself, she'd struggled with the nuances in which Monique had expected her to be proficient...the ones Tess had never learned because she'd never had to.

Not to mention she still dealt with hostility from Cecily, blowback from the artists and delicate intrapersonal relationships with Josh and Monique. The pressure Monique placed on her to bring in new accounts pulled at her day and night.

What would things be like if she'd stayed at Ullo?

Had her pride led her to greater hardship? Had it pointed her in a direction she was never meant to travel?

She didn't know the answers to any of her own questions, and unfortunately, her mother had been right.

Tess would have to walk the path she'd hacked out of the jungle of life on her own. Any missteps would be her own. Time to own her mistakes, suck it up and move forward. There were no do-overs.

But she could move forward with a better vision, accepting exactly what her mother had said—life isn't perfect.

To recognize the good, she had to experience the bad.

Tess rose, and like her mother moments ago, straightened her shirt, took a deep breath and gave the world a tremulous smile.

FRANK ULLO FORCED himself to sit up straight at the dinner table when all he really wanted to do was lie down. Some people who underwent chemotherapy didn't feel too bad. Some did. He was in the latter category, which made him angry. The least this bastard cancer could do was leave what little he had left of life alone.

His family chattered as if it were just another Sunday. He supposed it was just another Sunday to them, but to him it was the fourteenth Sunday since he found out he was dying. Thinking about the day that way caused an incessant pricking of his conscience.

How many more Sundays did he have?

Looking down the table, Frank settled his gaze on his youngest, who'd been awfully polite and quiet during the meal. He'd seen Maggie take her out for a talk. Part of him resented his wife's interference, part of him felt relief. He and Tess had gone too long without talking.

She lifted her eyes and caught his gaze. Holding it this time, rather than looking away, her eyes filled with tears. The sight ripped at his heart. Tess dropped her eyes and shoveled her food around on her plate before looking around at her brothers and their wives assembled at the table. The kids were all in the kitchen and the meal had passed without any bickering or spilled iced tea.

Clearing her throat, Tess asked, "Do you guys think I'm difficult?"

His sons stopped eating and looked at their much younger sister.

"What do you mean?" Joseph asked. This son was always calm and reasonable, repressing the dreamer he'd once been.

"I mean, do you guys think I'm hard to deal with?"

Maggie pressed her lips together and looked at him. Frank raised his eyebrows but said nothing.

Michael laughed. "What dude has told you this?"

Tess grimaced. "This isn't about a guy. I'm just wondering."

"Hell, yeah, you're difficult," Frank, Jr. said, jabbing a fork at her. "You always have been. Remember when she was teething, Ma? And we couldn't get her to stop biting everything? She bit the poor dog every time we turned around."

"And when she decided she was going to be a chef and made us those terrible cookies and brownies every day?" Michael made a face. "That kick lasted for months."

"Or when it came to her spelling?" Joseph smiled, joining in on the fun. "Or putting sunscreen on her? Or how about when she had to take medicine?"

"She's just like Granny B," Michael concluded, lifting a finger in the classic eureka pose.

Frank watched the aggravation gather on his daughter's face. She never should have asked her brothers if she was difficult. New tears gathered in her eyes.

"I'm not like Granny B, Michael," Tess said, not huffy like she'd usually get, but rather resigned.

"Yeah, you are," Frank, Jr. said, with an emphatic nod. "You might be worse. You've still got a lot of years left on you."

"Hush," Maggie intoned. Laurie and Beth also shot looks toward their husbands.

Frank looked down at his daughter. "Tess?"

This time she didn't ignore him. "Yeah?"

"You're worth the trouble, baby. Always have been."

His words caused Tess to burst into tears.

Michael pulled away from his sister as if she were a loathsome cockroach, shooting his dad a funny expression. "Why'd you go and do that for? We haven't even gotten to dessert yet."

For the first time in weeks, Frank felt a lightness bloom within him. He looked at his baby girl crying into her napkin and knew her anger had abated. Something in the way she'd looked at him had told him all he needed to know. Tess had forgiven him for his transgression. She'd seen things from his side of the table and had accepted in some small way that his view was valid.

Didn't mean things were healed between them.

But he could wait.

Didn't have a lot of time left in this world, but for the moment it was enough.

CHAPTER SEVENTEEN

TESS WALKED INTO her loft feeling as if she'd been washed twice and hung out to dry. Limp as a noodle, her conscience cleaner, she sank onto her couch and looked around the silent room. She'd tidied the place that morning, picking up the gold dress she'd flung on the chair the night before, scooping up the sandals tossed capriciously onto her fluffy area rug. Her cleaning service had come Friday and the apartment smelled clean. Everything in its place.

But it was lonely.

Picking herself up, she opened the fridge. Maybe she'd make supper. She closed the door. Or not.

Emptiness stared back at her when she spun around.

Her fingers seemed to reach for her phone as if they weren't even attached to her brain. Scrolling through her contacts, she found him.

Graham Naquin.

Her finger hovered over his number before she sighed and tossed the phone onto the counter.

A booty call? Really, sister, it's come to that?

So she wanted him? So she'd dreamed about him

all last night? So she'd regretted not finding an immediate exit so she could get busy with him in the parking lot?

Did that mean she had to call him and—

The sound of the buzzer interrupted her personal lambasting. Probably Gigi coming over to chat her up about the amazing guy she'd hooked up with the night before. She'd seen drunken pics on Facebook earlier. Or it could be food delivery or—

She pressed the button. "Yes?"

"Tess?"

"Graham?" A rush of pleasure, of anticipation.

"Hey, let me in."

"Not by the hair on my chinny, chin, chin," she muttered, before pressing the buzzer.

Ask and you shall receive.

Rifling through her purse, she found some breath mints. She hadn't eaten much of her mother's garlicky pasta, but she'd had a bite. After tossing a mint in her mouth, she tucked her hair behind her ears, giving her cheeks a pinch. She wished she'd had time for a shower, time to wash her face after bawling like a baby at the dinner table.

He knocked on the door.

Too late.

"Come in," she called, turning on the faucet as if she'd been about to start the…

No dishes in the sink.

Turning off the water, she grabbed a dishtowel

and dried her hands, spinning toward the door as it opened.

"Hey," she said inanely, her eyes working over every inch of his body. "What are you doing here?"

He closed the door. "Breaching your walls."

"Beg your pardon?"

Graham advanced, his gaze determined, his mouth set. "I'm about to breach your walls the only way I know how."

"I'm not sure what you're talking about. In case you haven't noticed, I'm not a lady in distress, and there isn't an actual castle."

He stopped in front of her, not touching her, but close enough for her to wish she'd popped a second mint. "You're a lady in distress if there ever was one."

Point taken.

"Maybe a little distressed, but I'm working through it," she said, studying his beautiful lips. How could a man have pretty lips? But Graham did. Graham had pretty everything. He was a walking dirty sex dream.

"Are you?" he asked, his eyes equally thoughtful and sinful.

"Giving it the ol' college try," she said, sucking in some air so she didn't pitch forward and cover his body with her own. That might happen later. God, she hoped it happened later, but right now there were questions. "Seriously, what are you doing in the enemy camp?"

"Can we shelve that? I'm tired of talking about why. I'm tired of it being you against me."

"Tired of being enemies?"

"You know we aren't enemies," he said, hands now propped on his hips, legs akimbo. "We're far from that designation."

"Okay, we're not enemies, but we're not playing for the same team."

"And whose fault is that?"

Tess felt aggravation hone in on the desire that had already overtaken her. "Are you here to fight?"

"Hell, no. I'm here for the opposite," he said, grabbing her by the hips, drawing her to him. She let him because she couldn't think of a good reason not to. Okay, she could, but she wanted Graham more than she wanted her principles at that moment. She'd think about those tomorrow. Along with all the other thoughts that had tumbled about in her head that afternoon. She didn't want to talk about why, either…or anything else, for that matter.

She crooked her head and smiled. "The opposite of fighting is—"

"Loving," he said, his head dipping toward hers. "After last night, I figured there's nothing else I can do to make things up to you, nothing else I can do to make you feel better…but be your sex slave for one night."

Tess caught him by the jaw just before his lips covered hers. "Who said it was your responsibility to make anything up to me?" she whispered.

"Maybe it's not. Maybe I just want to see you smile," he said, his blue eyes nearly violet as he studied her.

Tess smiled. "Sex slave? I think that's the best offer I've received in a while."

"Good," he said, one arm going around her. "Now stop talking."

"But what about tomorrow? What about when life closes in and we're back to the real stuff?"

"To hell with tomorrow. I want this moment, Tess. I want you," he breathed as he covered her mouth with his.

A beautiful sweet hunger swept through her. Holding his head in both her hands she took from him as much as he took from her. The kiss went from sweet to hot in seconds.

Tess moved backward, tugging Graham toward her bedroom, but she ran into the counter.

"Oh, let's go—" She tried to get the words out, but she couldn't seem to stop kissing him, to stop running her hands up and down his back.

He cupped her ass and lifted her onto the cold granite. Pulling back slightly, he tugged the shoulder of her blouse to the side but met resistance.

"Here," she said, grabbing the elastic bottom and jerking the shirt over her head. She'd worn a plain white bra that day, nothing dazzling or sexy, but Graham didn't seem to mind. His hands made short work of the clasp.

"Ah," he breathed as she shimmied out of the

stretchy cotton, her breasts jiggling with the effort. "I've dreamed about these."

Tess smiled and her eyes widened…and then shut as his mouth moved down her body, capturing one breast and sucking it into the heat of his mouth. "Graham."

"Mmm" was all he said.

Boneless, Tess fell back to her elbows, knocking some papers to the floor and hitting the empty fruit bowl. Graham ignored the clatter, choosing instead to shift his attention to her other breast and tugging her pelvis tight against his, unapologetically grinding his erection against her sensitive flesh.

"The bedroom," she gasped as he continued the delicious torture. At that moment there was nothing else but Graham, his magical hands and hot mouth.

He lifted her into his arms and she wrapped her legs around his waist. Raising his head, he kissed his way up her throat to her mouth and walked to her bedroom.

Graham set her on the bed and she reached back to catch herself, unwittingly thrusting her chest forward. Legs sprawled, back arched and breasts unbound, she likely looked like a calendar girl. He stepped back and caressed her with his gaze as he slowly raised his soft T-shirt, revealing a sculpted torso. Graham wasn't freakishly muscular, but he was hot. He'd gotten some sun since she'd last seen him, and the golden flesh made Tess's mouth water.

Unbuttoning his shorts, he allowed them to slide

down his legs, leaving only his tented boxers in place. It was a delightful striptease, made even humorous when he stood absolutely naked in front of her wearing only his running shoes.

"I like your look," she said with a wicked smile. "Are you jogging off somewhere as soon as we finish?"

His teeth flashed in the dimness of her room. "Ah, baby, it's going to be a long time before I leave."

Tess shimmied out of her shorts and tossed them across the room, leaving only a tiny pair of bikinis covering the area Graham's eyes zoomed to. Thankfully, she'd waxed a few days ago in anticipation of hitting the pool with Gigi. Finally, something she'd done right.

Lifting her arms, she reached for him. "Please."

He toed off his shoes, pulled off his socks and lowered himself to his knees, inching forward across the area rug toward her. "All in good time. You see, I've had these dreams, these memories of the way you feel beneath my hand. Memories of the way you smell, the way you taste, and the sound you make when you come. You can have your fun, Tess, but only after I've had mine."

With that, he gently pushed her onto her back, tugging her knees so her legs dangled off the side of the bed on either side of his body. Then he leaned forward and blew on the exact spot that throbbed for him.

"Ohhh," she said, her hips tilting toward him.

"Yeah, just like that," he said, his hands sliding down her equally smooth legs, lifting them so they draped over his shoulders. He hooked his thumbs in the waistband of her panties and peeled them off her. The smile he flashed when she lifted her head to look down at him made her shiver with anticipation.

And then Graham Naquin, the man who'd stolen her job, the man she'd tried to outwit in business, the man she'd fallen half in love with months ago made Tess scream his name.

GRAHAM RUBBED THE sweet melon-scented soap over Tess's breasts, enjoying the way the flickering candles played over her wet skin. "If we don't get out, we're going to get all wrinkly."

"Who cares?" Tess sighed, lifting her leg and using her big toe to shut off the hot water she'd turned on to warm the tepid. "I've never had a better bath. You're like a soft easy chair I can snuggle into." She wiggled against him, allowing her bottom to brush against his genitals.

When he laughed, the water sloshed over the hills and valleys of Tess's body which he liked. Clutching the soap tightly, he continued washing, lifting her arm and soaping the length of it.

She sighed again.

Best sound ever. No, second best. First was when she'd called his name and shuddered against him. He could go to his grave happy after hearing that one.

"So that's why you lured me over to your place," he teased.

Tess turned the head she had resting on his chest. "I did not lure you over. This wasn't my idea."

He made a face.

"So why did you come?" she asked, her voice suddenly serious. "Or maybe the better question is why did I let you in?"

"I'm a sure thing?" He didn't want to talk about whys. He wanted to live in the moment. He couldn't handle serious talk right now because serious talk set something between them.

"So confident," she said.

"I thought that's what you liked about me," he said, lifting her other arm and washing that one, too. Dropping it back into the soapy water, he wrapped his arms around her, locking her to him. She felt good against him. He could hold her this way forever.

"I like a lot of things about you," Tess said, laying her arms over his. "I like your confidence, I like the father you are to Emily and I like the way you fill out your running shorts."

He laughed. More water moving over her body. Beautiful. "Actually, I joked about confidence. I'm surprised that's a characteristic you like about me."

"Everyone has doubts, right?" she said.

At that moment he could see the doubts Tess carried and knew he could put at least one of those to bed. "Yeah, but my lack of confidence is what kept me from you in the first place."

Her head tilted and a piece of the honey-streaked hair she'd piled atop her head fell loose. "What do you mean?"

"Last year was tough. I lost my job and couldn't find another one. I was either too experienced or not experienced enough. My financial situation got pretty grim. Actually, when the headhunter repping your father called me, I was on the cusp of taking a job at a local electronics store."

Tess stiffened slightly—was she shocked or disappointed? "Things are tough out there."

He wanted to say "you wouldn't know that" but bit his tongue. At the very least, he had to give Tess credit for refusing to bend to her father's will and striking out on her own. She'd done pretty damn well, taking a fair chunk of Ullo's business with her. "Yeah, it is tough which is why when I landed this job—the perfect job—I was not as much ecstatic as relieved. I didn't really want to have to hawk big-screen TVs and routers."

"Hmmm," was all she said. He didn't know what to make of her response. Was she angry? Or did she pity him?

"And that's the real reason I didn't return your call. I had every intention of calling you when I got to New Orleans, but I wanted to get set up here, get caught up on my bills. I didn't want to come to you half a man. I was too embarrassed to tell you the real reason, so I let you think it was no big deal."

Tess sat up, water sluicing off her back as she twisted to face him. In the low light, he couldn't read her eyes. Her mouth drew into an outraged line. "You think having a hard time financially makes you half a man?"

Didn't it? He didn't know one man who would blurt out "I'm over-extended and I don't have a job. Wanna go on a date?" Hell, no. Dudes wanted to show they could afford a good bottle of wine and a filet. "I wanted to be stable, able to take you out for that night on the town I'd promised you without having to calculate the cost. Frankly, my pride stood in my way. I didn't want to be the loser I'd felt like for the last six months," he shrugged and shifted his gaze away. "I wanted to be good enough for you."

"You're joking, right?"

He glanced back at her, trying to figure out if she were angry or sympathetic. "Actually I'm baring my soul to you, something that's always been hard for me."

"Wait, you didn't call because you thought you weren't worthy of me? Did you think I was that kind of girl? Was there anything in my demeanor that said I need a man with money in order to fall in love?"

Love. She'd said the word he'd danced around for the past few weeks. Falling in love should be wonderful. It shouldn't be like this—fraught with difficulty and hurt.

"I knew what kind of girl you were. It was on me. I'm the one with the insecurity." He pulled her back to him, settling her against him, stroking her side as if he could take away the insult. Maybe she needed to understand him better; maybe she'd see he was insecure because of what he'd lost so young. "You have to understand—my father spent his life chasing dreams. There was always a sure thing on the horizon. He'd sink every bit of our money into the venture and then—nothing. I spent my whole life watching my old man get beat down. Then one day, he didn't come home."

"He left you and your family?"

"He left everyone. They found him hanging from a rafter down at a shack on the lake. It was supposed to be a piece of development land he'd bought, but that had fallen through, too."

Tess covered her mouth with a hand. "Oh, my God, Graham. I'm so sorry."

"He was a loser and not brave enough to admit his failings. He checked out rather than face reality, so living through that left a mark on me. I didn't want to come to you empty-handed. I thought if I got myself together, we could start over." He gave a wry laugh. "Things didn't exactly work out, did they?"

Tess moved her hand down to capture his. "No.

Who would have ever thought we'd tangle ourselves so well in a web of our own making?"

For a moment they both lay in the warm fragrant water, minds turning over the irony that had bound them together.

"What about now?" he asked, lifting her hand and kissing the tip of each finger. "Does this change anything?"

"I don't know. Professionally? No. Personally? I'm not sure. We could try to sneak around and see each other. Or maybe we could say the hell with it and make our relationship public, but what would happen? We work for rival companies and eventually there'd be suspicion. I already feel like Monique's heading that way. That's no way to start a relationship."

Graham wanted Tess so much, he didn't want to hear any argument against getting what he wanted, but deep down he knew she was right. When she was nestled in his arms in their own private world, he could believe in a tomorrow for them, but in the cold light of day, when the eyes of the world were on them, he knew it would be impossible. "So this is it? Tonight is what we have?"

Tess turned her head, her green eyes mysterious in the candlelight. "I think it has to be this way. At least for now. Nothing has changed other than...I know you." Her voice cracked a little.

He caught her lips, kissing her softly. Sadness settled around him. He'd found the perfect girl, but because he'd taken the perfect job, he couldn't have her. Bitter, bitter irony. Actual tears caught in his throat when he thought of this being the last time he held Tess.

"Life is not fair," he said, trying to keep sorrow from spoiling the time they had left.

"I'm beginning to understand that more and more. Come on. We still have tonight. I don't want to think about tomorrow." She stood and the water ran off her naked body.

And then he wasn't so sad anymore.

She was a goddess—not of the usual variety—but of the Tess variety with her trim legs, soft ass and perfect breasts. Girl next door meets Barbie. Freaking awesome.

Graham rose and pulled her against him. "Only tonight."

She kissed him. "A good policy for the moment."

Much later, after they'd made love again, Graham walked quietly out of Tess's bedroom where she lay dozing. He hadn't had supper, and after spending the last few hours quenching his hunger for Tess, he was ravenous. He rounded the bar and nearly slipped on the papers that had fallen when he'd lifted Tess onto the counter. He shuffled the papers into a haphazard stack and tossed them and the folder onto the bar before opening the fridge.

Eh, not much to be had. He grabbed a yogurt that had expired a week ago and found the silverware. In the low light, he leaned against the counter and made short work of the yogurt. Looking around Tess's Spartan kitchen, his gaze snagged on the only disorganized object—the stack of papers—and the drawings lying atop the folder he'd dropped.

He moved closer, lifting the first one so he could see it better in the light.

Stunning.

He picked up a few more and took them back to the light above the sink so he could see them better. Obviously they were the drawings done for Oedipus with their theme of "Song of the South." Instead of large bulky props, Tess had layers of numerous smaller magnolias over the sides of the "Belle of Bourbon" with a twisting oak sprawled across the middle of the float, holding fiber optic glowing magnolias and glossy poster board leaves. The second layer resembled a huge white plantation house. The design was elegant, elaborate and…way better than what Ullo had put together.

He flipped through the other sketches: "Paddling the Mississippi," "Ain't She a Peach" and "Bayou Dreamin'." All were artistic and—

"What the hell are you doing?" Tess said from the hallway.

Graham jumped, nearly dropping the computer-generated sketches. "I was picking up the papers we'd knocked down."

She crossed her arms over the large T-shirt she'd pulled on. "Way over there?"

Tossing the sketches back upon the folder, he

shrugged. "Everything fell out. I came to get something to eat and they caught my eye."

Narrowed eyes. Mistrust.

He held up his hands. "I'm only human. Those sketches are like porn to a fifteen-year-old boy. I can't not look."

"This is what I'm talking about. Competing against each other, minding our words, worrying about subconsciously sabotaging each other's work—this is why it can't work between us," she said, padding into the kitchen and stacking the drawings together before sliding them back into the folder.

"Does it help to say your proposal for Oedipus is…so good I'm breaking a sweat?"

Her head snapped around. "You're just saying that because I let you tie my hands to the bed and play Princess Leia and Han Solo a few minutes ago."

"Is that why you called me Han?" he joked, pulling her to him. "Baby, those are brilliant. Really beautiful."

"Those are the early copies, but probably won't be enough for Miles. He protects the integrity of the parade, but he's more a nuts-and-bolts guy. He'll appreciate working with you," she said, relaxing against him, even as her gaze stayed on the folder. "I don't want to talk business. I want to go back to bed with you, feel you against me. Morning will come soon, and until the first ray peeks over the sill, I need to stay in the world we've created."

Ducking his head, Graham placed a gentle kiss atop her head. He wanted that, too, but he wanted it to last past morning. But at 1:17 am, his brain was too fuzzy to figure out how to make that happen…and his body had gone from boneless to hard while holding Tess.

There were better things to do than contemplate the morrow.

Daylight would come soon enough and pop the bubble of contentment that enveloped them.

Like that Scarlett O'Hara chick, he'd think about another day.

CHAPTER EIGHTEEN

MILES BARROW'S OFFICE held a huge desk, a huge blue marlin mounted on the wall, a huge plate glass window overlooking Magazine Street and a small assistant twitching nearby like a bluejay guarding its nest.

"Julian, sit down or go fetch more coffee. You're driving me batty with your hovering," Miles said, leafing through the contract Graham had brought, his legs stretched in front of him, huge leather desk chair tilted back.

"I don't hover," Julian drawled, pressing his hands down the skin-tight chambray jacket. Slim white trousers tailored down to classic oxfords. A jaunty bowtie, moused faux hawk and dark edgy glasses completed his dapper look. "But I will go for coffee if you want. Mr. Naquin?"

"None for me, thanks," Graham said, waving a hand and trying to look at home while his gut clenched awaiting Miles's response. This deal meant the difference between a decent 2016 and a subpar one...and he'd seen what Upstart had delivered.

"I don't need the caffeine anyway," Miles muttered. "Just work on the Happy Burger case."

Julian held up a hang loose sign and then the door snicked closed, leaving Miles to continue his *hmm*s after reviewing each page.

Finally, the large man set the contracts followed by the numbered float specs on his desk and looked up at Graham. "Interesting."

"I think so, and I think it's a solid proposal. Dave Wegmann, our art director, took your vision and created something over-the-top, and we're offering you more perks than we've ever offered another krewe. Frank Ullo wants to keep you happy, Miles."

Miles nodded, making a teepee of his hands atop his large stomach. "And I like that. But this isn't brain surgery, right? I like the relationship I have with Ullo. We've always used you guys, but I gotta admit there have been some issues in the past with labor costs and parade day glitches. This new outfit Frank's daughter is working for has promised me those bumps will be smoothed out. Her floats aren't exactly what I was looking for, but sometimes the experience with prop builders is more important."

"Not what you're looking for?" Graham said, leaning forward, his emotions mixed. Something within him hitched at the thought of Miles not liking what Tess had created for Oedipus. How could anyone not appreciate the designs she'd created? "I actually saw a few of them. Too elaborate?"

Miles made a face. "Since when has an artist for a rival company ever showed her designs? And, no, that wasn't the issue. Not detailed enough, in my opinion."

Something prickled on the back of Graham's neck. "I won't comment on how, but I thought they were exquisite, detailed and, honestly, better than ours." He pressed a hand against his head and mumbled, "I probably shouldn't have said that. Stupid."

Miles chuckled. "Look, guy, this ain't Wall Street and though business is business, you know how things are run in New Orleans. I don't hold nothin' against you as long as it don't affect me."

Graham rocked back in his chair, discomfited, as Miles spun his chair. An attorney by day, krewe captain by whatever was left over after billable hours, Miles didn't seem to be the most organized of men. Which is probably why he spun back around empty-handed and pressed a button on his phone. "Julian!"

"You don't have to yell into the phone, Miles," Julian drawled like the smart-ass he obviously was.

"Get me the Upstart proposal," Miles said, ignoring Julian's tone.

"As your generation says, '10-4,' big guy," Julian responded.

Five seconds later the assistant entered and handed off the bonded proposal. He turned and winked at Graham.

"Don't mind him. Bold as the devil, but the best

legal assistant I've had. He's taking the LSATs next month so I'll probably lose him," Miles said, opening the proposal. "This is what the courier brought."

He passed it to Graham who flipped through quickly. None of Tess's designs were in the proposal. Graham snapped it closed. "I'm confused."

Miles lifted his wooly eyebrows. "Why?"

"These aren't the sketches I saw."

The big man shrugged. "This is what I got."

"Hmmm," Graham said, shaking his head. Something was rotten in Denmark. He hadn't prodded Tess any further about business—they'd been busy exploring other pleasurable things, and when they'd parted this morning, they'd agreed to go back to whatever it was they had before, each agreeing it had to be over for now. Tess had given him one night, perhaps relying on their lovemaking as a time-released medication, working long enough to get her through the next few weeks. Or maybe it was merely a last-ditch effort to get him out of her system. Or maybe he didn't know what it was other than it had given him another taste of something he wanted so badly, and that would have to do him for a while.

But he had a bad feeling about what Monique had obviously done. His ex-partner and lover used Tess to bring in business, like a prized carrot dangled in front of krewe royalty. But if Monique didn't value Tess as part of her team beyond some honeyed trap, there was going to be an issue. Tess deserved to be valued as a designer…as a team member. Monique had quite deceitfully hog-tied her, subbing what he was quite certain were his ex's own designs instead of Tess's. Monique's biggest flaw had always been her hubris. Unable to let go of her need to control every aspect of Upstart, she'd submitted her own designs rather than better ones.

Here was the reason Upstart would never rise above midtier. If a CEO wasn't willing to toss his or her own pride aside and rely on the person best for the job, then all the efforts to nab new business would be for naught.

This was where Frank Ullo trumped Monique.

"Miles, if that's so, you should know Tess's designs are ten times better than what's in this proposal," Graham said, slapping the Upstart proposal on the oak desk. "And they're better than my proposal. God help me."

Miles narrowed his eyes, looking confused. "So why? If Monique wanted the Oedipus contract, why wouldn't she give her best?"

Graham licked his lips and thought how to say what needed to be said without sounding crass. "There is much to admire about Monique, but she's, how do I put this, wrapped up in herself?"

Miles nodded. "Egocentric, sure, but still. These are good sketches, nothing wrong with them, but if she knew—"

"She wouldn't. She can't look beyond her own nose. Monique likes to control every aspect of Upstart. Not a bad thing, but team player she ain't. So in her mind, she gave you what she believed were the best sketches—hers. The world revolves around Monique. That's about as nice as I can say it."

Miles sat, silent and taciturn.

"Look," Graham said, closing his eyes briefly before opening them, "I can't believe I'm saying this, but you need to call Monique and ask for Tess's set of designs. You don't have to tell her how you know what you know, but give Tess a shot at landing your business. Her design work is better. Plain and simple."

Miles Barrow hadn't been born yesterday. He shifted his gaze to a plant that needed a good watering and sat still for a moment before returning his gaze to Graham. For several seconds Miles studied him. Graham didn't like the perusal, for the man seemed to possess the uncanny ability to see within to the soul. After a moment, recognition sparked within the depths of the man's eyes. "Okay. Tess is a good girl. Things ain't been grand for her lately, so I think you're right. She deserves a shot even if I have to tangle with Monique for it to happen."

Graham didn't know whether to punch himself in the face or pat himself on the back. He'd just wrapped a ribbon around Oedipus and given it to the competition.

God, he was a fool.

Or maybe he'd righted the wrong inadvertently done to Tess Ullo.

Miles stood and offered his hand to Graham. "Damn, man, I can't say you're a good businessman."

Graham's ego shrank a bit.

"But you're a good person." Miles gave a hard squeeze. "And in the game of life that's always more important."

"Tell that to Frank."

"Frank knows. Your company is only as good as the person running it. There's a lot you can learn from Frank Ullo. He's a good businessman, and though many don't know it, he's a good person. Not everything is out for all to see, you know what I mean?"

Graham dropped Miles's hand. "I do know."

The big man came around the desk and slapped a hand on Graham's back. "I'll have a word with Monique and be in touch."

Graham gave Miles a final handshake, a wave to Julian and then stepped out of the tidy shotgun house that had been converted into an office and inhaled the humid air.

Next week he might be out on his ass, tossed there by Frank Ullo for destroying any chance the company had to revitalize the business.

But for the time being he'd cherish the idea he'd done something honorable. He'd done something brave. One step closer to his goal of being a better man…and one step closer to losing the job he loved.

TESS LOOKED OVER the notes the captain of Icarus made on the prop rotations she'd suggested and glanced at her inbox. Monique had been out of the office all afternoon and hadn't answered when Tess had texted her about the new guidelines the city had put out regarding rider-safety harnesses. She wanted to make sure Upstart had already made them on the 2015 floats because the penalties assessed for failure to comply were stiff. The krewes would expect the builders to get that right.

Spinning in her chair, she closed her eyes and sighed.

All morning she'd tried to get serious work done instead of reliving Sunday night in her mind.

Being with Graham had been good…almost healing. After weeks of feeling so alone, having him beside her connected her, gave her a glimpse of what it would feel to be in a relationship with him.

Oh, it wasn't just the sex—which was amazing, of course. Their conversations stimulated and comforted just as they had from the first time she'd met him on that barstool at Two-Legged Pete's. She wanted more than what she currently had with him which was…nothing.

Okay, they were nothing on paper, but maybe they could—

"What the hell, Tess?" Monique growled from the open doorway.

Tess spun. Oh, God. Monique knew about her

and Graham. But how could she? Unless the woman had been following him around. Or maybe she'd hired a private eye or something. Sometimes women did that in custody cases…but she and Graham weren't in a custody battle, were they? "What do you mean?"

"You know exactly what I mean," Monique said, framed in the doorway, looking like she might spit fire. Tess's office masqueraded as a broom closet, so Monique stood close, her eyes snapping, her dark hair slicked back into a low ponytail. Dressed in a black minidress and fishnet stockings, she was the epitome of every Disney villainess. Sorta scary.

And right on cue, her lackey Cecily popped her head over Monique's shoulder, self-satisfied half smile on her face.

"I really don't know what you're talking about," Tess hedged, hoping it was something other than the fact she'd had sex with the competition.

Like, three times.

"Miles Barrow called me and wanted a meeting. Basically, we've landed the Oedipus contract with the stipulation you take the lead," Monique said, her eyes still narrowed to slits. For someone who should be over the moon, she was decidedly aggravated.

Tess, relieved this wasn't over Graham, made a face. "I don't understand why you're upset. That's wonderful news."

"Miles wants your float designs."

"Well, yeah." Tess couldn't grasp the conversation. She felt as if she'd fallen into some parallel dimension where bad news was good news and vice versa. "That's what we gave him."

"No."

"No?" Tess sat back in her chair. "You didn't sub my proposal? You subbed yours?"

"Exactly. But somehow he knew about yours."

Monique moved inside the office and Cecily took up her former position at the door, looking gleeful, as if she were watching an execution.

Tess gripped her chair arms, and she wasn't sure if it was because she wanted to punch Monique or needed the support. "I never talked to Miles about my designs and, frankly, I'm pissed you chose yours over mine."

"Why? It's my company. I can submit whatever I wish."

"And yours weren't better than hers anyway. You've never been told no, have you, princess?" Cecily said, with another greasy smile.

Tess stared at both the women wondering if this was a joke, and then the situation really hit her.

Monique had not given Miles Barrow the designs Tess had slaved over.

Instead the woman had submitted her own substandard float designs. Monique had allowed Tess to play at design much like she'd given Emily a made-up project to keep her occupied, never intending to use Tess's work in the first place. Fury flooded Tess. She stood.

"Wrong. My designs were the better of the two, and you know it." Tess peered over Monique's shoulder. "And your fairy godwitch knows it, too, but she's too busy with her nose in your ass to tell you the truth."

Cecily gasped but Monique laughed. "Ah, there's my tiger."

Tess hadn't expected the amusement cropping up in Monique's eyes. God, the betrayal the woman had just exercised was almost as bad as what her father had done. Monique hadn't valued her in any way beyond her family's name. She'd used Tess and the Ullo reputation to her own advantage, lied about the designs and then had the gall to laugh about it.

Monique patted her cheek and Tess swatted at her hand. "Don't be mad, Tess. Maybe you're right. Yours might have been better, but you have to know I will always have final say," Monique said, not looking even slightly guilty.

"But you purposefully deceived me." For once Tess was glad she was bigger than Monique. She crossed her arms and became her father—cold, businesslike and pissed a person could treat an employee so shabbily.

"I merely decided at the last minute I liked the original proposal." Monique rolled her hand, very nonchalant even though in her gaze Tess could see a prickling of uncertainty. "So how did you know?"

She hadn't. And she had no idea why Miles insisted she take the lead beyond what she suspected—the man trusted her because he'd worked with her before.

Not saying a word, Tess stared at her boss, trying to make her uncomfortable with the way she'd behaved.

Monique shrugged, seemingly unaffected. "But know what? It's fine. Not a bad idea to give him choices. I just wished you'd have consulted me before proceeding with Miles. He's signed the contract stipulating we use your designs and that you oversee the production. You're his contact person and now wholly responsible for Oedipus. I'm half pissed at you and half proud of you for going after what you wanted."

Tess opened her mouth but this time nothing came out. Yeah. Speechless.

"I'll send all the information over to you. Miles wants a few adjustments on your Gulf of Mexico float, but beyond that, he trusts your vision. Congratulations." And with that, Monique left. Cecily stood openmouthed as Monique passed.

Tess sat down before her trembling knees buckled. She couldn't grasp what had just happened.

Cecily's drawn-on eyebrows rose toward her thinning hairline. "You don't get where your bread is buttered, do you?"

"Stuff it."

Cecily scoffed. "You didn't get your way so you ran off and played poor little rich girl with Miles."

"I had nothing to do with this."

"Bullshit," the woman said, her mouth curling into a half snarl that would have made Elvis jealous. "You're cut from the same cloth as your old man—you do whatever it takes."

"Don't even speak his name. Besides, I don't need the approval of a woman who stoops so low to accomplish her goals. You're pathetic. Now, don't let the door hit you in the ass when you leave," Tess said, making a shooing motion toward the older woman.

"She won't keep you on, you know. Don't think you didn't piss her off. She'll use you and then toss the accounts your name nets us to me." With that said, Her Creepiness slunk out, closing the door behind her.

Tess released the breath she'd been holding for the last few seconds and tried to center herself. Anger galloped like a stallion through her body, pounding through her blood, leaving her trembling from the sudden adrenaline rush.

How dare Monique?

Tess spun toward her computer, moving her mouse, automatically clicking on her email out of habit, while her mind raced and the anger continued its steadfast course through her body.

A little ding announced a new email as the window popped open and there it was—all the information forwarded by Monique regarding the Oedipus account.

Un-freaking-believable.

Her bitch of a boss hadn't even submitted Tess's designs. And they were so much better. Why had she done that?

But deep down inside Tess knew. Monique had a sort of egotistical insecurity that prevented her from seeing the truth in front of her. She'd felt threatened and less important, so she'd made sure she would get the credit. Tess was fairly certain Monique needed some intensive therapy to deal with her Napoleon complex.

Monique won't keep you on, you know.

At that moment, she understood everything about Monique's intent. She didn't want a team at Upstart—it was a dictatorship. Tess was an instrument to be used…but not valued.

Here's our Tess. You know she's an Ullo, right? Works for us now because she realized her father's company was a sinking ship. Utmost quality is what we offer—even an Ullo can attest to that. Her mark is on everything we do.

Yeah, right.

More like *Here's Tess Ullo. She does nothing but smile like a moron, and we lie to her and tell her what she wants to hear because it behooves us.*

Clicking the mouse, Tess reviewed what Miles wanted, feeling only a smidge of pride at the clause stating Tess Ullo must be attached to the project as director or the contract was subject to a renegotiation of terms or a forfeit of agreement between the two parties. At least *Miles* valued her.

But how had he known?

Tess liked to sign her name to her renderings much as any artist. Perhaps Miles had glanced down at the signature and not recognized it as Tess's? She was certain she hadn't mentioned specifics at the mixer.

So how had Miles figured it out? Maybe...

Couldn't be.

Other than Monique, Graham was the only other person to see her execution for the floats, and he would have to be dog-assed stupid to mention her designs to Miles. Losing the Oedipus account would piss her father off. Sick or not, her old man wouldn't suffer the loss of Oedipus. In fact, he'd likely fire Graham for losing so much business his first month as CEO...even if he did like the man.

And with Graham out of the way...

Oh, God, Tess. What the hell are you thinking? Do you want control of Ullo Float Builders so badly, you'd wish ill-will on the man you lo—

She mentally clamped down on that thought.

No.

Deny that word. Contradict those feelings. The fact was she didn't want control of Ullo enough to stoop to Monique's tactics. If anything came of this experience, it was that Tess knew better who she was. Tess was tough, stood up for her beliefs and recognized she did indeed have weaknesses. She could sweet-talk a city inspector, she could coach a gaggle of seven-year-old future soccer stars and she could cry on someone's shoulder, allowing herself to be vulnerable.

She could also learn she was wrong.

Wasn't easy for her to admit it, but she'd been off base in thinking she'd be capable of running Ullo at present. Perhaps she could have slipped right into her father's Hush Puppies and never missed a beat, but then again, maybe those shoes wouldn't have fit. Perhaps they never would.

Maybe she'd never be part of Ullo again so all this self-discovery wouldn't matter for shit. But now she knew being at Ullo meant being part of a team—a team that affirmed her and allowed her to shine. Her family company wasn't perfect, but with failure came a chance to learn.

She'd been wrong about so much.

Rising, she grabbed her purse and looped it over her shoulder before turning back to the computer and quickly transferring the Oedipus file to her personal email account, carbon-copying it to Gigi. She'd text her friend and see if she could give her a crash course on reading through contracts. Tess didn't have much experience, always leaving legal matters to her father. He'd break it down, review it with their attorney and then report back, giving her the nuts and bolts about what each krewe expected for their floats. Another weakness Tess had discovered—she didn't know diddly poop about contract negotiations.

She flipped the light switch, prepared to tell anyone who tried to stop her to go to hell.

"Hey, Tess," the small voice came from the makeshift break area sitting outside the painting bay.

Tess turned to Emily with a forced smile. "Hey, Em."

The little girl sat at a table, eating powdered donuts, swinging her untied sneakers back and forth beneath the table. "I'm doing my homework. Just finished spelling and now I got a worksheet on subtraction. Yuck."

"Yeah, subtraction stinks," Tess said with a shrug, "but yay for finishing your spelling. Oh, and don't forget you have to work on a Ladybug chant. We have practice tomorrow."

Emily's eyes lit up. "I already got one. Dad helped me make it up. Wanna hear it?"

"Sure," Tess conceded, moving closer to Emily while eyeing the unhealthy half-filled bag of donuts.

Emily leaped from the chair and spread her arms out wide. "Fly, fly ladybug, give it all your might. Fly, fly ladybug, show 'em how we fight. Red and black dynamite, we run, kick and score. Lake End Ladybugs, hear the crowd roar!"

During the chant, the child had waved her arms, kicked her feet and performed a little wiggle with her rump. Like a giant fan, Emily's antics cooled the ire raging inside Tess.

As she watched, trying not to giggle, something quite wonderful struck her. Here was Monique's daughter—a piece of the woman who'd so callously used Tess for her own gain. And here was Graham's daughter—a piece of a man who'd waited so patiently for Tess to find her way. Two parts of a whole.

Emily, with her lopsided bow, mouth ringed in powdered sugar and shirt too tight across her middle. She was part of those two, imperfect and wonderful all at the same time. Innocent of the machinations employed by those in her life, Emily hungered for attention and acceptance.

Just a little girl who loved her daddy and wanted to please him. Not so unlike Tess herself.

Finishing her final spin, Emily struck a pose and blinked up expectantly at Tess.

Sudden tears pricked Tess's eyes.

"Oh, man. It was terrible," Emily said, her small head tilting down.

"Are you kidding me?" Tess said, bending down and sweeping Emily into a huge hug. "It was the best cheer I've heard in forever. It was perfect."

"Really?" Emily leaned back and studied Tess's face as if she were a police detective. "You're not just saying that? Mom said it was pretty good, but Dad thought it rocked. He helped me with the motions, too, but he looked really weird doing them."

Tess laughed. "I can only imagine."

"Tess, do you like my daddy?" Emily asked, suddenly earnest. Suddenly looking older than her seven years.

"Sure I do. He's been a pretty good assistant coach. I never have to yell at him for not having our water bottles filled," Tess joked, not sure how much Emily understood about the relationship between a man and woman.

"No. I mean like love stuff. I think Daddy likes you. You know, he wants to kiss you." Emily averted her gaze, suddenly finding the ancient coffeepot fascinating.

Tess straightened. "What makes you think that?"

Emily shrugged. "A few of my fish died."

Uh, what? Tess looked at Emily with a blank expression. She had no clue. No innate mothering skill to enable her to peer into the wackiness of a child's brain. Fish and kissing. How in the hell did that relate?

The girl made a face. "When Daddy moved here, he said he wanted to be a family. He can't marry my mom. She's already married to Josh. But I'd really like a baby brother, you know."

"Uh, I'm not following the fish thing," Tess said.

"Well, I said maybe we could get a kitten to help us be more of a family, but Daddy said no. He said we have to start with fish. So we got us some, but the yellow one and two of the blue ones with the pretty tails died."

"Oh," Tess said. "Uh, I'm sorry."

"So maybe you could just marry my dad? Maybe have a baby or something? There's a swimming pool at his new place." Emily smiled encouragingly, her blue eyes half full of pleading, half full of "this is a great idea."

"People don't just get married."

"They do on TV. I watched that bachelor show once. Those girls were just happy with a hot tub. And they kissed a bunch," Emily said, nodding her head this time like she'd figured out the entire formula for falling in love.

Yeah. A hole with water inside.

Tess thought about arguing with the child, but then thought better of it. "Okay, I'll keep that in mind. You keep practicing your chant, get that math homework and lay off the donuts—you're in training."

"For what?"

"Being a Ladybug," Tess said, giving Emily a wave.

"Oh, yeah," she said, hurrying back over to her chair and folding the bag closed. "I gotta be able to run fast."

And Tess walked briskly out—proud of herself for not running.

THE GODDAMN SWEAT rolled down Frank's back as he sat like an old bullfrog on the patio out back. Maggie had gone to Peggy Garland's house to take a pound cake for the visitation. Her choir friend's mother had passed. Frank wondered if Peggy would return the favor when he passed. What was it with frickin' pound cakes anyway? In his opinion most tasted like crap. Give him a good piece of coconut cake. Maybe he'd send Peggy a note and tell her he wanted to be honored with something more than pound cake…but that might be too morbid.

Middle of May and already it was sultry. A breeze made a half-assed attempt at stirring the leaves, but it wasn't enough to stop him from sweating.

And then he felt the first mosquito.

Christ. Nothing like feeling good enough for some fresh air and then having to battle Louisiana.

He'd finally finished the last round of chemo, had a PET scan next week to see if anything had worked. The doctor had talked about some kind of surgery if there hadn't been any progress, but Frank had told him to go fly a kite. No more pain, no more puking and no more last-ditch efforts.

He craved peace.

The only thing stopping him from surrendering— No, wait, he wasn't giving up on himself or the medicine yet. But he could relax into his fate better if he and Tess could talk. Her gaze last Sunday had told him her heart had changed, but the words had not been spoken.

He and Tess had things to say.

"Dad?"

Frank snapped out of his reverie to find the very devil he'd been thinking about standing in front of him as if his thoughts had summoned her. Tess didn't look like anyone who could bedevil with her benign honey hair and sweet face, but this one had never been an angel. Just his Tess—perfect in his eyes.

He squinted against the sun slanting in through the oak's canopy. "You okay?"

She shrugged. "Drove around for a while, looking for a spot I could breathe in. My car took me here."

Thank God. Frank patted the bench. "You can sit."

"I'm good. How are you feeling?"

"Like I've been pumped full of chemicals."

"Yeah," she said, her brow furrowing. "Mom said the doctors haven't said much."

"Gotta do a scan to check on the cells or something like that." He brushed the matter away with his hand. He didn't want to talk about being sick, but he didn't know how to bring up what sat between them.

"I'm sorry, Dad."

For what? His cancer? Quitting Ullo? Not speaking to him for over a month?

"About a lot of stuff," she clarified, looking down at her hands. Then she glanced around. "Guess our backyard has always been the go-to place when you need to talk. When you need to think. Maybe I knew I could breathe here."

Frank looked around. "And sweat. I'm about to burn slap up sitting out here and the mosquitos are eating on me. Wanna go inside to the other place where family problems are solved to have this conversation?"

"The kitchen?" Tess asked, a small smile creeping out.

Frank struggled to his feet, and Tess rushed to grab his elbow. He patted her arm. "I'm good. A little weak still, but not as bad as I was last week. This shit really did a number on me. Guess I ain't too tolerant of chemo."

Tess's face crumpled. "Dad…"

"None of that. We gotta talk about what happened, Tess. We got a lot of words to say and I can't say 'em if you start blubbering. You know what your tears do to me."

Tess managed a shaky smile. "Think that's the problem to begin with, huh?"

"A little."

Together they moved toward the back door, each with much to say, but for a moment content to feel the other's presence. Shoulder to shoulder, they walked. Father and daughter—more alike than either wanted to admit.

CHAPTER NINETEEN

TESS POURED SOME lemonade in a tall glass and handed it to her father, glad to have something to occupy her hands. He waved it away, sinking on a bar stool with a small sigh.

He didn't look good, but she supposed after all the rounds of chemotherapy he'd undergone, he wasn't supposed to. His body was at war, so he wasn't exactly up for running marathons. His craggy face with the large Italian nose, so dear to her, held a pall, the wrinkles more pronounced, and his salt-and-pepper hair more salt now.

She knew why she'd come. After the drama in her office with Monique…after the realization of what she'd given up, she'd come home not to lick her wounds but repair one still bleeding.

Or maybe it was more she needed to loosen the knots she'd tied around herself, but she wasn't here to ask her father to fix anything in her life. She was here to make things right.

"Mom and I had a long talk," Tess said, pulling the cool glass to her place as she sank onto the stool opposite her father.

"She told me but didn't say much else," Frank said, playing with the bobbing rooster her mother had bought at a flea market one summer. "I didn't ask her. I knew you needed some time to figure things out."

"I've had plenty of time," Tess said, in the quiet of the kitchen. "I'd graduated into avoidance. Sorry I didn't return your calls. I didn't know what to say."

Her father looked at her. "None of this has been easy, has it? I'm still trying to get my footing. Thing is, I may never be rock-solid again."

Tess put her hand over his worn, calloused one. "Don't say it like that, Daddy."

"Baby, I ain't afraid of dying. I just don't want to leave all of you behind. But the good Lord might just be ready for me up there. I've come to terms with that, Therese. I have."

"I haven't," she said. His words ripped into her, shredding her heart. She couldn't grasp the concept of her father dying. She refused to.

"I know, honey, but dying isn't as scary as living sometimes. I have faith there's a place for me, and I'll be waiting in glory for all of you. Maybe not my own mama 'cause she might not make it past St. Peter." He gave her a sad wink.

Tess managed a small smile. "She'd probably tell God how to run the joint. You know she still writes her congressman about daylight saving time?"

For a moment they both smiled through the pain.

"But I'm not just sorry about your getting sick,

Daddy. I'm sorry about everything that happened when you gave Graham the position of CEO. I didn't think before I acted, and, honestly, put myself in a bad situation."

Frank shook his head. "Ah, Tess, I didn't handle it right, either. I was a coward, plain and simple. Everything in life was suddenly so hard, so scary. I knew I couldn't undergo all the procedures and chemotherapy and still run the company. It broke my heart." Her father's voice quivered and Tess couldn't stop a lone tear from trailing down her cheek. Swiping it away, she realized she'd never stopped to think about how hard handing over his company, virtually his baby, must have been for him. She'd never even considered how being given a virtual death sentence had affected her father. She'd only thought of herself.

"I didn't know, Dad."

"I know you didn't. Once I found out about the cancer, I didn't tell anyone for several days…not even your mother or Joe. This horrible thing grew inside me, twisting around this selfish need to pretend like everything was okay. At first, I planned on not telling anyone at all. Just thought I'd ride it out until the end and then cash my check. I didn't want to put anyone through all the crap that comes with the fight. But I changed my mind the day we rolled Bacchus out. You remember?"

She did. That Sunday had been perfect. Maggie had brought them a big picnic basket and she and her father had sat in the parade stand, each connected with their guys coordinating the tractors. Last-minute emergency work was handled by Red Jack and Bennie B so Tess, Dave and her father had been able to enjoy the fruits of their labor. All her brothers and their families had been there, each bringing a picnic basket full of New Orleans favorites, including a huge cinnamon-and-sugar king cake. The weather had been mild, no floats had broken down and the excitement in the air had been electric. It had been a while since Tess had enjoyed herself like that at a parade. "It was perfect."

"Yeah, the floats looked great and there were so few hiccups. I laughed for the first time since the doc sat me down with that news." Frank smiled as if sucked back into the memory. "You laughed a lot, too, and it was good to see you happy. That Nick fellow had pissed you off over Christmas and then the season hit and we were too busy to think, much less smile. I remember watching you and your mama that day, flirting for beads and dancing to the music. At the end of the parade, you laid your head on your mama's shoulder and she kissed your forehead. That was when I knew I had to fight, and I knew I'd have to make some tough decisions."

Tess dropped her gaze because it hurt to think about that moment, hurt to know the burden her father had carried.

"I've always been proud you wanted to do what I do, Tess. We make magic. We make people happy.

That's a satisfying feeling. I hadn't planned on retiring this soon, and I'll be honest, I thought with a little more tempering and the right crew around you, you'd be fine running the company. But I didn't think you were ready. I'm not saying you had to have a business degree, but you didn't have a clue what I do on my end. I thought if I could find a guy—"

"Or girl?" Tess added.

"Maybe. There aren't many women in this business, Tess. Well, at least not many running the show, no how. But I wasn't against hiring a woman—I wasn't against anyone who could do a good job. I wanted to find someone who could easily do what I do and leave you to do what you do." Frank spread his hands, and Tess was able to climb over the fence and see it from his side. He hadn't wanted her stressed. He'd tried to take care of her even then.

"So when the headhunter guy called me and sent me Naquin's resume, it was like being handed a lottery ticket with the winning numbers. He was a perfect fit—young, experienced and had listed New Orleans as his ideal relocation area. I thought I was doing you a favor, keeping you from worrying so much when I wasn't around. But I also knew you'd be mad at me. And that's when I got chicken."

"But you should have told me. You should have given me the benefit of knowing before he got there, not send me off with Granny B so I wouldn't know."

"Yeah, I should have, but I think, as your mother told you, I'm not good at telling you no, baby. You've talked me into about anything you've wanted all your life. I gained five pounds one summer on those Plum Street Snoballs alone. What you wanted, you got."

She'd gotten on a Snoball kick one summer between seventh and eighth grade, wanting one after every soccer practice. Her father had dutifully driven her to get her blackberry with crème.

Frank continued. "I loved giving you things, but when you're facing a crypt down the road there—" he pointed toward the huge cemetery sitting a few miles down Metairie Road "—you start looking at things differently. You start doubting all the decisions you made, wondering if you'd given your kids and wife what they really needed all this time."

For a moment he paused. "I don't think I did that bad. I'm not perfect and, yeah, I screwed this the hell up, but when I thought about just giving you the position, it felt wrong."

A fishhook of hurt snagged inside her soul. "I wanted to be good enough."

"Ah, Tess, you know that's not it. Don't make it that. You're brilliant at what you do, but I decided as soon as you came aboard, this was a business that needed a partnership to run it. You taught me that, so I thought I'd replaced myself with a guy who could balance you out. He seemed a lot like me. Determined and smart, but not too hardass."

Tess's heart leaped at those words. A partnership with Graham.... It fit in more than just a business sense. What if her dad had seen beyond the business to who she needed in her life—a man who balanced her?

Not a pretty rich boy with little stickability like Nick. Not the half dozen other guys she'd dated—an attorney in Gigi's office, a hairstylist from the Westbank or the guy who said he was an officer in the Navy but really just worked at the base—but a guy who had a passion for doing what she did. A guy who balanced out her creativity with a nose for business. A guy who looked pretty damn spectacular in the buff, loved his own daughter above all else and wasn't as confident and capable as he portrayed. Like Tess, he wasn't perfect.

But maybe Graham was perfect for her.

"I've screwed up so badly, Dad," Tess said, emotion snagging in her throat. She couldn't undo what she'd done. She couldn't expect her father to fix what her pride had led her to.

"Maybe not. But you landed a job on your own, and I bet you've learned more working for a smaller company than you ever did working for a bigger one. No one to hand things off to—you had to do it yourself. And Monique's an interesting woman."

"Monique is a bitch, Dad."

Frank laughed and for a moment he didn't look sick. Color bloomed into his cheeks and his eyes sparkled. "She's ambitious. I respect that about her.

Personally, I never cared about her politics when it came to doing business, but I'm sure she didn't care for mine. She's broken new ground for women in this business and made a better way for you and other little girls who want to build floats and play with the big boys."

Tess nodded, still miffed over the way Monique had handled the Oedipus deal. "Fine. I'll give her that. She's definitely interesting."

"So, Tess, do you forgive me for hiring Graham?"

Tess nodded. "Yes. I've had to swallow my pride and admit I can't do all I thought I could. Working for Upstart has taught me a lot about myself. But most of all, I've learned to accept my flaws and to just keep swimming when the current gets rough. Never had to do that before."

Frank lifted his hands and beckoned her. "Come here, my Tess."

Tess swallowed the lump in her throat and walked around the end of the bar. Her father enveloped her in a strong hug and for a few seconds, Tess lay her head on the man's shoulder, inhaling the Hugo Boss cologne he'd gotten for a "song" at T.J. Maxx and the lavender fabric softener her mother used in the laundry. He smelled like her father. He smelled like all things safe. He smelled like her past and present. Like home. But he'd also given her the scent for her future.

Inhaling once again, she took the deep breath

she'd been looking for and exhaled, determined to fix the other parts of her life she'd mishandled.

GRAHAM SAT AT his desk and stared at the stapler. He'd chosen that particular item at random. He could have stared at the nameplate Billie had stuck on his desk the day before as if she were placing a tiara on the head of a beauty pageant winner. But he didn't want to stare at it. It seemed indefinite, like he might have to toss it in the trashcan at any minute...along with his short-lived reign as CEO of Frank Ullo Float Builders. So the stapler would have to be his focal point while he contemplated his future.

Like he did most days around the end of the workday, Dave popped his head in. "You busy?"

"No. I should be, but I'm contemplating what I'll be qualified for when Frank tosses me out like last week's Chinese."

Dave settled in the chair opposite him. "Nah, Frank has faith in you, and after your speech last week, we all have that faith in you."

Had it only been last week? Seemed long ago he'd rallied the troops around pizza and a common objective. "We lost the Oedipus account to Upstart. Miles Barrow just called me."

Dave's eyes popped wide. "Oh, well, in that case, I'll go get a box for your things."

Graham shifted his gaze back to the stapler. "Yeah, right."

Dave sighed. "That's really shitty news. Tess snaked us, huh? I taught that girl too well."

What to say to that? He didn't want to admit he'd handed over the contract to Upstart by telling Miles about Tess's designs. What stupid-ass CEO would do such a thing? Miles's kind words about his intent and about how Frank would understand did little to buffer the sting of the call he'd just received. He'd known it was likely coming, but the finality of it suckerpunched him in spite of it. "Yeah, she's good. I wish she were still here doing work for us. I tried to talk her into coming back but it did little good. Her pride was pricked and I likely wasn't the right person to persuade her."

Dave's laugh was bitter. "No kidding. But I'm impressed you went to her and asked her to come back. I like that about you. A little humbleness is welcome around here, you know?"

"All I got left is humbleness," Graham said.

"Nah, we got plenty of business. I talked to some krewes out of Houma and Lake Charles today that want new marque floats and we're working hard to keep our regular customers happy. I won't lie and say Oedipus wasn't a loss, but we'll be okay." Dave stood and perused the schedule board Graham had mounted on the wall. "Might not be the best of times to ask, but we really need someone to help me. Honestly, the part of the job Tess did as liaison with the other directors and captains was never something I wanted to do. Tess was good with them, keeping them happy, making sure the vision fit actuality, so if you could shift that job requirement over to the new guy, I'll keep the lion's share of the design work. And my pay raise."

Graham rubbed a hand over his face. "Anyone in house capable of doing the job?"

"Not really, but Billie sent an ad to some local websites, and Red Jack posted it on some NOLA message boards for artists. He's into all that crap."

Graham stood, offering his hand just as he'd done for the last few days. Having Dave on his team felt good. Billie, too. He'd finally gotten some decent coffee. "I'll pull any resumes Billie has and set up some interviews at the beginning of next week."

"Good man," Dave said, taking his leave for the day.

Graham sank back into his chair and pulled out his cellphone. Tess still hadn't called him back.

His work life might be in shambles, but, damn, Sunday night had been incredible. He'd called her earlier in the week and left a message. Then texted her right after the Oedipus meeting, hoping the magnanimous gesture of giving Miles the real skinny had lined the stars up in his favor.

But she hadn't called or returned his text.

In her eyes, they were over.

He could see her point, being rivals and all, but after the tender way they'd parted, he'd hoped she relented and considered a tenuous relationship.

Damn it all, didn't they deserve to see if what

they had was the real thing? Bad blood or no, he knew she'd fit him like a latex glove—no room for anything else. Just skin on skin—the way he liked it between them.

He pressed the email icon and sighed. No email, either.

Frick.

He picked up the desktop phone and hit the red button that would page Billie.

"What's up?" she said.

"We have any resumes for the art director gig?"

"Four."

"Can you get them to me?"

Billie sighed. "Can a woodpecker peck wood? Check your inbox in thirty seconds. No, wait. Make that a minute or two." She clicked off and Graham went through his other messages, waiting on the resumes.

Waiting on Tess.

CHAPTER TWENTY

AFTER LEAVING HER parents' house, Tess headed back into the city, phoning Gigi because she'd emailed her friend the contract terms Miles had sent Monique, hoping Gigi could do a quick look-see.

"What up, homey?" Gigi drawled into the receiver.

"I know you're super busy, but I sent you an email—"

"Already got it, and I'm charging you the usual friend rate," Gigi said, moving around some papers or something in the background.

"A night of binge drinking and then holding your hair back while you puke?"

"Exactly." Gigi laughed and it sounded like little bells tinkling. Seriously, how did someone have a magical laugh like that? "So when do you want to go out and shoot Jagermeister?"

"I could use a drink now, but I think I need a clear head this afternoon."

"You okay? You sound stopped up."

"It's been an emotional couple of days. I finally talked to my dad and got things straight with him.

Now I'm facing down this whole career decision I made."

"Yeah, I feel sort of responsible for that, so I've already read through the contract. It's fairly standard stuff in regards to business contracts. But there's this huge loophole. Like, I'm talking big-as-a-cloverleaf-in-LA huge."

"About my being the project manager?" Tess switched lanes and headed deeper into the city.

"Exactly."

"So if I quit Upstart…"

"Let's start with the contract I drew between you and Upstart in regards to your employment. See, when you and Monique agreed upon the three-month provision, I intentionally left the language loose. That's not to say you take any business you score for Upstart with you if you part ways, but I made sure you own your work and that it becomes the property of Upstart while you work for them. Intellectual rights stuff can get pretty complex, so I won't wade into that."

"My head's getting muddled just thinking about it," Tess said.

"So if you were to, say, leave Upstart, you would not be able to take any of the designs you created for Upstart with you. They would belong to the company because you were employed by the company. You dig?"

"Yeah. Sort of."

"Okay, so this Oedipus deal is different. Miles

Barrow is sharp as a pressed suit. In the contract he signed with Upstart, he designated that you, Tess Ullo, must be attached to the project in order for the contract to be valid. In other words, if you walk, he walks with you. In a roundabout way, he signed a contract with you, but because you work for Upstart, they get the krewe's business."

Tess hit a pothole and her teeth banged together, even as something radical bloomed within her. "So I'm the key to Oedipus?"

"Pretty much."

"Why would Monique agree to these terms knowing I could leave Upstart during my interim period without any repercussions, taking Miles Barrow's business with me?"

"It's risky, sure, but you said her ego is as big as Dallas, so maybe she's hedging her bets. After all, she believes you're out for revenge against your father. She might feel secure in the idea you won't leave a perfectly good job. Besides, I'm pretty sure she owns your designs. In other words, you can leave and take Oedipus with you, but you can't take the designs because those belong to Upstart."

"But those weren't the original designs submitted by Upstart," Tess grumbled, disappointed that her best work belonged to Monique…and the woman hadn't even appreciated it enough to send it out.

Gigi's lawyer signal kicked in. "What do you mean?"

Tess went over what she'd learned about the original proposal subbed to Upstart.

"So how did Miles know the designs weren't yours? Do you have some sort of trademark design I don't know about?"

"No. The only thing I could think of is that Miles saw the signatures or something on the designs Monique submitted that told him they weren't mine. He knew I had worked the account because I told him as much at the mixer."

"Hmmm…" Gigi said, her wheels obviously spinning. "My advice is to call Miles and see what's up."

"Is that official legal advice?"

"Yeah, totally free as long as you invite me to Sunday dinner when your ma makes Bolognese sauce."

Tess smiled. "Will do."

Clicking off with Gigi, Tess had pulled over to Cuppa Joe's, her mind reeling with this new information. Something in her was exhilarated at the thought of having Monique by the balls. She'd call Miles from the coffee shop and grab a cup of soothing tea to calm her shot nerves.

The place wasn't too busy and she quickly found a table and gave Miles a call. Of course, he wasn't available.

"Well, this is important, so I'd really appreciate it if you would give him my cell number and have him call me ASAP."

"All his calls are important, so you'll just have to hold on to your britches," Julian said.

"Julian, this is Tess Ullo. I sent you the gift certificate to Emeril's last year. This is me calling in my favor."

"Missy miss," Julian said, and Tess could picture him rolling his eyes. Probably clad in poplin and a bow tie. "I'll have him call you. Don't have a hissy."

Tess grumbled an "okay" and then hung up. Settling back to wait, she watched the people coming in and out of the coffee shop. Her city was such a diverse one—the doors swung open to a teen girl with piercings and a tattoo wrapped around her neck, a soccer mom in Lululemon, a businessman barking into his Bluetooth and a gaggle of kids who'd obviously been tap-dancing in the quarter after school. They paid in wadded up dollars and change, counting it out carefully and sucking down the sweet, icy coffees.

Finally, her phone rang.

"Ma chère," Miles crowed into the receiver. "I've made you a happy woman, eh?"

"Yes, Miles. I appreciate your liking my designs so much," Tess said, cradling the dainty cup she always requested for her tea.

"Good, good. So why the frantic call? You had Julian doing flips trying to get me off a conference call with a disgruntled, and might I add, burned, employee of Happy Burger."

"Sorry, I had a few questions," Tess said, unsure

as to how to basically ask if he were aware her boss double-crossed her. "The first proposal Monique submitted wasn't mine."

"I know," he said, with a smile in his voice. "That's why I called her and asked her to take a meeting with me. I didn't understand why she would hire the best float designer in town with the best name in Mardi Gras and not use her the way God intended."

Because Monique couldn't give up the slightest bit of power to anyone? Because she was scared? Because she was a bitch? Because she was a blooming idiot? Pick one. Any one.

Tess didn't say that, of course. "How did you know the design wasn't mine?"

"I didn't. The first proposal was fine, but to be honest, I had decided to continue with your dad's company. I've been with Ullo a long time and what Monique gave me wasn't enough to make me want to switch. They were very competent and professional, but I needed fantastic to make that switch, you know? So this morning, I met with Graham Naquin and prepared to sign on the dotted line."

Graham again.

The man popped up everywhere—in her thoughts, dreams…her life.

"So…" she prompted.

"Well, in the course of my conversation with Naquin this morning, he said something about your design that didn't mesh."

"He talked about my design?" Something not so warm climbed within her. He'd been poking through her things, had seen her designs, giving himself a leg up on what the competition planned.

But then the rational part of her remembered who Graham was. He wouldn't have trashed her. Wouldn't have good reason to mention her at all.

"In a good way. He said something to the effect of having seen your designs and sweating our contract negotiations. Something about that didn't sit right with me."

Another long stretch of silence.

"Miles?"

"Yeah. Okay, here's the deal. You know I'm a man of my word and you know I'm not under-handed in the slightest. Well, at least not much. But I showed Graham the designs Upstart had submitted. Now, don't you go telling Monique. I don't need her riding my back, implying I'm unethical. I've never done nothing like that before, but I can smell when something ain't right.

"So, I hand over the proposal to Graham and he gets this funny look on his face. Finally, he tosses the proposal on my desk and says it isn't your work."

Tess sat back so hard in her chair she scared the man reading the paper sitting behind her. "What? He…uh… I can't—"

"Yeah, I couldn't believe it, either, but he said they weren't yours, and that I couldn't ask him how he knew, but he knew. Then he did the damnedest thing I ever saw in the business world."

Tess knew what Miles was going to say before he said it. "He told you my designs were better than his."

Miles laughed. "Yeah, the bastard did. He said I should call Monique and tell her to send your stuff over. He said you deserved a shot at my business."

Tess dropped her head to her chest as a huge wave of mixed emotion washed over her—guilt, shame, pleasure, gratitude and love were only a few of them. "Why would he do that?"

"I don't know. He's either the most honest man in the world, or he had a really good reason. But he was right. Your designs are better than any of the others I've received. I don't understand why Monique didn't sub them. Well, I've met her a few times and actually I do."

Tess couldn't comprehend what Graham had done. Why had he destroyed his chance to secure the krewe of Oedipus's business? It didn't make sense for him to hand over the golden apple, a very lucrative, point-of-pride golden apple. Integrity was one thing, being stupid in business another.

Maybe her father had been wrong.

Or maybe Graham had a different motivation. Maybe Graham was more like her father than what she wanted to admit.

"Okay," Tess said, nodding her head though only

the man who'd gotten up and moved to another table could see her. "That's what I wanted to know."

"Hey, Tess," Miles said, his tone growing more serious. "I'm not saying anything against Monique, but I will note this. I don't like she didn't present your work over the proposal she sent over. Any fool could see your design was better, but I gathered she thought her design work should stand before yours. A good business owner never lets her ego get in the way of doing what is best for the company. The only reason why I signed on with Upstart, for one year only I might add, was because of your designs. Monique wasn't overly happy with contract terms."

"Yeah, so I gather," Tess said, walking toward the bar and sliding her cup over to the barista. "I thank you for being forthcoming with me, Miles."

"See ya, Tess."

Tess hung up, took a deep coffee-scented breath and pushed back out into the humid New Orleans air.

Finally the pieces of her life were snapping into place. She had learned more about her boss in ten minutes than she had the entire time working for her. Tess wasn't cavalier enough to overlook the blatant lack of professionalism her boss had displayed. Nor was she willing to play backup to Cecily. She'd made peace with her father, and in doing so, made peace with her own faults. And finally, she'd come face-to-face with Graham's selflessness. Maybe not the shark her father had hoped for, but the man had a heart of gold and an undeniable sense of honor.

Her pride had brought her to where she now stood, but love would take her where she belonged.

Tess climbed in her car and drove straight to Upstart. At the office, the workday had wound down, but Monique still sat at her desk, phone to ear, fingers clicking on her keyboard.

Josh wasn't lounging around anywhere, and Emily didn't seem to be around, either.

Perfect time to quit her job.

Tess didn't belong at Upstart...and never would.

Monique sat the phone in the cradle, not bothering to meet Tess's gaze. She said, "What's up?"

"Can I talk to you?"

"You are talking to me," Monique drawled, the glow of the computer illuminating her perfect features.

Yeah. And there was the whole "make Tess feel stupid" thing Monique had going.

"I'm not going to stay."

Monique's brow furrowed and still she didn't look at Tess. "You don't have to. I'm not checking your hours. I trust you."

"Wow, that's unexpected," Tess said, placing the copy of her contract on the desk. "But what I'm trying to say is that I don't think my job here at Upstart is going to work out."

Monique finally looked at her before slamming her hands onto the desk. "No. Unacceptable."

"I can't stay, Monique."

"Is this because of what happened earlier? It was a disagreement, Tess. Please don't tell me your skin is that thin."

"It's not just about today. It's about realizing I will never belong here."

Eyes blazing, Monique leaned back. "I guess you're not the woman I thought you were."

"I guess I'm not," Tess said. "But you can't deny I don't fit here. I've learned a lot from you, but I think it's better if I don't continue."

Looking down at the contract, Monique sighed. "I knew I shouldn't have agreed to that ninety-day trial period. Damn it."

Tess sank onto the same chair she'd sat in over a month ago. "I don't think you're happy with me, either. You're accustomed to running things, and I am, too. This was the first clash we've had, but it wouldn't be the last. Upstart is a good company, and you were doing fine without me."

"We're doing better with you," she said.

Tess nodded. "Maybe for a while, but the Ullo name only does so much, Monique."

"Is this about Graham?"

Tess jolted at the thought of Monique seeing so easily through her. "A little, but mostly it's about me. This past month I've had to take a hard look at myself. I left my father's company because of arrogance. I took this job because I wanted to punish him. None of those were good enough reasons.

From the beginning I knew I'd made a mistake, but I was too stubborn, too prideful to admit it."

"Nothing wrong with being tenacious or having self-respect."

"Maybe not," Tess said, looking around Monique's office, seeing nothing of a personal nature. Not even a drawing by Emily or a photo of Josh. Nothing. Empty. "Can I say something to you that might be a little out of line?"

Monique snorted before rolling her eyes. "I know what you're going to say. I'm a bitch. I'm underhanded, merciless, sneaky. Go ahead. I've heard it all before."

"That's not what I was going to say," Tess said, with a small smile. "I wanted to tell you how talented you are, and how much I admire your determination to make it in this business."

"But…?"

"I think you're scared."

Monique flinched. "I'm not scared."

"You conduct business like you're scared. Like you're afraid someone won't think you're good enough. That's what that whole sketch thing was about—control and ego."

"That's ridiculous."

Tess shrugged. "Maybe, but you're only as good as the people around you. My father taught me that. I hadn't even realized it. And it's not just your employees, it's Josh. It's that wonderful, funny little girl who draws you pictures every day." Tess looked around the austere office again and arched an eyebrow at Monique.

Monique pulled out a plastic container of drawings from a drawer. She took the top one, a picture of what looked to be a person playing soccer. "This one is of you, I think." She passed it over.

Tess took the drawing and smiled at the little girl's interpretation of the soccer field and the overly long prongs on the soccer cleats.

"Whatever anyone may think about me, I love my daughter." Her tone wasn't defensive. It was sad.

Tess nodded. "I know you do."

"I'm good at running this place. I'm just not good at being a mom." Not knowing what to say, Tess handed the drawing back.

"It was easier when she was a baby. Feed her, change her, rock her. I didn't worry about messing up, but as she grew, I felt more and more helpless. Josh is actually better with her than I am." Monique snapped the lid closed and placed the box back in her drawer. "I'm sorry. I shouldn't have even gone there. I guess I didn't want you to think I'm some unfeeling monster."

"I don't think that, Monique."

"Well, I feel that way sometimes," she said with a sigh.

"My dad built Ullo from nothing, just like you, but it's easier for a man. He had my mother at home taking care of carpool, homework, snacks—the stuff all parents have to deal with. He worked hard to build Ullo but he never put his business before his family. Never. I think that's a good policy."

Monique twisted her mouth and shifted her gaze, seemingly thinking about what Tess said. "Maybe so."

"My father's dying, and in these final months, he's let Ullo go…but he's gathered the people he loves to him. It's not about contracts—" Tess tapped the paper "—or specifications. It's about people."

Tugging the contract from beneath Tess's finger, Monique tossed it in the trash. "Okay. There. I'll start with you."

Tess gave her a puzzled look.

"I'm not going to read over the fine print, talk badly about you for changing your mind or pitch a fit over the Oedipus bid. I'm going to let it go so I can go home early and watch Josh and Emily kick balls into the net Graham bought her. The thing takes up our whole backyard." Monique gave her a shrug and a slight smile. "I don't want to lose you, Tess, but I'm not going to stop you. Hell, I can't stop you anyway. I agreed to that damn waiting period."

"Thank you," Tess said, standing and extending a hand. "And I'm sorry if I got preachy on you."

"Maybe I needed a little preaching. Maybe I need to quit trying so damn hard. Miles actually said something like that to me, too." Monique took her hand.

Miles and Oedipus. The conversation between her and Monique had taken a turn off course, and

Tess hadn't addressed the contract clause Miles had placed in the agreement with Upstart. "You need to talk to Miles and renegotiate the contract. I'm not staying, but my Oedipus designs belong to you."

Monique released her hand. "I'll call him."

Tess turned and started for the door.

"Hey, Tess," Monique said.

Tess turned around. "Yeah?"

"I never said I was sorry, but I am. I shouldn't have allowed Cecily to tell me my stuff was better when it obviously wasn't. You're right about my issue with control and wanting affirmation. I need to deal better with that. I don't want you to leave Upstart, but I understand about belonging."

"Thank you for the apology. I learned a lot about myself working here."

"Like what not to do?" Monique lifted one corner of her mouth.

"I learned it's okay to fail, to be wrong and to accept who I am." Tess gave Monique a smile and then walked out of Upstart. When she got to her car, she dialed the number she hadn't dialed in almost two months.

"Hey, Billie, it's Tess. I'm wondering if Mr. Naquin has filled my old position yet."

She listened for several seconds, covering the mouthpiece to keep from laughing in relief.

"In that case, I'd like to make an appointment for next week."

CHAPTER TWENTY-ONE

THE FOLLOWING MONDAY came with little relief from the now summerlike heat or the ache in Graham's heart. He had seen Tess Thursday at Ladybug soccer practice, where she treated him with polite professionalism.

Hell, he'd rather she rubbed in the fact she'd scored the Oedipus floats for 2016 than treat him as if he were just another parent. He'd gotten the message last Monday when they'd parted—they'd had one more night of magic together and then it was business as usual. He didn't like it at all.

The entire time he watched her work with the little girls on the soccer team, he kept thinking, "She's mine."

But she wasn't and likely never would be.

She'd never responded to his call or text, and now he knew how she'd felt months ago. Made him feel used and not worth bothering with.

Pair all that with the fact he'd lost the Oedipus account and the shipment of industrial foam was on back order and today was about as shitty as they came. The only upside was that Emily had stopped bugging him about a kitten. Of course, she'd replaced it with wanting him to get married and get her a baby brother, so it really was lose-lose.

"Hey," Billie said, knocking then immediately popping her head in. "Your first applicant for the art director position is here. Where are you planning to hold the meeting?"

Graham closed his eyes for a moment and rubbed a hand across his face. A dull headache pounded behind his eyes. Cracking open an eye, he saw the clock read 10:00 a.m. Still had a long way to go to finish the day, which would end with a meeting at Frank's house.

"Uh, I suppose we can do it here."

"Okay. I put the applicant in Frank's office, but I can—"

"Nah, that's fine. His office is nicer. Now which one is this? The one from Mobile?"

"Oh, I don't think I gave you the file on this one. I'll grab it and bring it to you," Billie said.

Graham waited for ten minutes, buzzing Billie intermittently, but she didn't answer or return with the folder.

Damn it.

He didn't like to keep people waiting. He'd certainly never appreciated such tactics when he was being interviewed, so he didn't like to do the same with others.

Rising, he peered out into the recesses of the

outer office. Billie wasn't at her desk and Dave's door was closed.

"Hell," he breathed under his breath, walking toward Frank's office. He'd have to wing it. No other recourse.

Opening the door, he donned a polite smile. "Hi, I'm sorry to keep you waiting." As he shut the door all he could see of the person waiting for him was the top of her bun.

Rounding the desk, he focused on the blotter to see if perhaps Billie had left the applicant's file for him before she disappeared. "I'm sorry I'm a bit late. I'm afraid I don't—"

"That's okay," the applicant said.

Graham snapped his head up. "Tess?"

She smiled politely, humor tipping the corners of her mouth as she extended her hand. "I'm Therese Ullo."

If the door had blown down and he'd found himself surrounded by a legion of gladiators he wouldn't have been more shocked than he was now.

What in the hell was she doing there?

"What in the hell are you doing here?"

She arched an eyebrow. "We have a ten o'clock appointment. An interview for the Head of Operations position."

"An interview? Head of Operations? I don't think—"

"Yes. I saw the ad on the NOLA artist forum. It said you were looking for an assistant art director, but when I called I was told it had changed to Head of Operations with art direction being only part of the tasks involved. Don't worry. I'm qualified for both." She folded her hands in her lap and looked at him expectantly.

Graham sat in her father's chair a little too hard. For several seconds he stared at her, trying to figure out if this was for real.

She looked the part of interviewee in a crisp white blouse, knotted at the neck with a huge bow and a tight black skirt that went to midcalf. Her shoes were low-heeled and conservative, as was the honey-brown hair she'd pulled into a knot.

"You're here to interview for a job?" he asked again.

"Yes," she said with an emphatic nod.

"Because you don't have one?"

"Right."

Graham stared at the historical float plans which Frank had hung on his walls, trying to figure out what was happening. "Okay then, let's get started. So, tell me a little about yourself, Miss Ullo. Wait, it *is* Miss, correct?"

"Yes, I'm unmarried. In other words, I'm single."

"Good," he said.

"I'm twenty-seven years old, turning twenty-eight in August, and I have worked in the float building industry all my life. I have a bachelor's degree in industrial design from Carnegie-Mellon and almost ten years' experience working in the field, starting with my first job in high school. I'm a former employee of this company and most recently Upstart."

"Former employee of Upstart?"

"Yes, former. Unfortunately, I found I wasn't a good fit there."

"May I ask why you chose to leave your former position?"

Tess shifted her gaze from his and studied the same stapler he'd studied a week ago. "Creative differences were part of it, but also, in the course of working for that company, I learned enough about myself to figure out where I belong."

"And that is…?"

"The reason I'm interviewing for this job." She smoothed her hair and rubbed her delicious lips together. "I find I'm more suitable for a company that emphasizes teamwork."

Graham wanted to laugh. He wanted to round the desk, clasp her to him and spin her around. But it was a job interview so he had to be professional. "I see. So tell me why I should hire you, Miss Ullo."

"I'm punctual—" she raised her eyebrows as if to point out his tardiness for the interview "—and I play well with others."

"Do you, now?"

Her smile was pure siren. "Oh, yes. I have a particular skill set. Never had complaints before. I'm highly imaginative in the office…and out. I'm confident, but I've also learned over the past few months, I'm not always right. Hmm…guess that means I'm flexible. In the office…and out."

Graham grew aroused thinking about her flexibility and particular skill set. Thank goodness he was behind the desk. "You sound like an interesting candidate, especially the flexible part."

Tess lifted one shoulder in a sexy shrug. "I'd be happy to prove it to you, um, that is, if I get the opportunity."

Graham swallowed and looked at his hands. "How soon would you be able to start?"

"When do you want me?"

Morning, night and day. He cleared his throat. "As soon as you're ready."

Tess's eyes deepened. "I'm ready now."

His heart literally started beating faster. Was this merely about working for Ullo, or was this about something more? With him? God, please let it be about more than a job.

"Good," he said, rising slightly and offering his hand.

She rose and placed her hand in his. Perfect fit. "So does this mean I have a future here?"

"I believe it does."

She rubbed her glossy lips together again. "Do you have an office policy on employees dating?"

"You'll need to fill out a disclosure statement. We like to be aboveboard here." His thumb stroked the curve of her finger.

Tess jerked her hand away. "Good to know."

Then she turned, shouldered her attaché case and walked to the door.

Graham dropped his hand. "I'm guessing you think the interview is over?"

She spun around. "I was simply locking the door."

Graham laughed.

Tess shook her head. "I'm kidding, of course. Another one of my good qualities—a good sense of humor."

"You were kidding?" Graham didn't want to look so confused, but he knew he must have.

"This is a job interview. Business only." Tess looked at him like he was stupid.

Something in his stomach sank. "Right."

"But I was hoping you could recommend a place for drinks. I'm thinking I want something local... and close by," she said with a Tess-like twinkle in her eye.

Graham couldn't stop the bubble of happiness that sprang to life inside of him. "Well, there's this place called Two-Legged Pete's—"

"Two-Legged?" she cracked.

"Yeah, the guy who owns it has a sense of humor, I guess. It's not far from here and I hear they have great stuffed mushrooms and will turn the TV to baseball if you ask nicely."

She tilted her head. "I love baseball. Think I'll stop by there around—" she looked at her wrist where her Cookie Monster watch popped out from beneath her blouse "—five-thirty?"

"That's a great time to go to Two-Legged Pete's. I met the woman of my dreams there once."

"You don't say," she said, a smile creeping over her face. "Well, then I'm definitely going so I can meet the man of my dreams."

Graham grinned like a goober, but he didn't care. "He'll be there."

"That's what I'm hoping for."

AFTER LUNCH WITH Gigi—where Tess bought all the drinks—and an afternoon of finding the perfect black dress and killer pumps covered in black lace, Tess walked into Two-Legged Pete's. She looked about as good as she ever had. The dress was tight, classy and made her legs look awesome. Or maybe it was the shoes that did that. She'd sprung for a manicure and the technician had even applied her makeup after suggesting a few things to do with her eyes.

As a result, Tess knew she didn't look like the girl Graham had met at Two-Legged Pete's that Monday night months ago.

"Hot damn, you look good, girl," Ron declared from behind the bar where a string of customers lined up. The place was busier than usual, but Tess found Graham immediately. He'd turned and watched her as she entered the bar, a beautiful smile on his gorgeous face.

"I try sometimes," Tess said, with a flirty smile. As usual Ron ate it up as he reached for the gin. "How's that little one?"

Ron set down the Hendrick's and reached into his back pocket. Tess pointed toward where Graham sat and Ron raised his eyebrows. "Okay, then. I'll show you later."

Tess made her way down to the very end of the bar where sitting right next to the trivia machine was her new boss.

And, God willing and the creek didn't rise, her new man.

Graham hooked his foot around a stool against the wall and pulled it over close. "Would the lady like a seat?"

"She would," Tess said, sitting.

Graham smiled at her and she remembered the last time they'd sat in this very bar. There had been an aura of mystery, of excitement, of crazy attraction. All of that was still there, but joining those feelings was a certainty she'd found the right man for her.

Finally.

Ron set the drink in front of her and slid Graham another of what he was having. "I suppose you two want to watch baseball," he said with disgust.

Graham hadn't taken his eyes off her. "Nah, man. We're good."

"So I see. What started months ago seems to have ended," Ron joked, and swaggered off to wait on more customers and drive up the tips for him and his new family.

"He's wrong," Graham said softly.

"Oh?" Tess asked.

"It's a new beginning. The one we should have had after that night."

"Well, I'm wearing my black dress."

"Very well, too, I might add," Graham said, his eyes sliding down her body. "Very, very well."

She wanted to say so much to him, and yet at the same time she wanted to say nothing at all. She was so tired of all the drama. Complicated was so overrated. "I'm sorry."

"I'm sorry, too."

"I want to start over—with a clean slate. No more grudges, blame or wounded pride. No more embarrassment over who we are." Tess reached out and touched the rugged hand cupping the sweating tumbler.

Graham turned his hand over and clasped hers. "Agreed. I'm ready to start clean."

"And I'd also like to say thank you."

He arched a dark eyebrow. "For what? Telling Miles the truth? For hiring you? Everything I did was aboveboard. You're deserving of all those things."

"No, though those things are nice." She swallowed the anxiety that cropped up. She needed to just say it. Do what she'd said she would do when she told Monique she couldn't work for Upstart…

when she'd strolled into the warehouse she'd vowed never to step into again months ago. "I wanted to thank you for loving me in spite of my being a complete asshole."

Graham started laughing.

Tess gulped. "I mean, I love you. I shouldn't necessarily presume you—"

His mouth shut her up.

Tess swallowed the stupid words and kissed him, her heart breaking apart and knitting back together at the sheer rightness of this man kissing away her fears.

Pulling away slightly, he smiled at her. "You can shut up now."

"Is that all you have to say?"

"No, I got tons to say, but I'm only going to say two key things. Are you ready?"

She nodded.

"First, tonight we are going to have a real date. I'm going to take you out for a nice dinner, we're going to drink wine, maybe dance beneath the stars then go to your place and make love until the sun comes up."

"Sounds good," Tess said. "But I need to remind you, I have a new job to start tomorrow."

"Sleeping with the boss has benefits," he joked, before becoming serious. "I'm not really your boss, you know."

"I know. You're my partner. My dad ordered you up for me. I just didn't realize it."

Graham kissed her hard and fast.

"Now, two." He held up two fingers, making sure she focused on him.

"I'm listening."

"Therese Ullo, I want to spend the rest of my life loving you. I'm not talking about a fling. I'm talking about forever. My partner in every way. I love you."

Tess's heart burst and she tried not to cry because she didn't want to mess up her makeup. It really looked good for once. Sweeping her bottom lash with a finger, she stopped the tear from falling. "You do?"

Graham grasped her face between both hands and kissed her before looking deep into her eyes. "You make me crazy, but I love it. This is a forever thing."

Tess smiled. "You don't know how good that sounds."

"You don't know how good it feels."

They smiled at one another, laughing as they heard Ron tell someone how he'd brought them together one rainy night months ago. And how he totally knew they were meant to be when he saw them together. And about how he was certain his daughter would be just old enough to be a flower girl when they wed.

"He's got plans for us," Tess said.

"They sound like good ones," Graham said.

And then she kissed her forever guy again.

EPILOGUE

Three months later

GRAHAM PROPPED HIS foot on the ottoman holding a stack of *Glamour* magazines and moved his arm so it wouldn't go numb. Tess sighed in her sleep and shifted so her head dropped into his lap.

Her tear-streaked face was slack and peaceful in the late-afternoon sun streaking in the loft windows. Across the room Emily, also asleep, curled in an armchair with her new kitten's head tucked against her.

Frank's funeral was held earlier and they were all worn out from the grief. Frank had passed peacefully three days ago with the family gathered around him—a family that now included Graham. Tess's father had been at home and in good spirits, his hospice nurse close by, rolling her eyes at Frank's bad jokes and monitoring his pain.

At one point when everyone had gone to the kitchen for tea and cookies or whatever else Maggie had baked, Graham borrowed a moment alone with Frank.

"Frank, can I talk to you a sec?"

"Quick. That's all I got," Frank cracked, gaunt and pale in his bed, but smiling nevertheless.

"Bad joke."

"I'm full of 'em," he said. "Is this about business? 'Cause if it is, I want you to know I trust you."

"No, it's about Tess." Graham swallowed the sudden tears that pricked in his eyes. "I wanted to ask your permission to marry your daughter."

Frank smiled. "Oh. My Tess, huh?"

"I love her."

"I know you do. I can see it in your eyes. Just the way I've always looked at Mags. It's precious, you know. Love. So many people let it die, allow their pride to stand in the way. They allow the world to interfere, to tell them what love should or shouldn't be. Bah. What does the world know?"

He drifted a bit, wincing and sucking in air.

"Frank?"

"Still breathing," he muttered and opened his eyes again. "I knew there was something about you. Didn't know this was about my girl. Thought it was just about business, but the good Lord knew. He sent you here for a reason."

"Yes," Graham agreed, easing a hand onto Frank's shoulder.

Frank covered Graham's hand with his own. "Can't think of a better son to add to this family. Marry her, have babies, name your first son Frank."

Graham laughed. "Thank you. I will treasure her always."

"I know you will," Frank said. "You're a good man."

And at that moment, Graham finally believed he was a good man. In that reverent moment, Frank had given him something his own father never had—a sense of belonging.

Tess moved against his arm now, opening her eyes, drawing him to the present.

Yawning, Tess sat up. "I fell asleep."

"You're tired," he said, brushing a hand over her head. "It's been a long day."

"We did him justice, didn't we?" she asked, her voice soft in the quiet of the room.

"He was there the entire time. In every conversation, bigger than life—"

"And very pleased no one brought pound cake," Tess said with a smile.

"Yeah, and he's still here now. He'll always be with you. He'll always be with us." Graham gathered her against him.

"It's such a sad day but it was beautiful, too. All those flowers and the way the sun shone like Daddy was already in heaven, maybe even organizing some parades."

"I got something for you," Graham said, digging in his pocket.

He brought out a small tin that looked like a pillbox.

Tess took it from him. "What is it?"

"It was your Grandmother Bella's. Your father kept it in his sock drawer."

Tess made a face. "How did you get it?"

"He made me get it out about a week ago…when I asked him for your hand in marriage."

"Marriage?" Her eyes widened as she looked at the box. Then she lifted her eyes to his. "You asked my daddy?"

Smiling, Graham brushed her lips with his and then slid to the floor. "Today we buried your father, Tess, but he and I talked. He loved you beyond anything imaginable. The way I love her." Graham glanced over at Emily.

"Oh, God, Graham." Tess breathed, dampness gathering in her eyes. "I can't cry anymore. Please don't make me cry. I'm empty."

"No more tears. Today isn't just about sorrow. It's about love. Your father wanted you to have this as your engagement ring." Graham laughed. "He said he had to steal it from your grandmother's safety deposit box so you can't wear it around her."

Tess jerked her head up, eyes widening.

"He was kidding. You know your dad."

That made her smile.

"So Therese Ullo, will you do me the honor of becoming my wife?"

He opened the box displaying a beautiful silver filigree ring with a small diamond winking within the lacy design.

"Oh." Tess brushed her finger over the antique ring. "It's beautiful."

"Just like you."

Then she kissed him, pulling back only to say clearly, "Just try and get rid of me."

And in the moment, Graham knew he'd finally come home.

* * * * *

Look for the next
Harlequin Superromance book from Liz Talley!
Coming in August 2014.

LARGER-PRINT BOOKS!
GET 2 FREE LARGER-PRINT NOVELS PLUS
2 FREE GIFTS!

H HARLEQUIN®

super romance®

More Story...More Romance